THE OFFICIAL MOVIE NOVELIZATION

Also available from Titan Books

WAR FOR THE PLANET OF THE APES: REVELATIONS
The Official Movie Prequel
By Greg Keyes

DAWN OF THE PLANET OF THE APES: FIRESTORM
The Official Movie Prequel
By Greg Keyes

DAWN OF THE PLANET OF THE APES
The Official Movie Novelization
By Alex Irvine

THE OFFICIAL MOVIE NOVELIZATION

GREG COX

BASED ON THE SCREENPLAY
WRITTEN BY MARK BOMBACK AND MATT REEVES
BASED ON CHARACTERS CREATED BY RICK JAFFA & AMANDA SILVER

TITAN BOOKS

WAR FOR THE PLANET OF THE APES: The Official Movie Novelization
Print edition ISBN: 9781785654749
E-book edition ISBN: 9781785654756

Published by Titan Books
A division of Titan Publishing Group Ltd
144 Southwark Street, London SE1 0UP

First edition: July 2017
1 2 3 4 5 6 7 8 9 10

A CIP catalogue record for this title is available from the British Library.

Printed and bound in Great Britain by CPI Group (UK) Ltd, Croydon CR0 4YY

Did you enjoy this book? We love to hear from our readers.
Please email us at readerfeedback@titanemail.com or write to us at
Reader Feedback at the above address.

To receive advance information, news, competitions, and exclusive offers
online, please sign up for the Titan newsletter on our website
www.titanbooks.com

THE OFFICIAL MOVIE NOVELIZATION

ARMED FORCES BRIEFING REPORT — CLASSIFIED

TO: COMMAND
FROM: [REDACTED]
TOPIC: HISTORY OF APE CRISIS

Fifteen years ago, a scientific experiment gone wrong gave *rise* to a species of intelligent apes… and a virus that nearly destroyed the human race. The SIMIAN FLU, as it came to be known, brought humanity to the brink of destruction. The survivors—the few who were immune to the crisis— came to envy the dead, while the apes continued to thrive in the safety of the woods north of SAN FRANCISCO.

With the *dawn* of their burgeoning civilization, the apes flourished in the absence of human contact, until they were discovered by a small band of desperate survivors striving to establish a colony of their own. The colonists and apes struggled to coexist, but their fragile peace was shattered by KOBA, an insurgent ape who sought revenge on his former captors. CAESAR, the reputed leader of the apes, attempted to restore order.

But there was no turning back from the brutal fighting that had already begun.

The embattled colonists sent out frantic distress calls for help, unsure if anyone was even out there to hear them. The signal was received 800 miles north at JOINT BASE LEWIS-McCHORD, where hundreds of soldiers had taken refuge after the viral apocalypse. These men and women were all that remained of the U.S. ARMED FORCES. Responding to the call, a hardened fighting division, led by [REDACTED], a decorated colonel of the Special Forces, was sent down to join the battle. Caesar and his apes retreated to the woods, but the human forces pursued, determined to destroy the apes once and for all. For two years, the soldiers have been searching in vain for Caesar, who is rumored to be commanding his apes from a base hidden somewhere deep in the woods.

And the *war* rages on…

1

The vast redwood forest had survived the end of the world. Civilization may have collapsed, but the woods endured, unchanged by the plagues and riots and upheaval that had brought humanity to the brink of extinction. Towering trees, rising as much as three hundred feet above the shady forest floor, seemed to mock mankind's precipitous fall, while the primeval scenery was just as it must have been twelve years ago, before everything went to hell, or fifty years or a hundred or five hundred. Sunlight filtered through the dense green canopy overhead, which was filled with birdsong along with the ceaseless chattering of squirrels. A brisk winter wind rustled leaves and branches and ferns. A damp misty haze chilled the air.

Nature endured. Whether humanity would was another question.

Footsteps, moving stealthily through the woods, intruded on the sylvan domain. Fallen twigs and leaves crunched beneath the tread of multiple army boots as a platoon of human soldiers made their way up a steep, thickly wooded hill as quietly as they could manage amidst the profuse vegetation. The soldiers moved without speaking, even their breathing hushed. Grim-faced men and women clutched rifles or military-grade crossbows tensely. Wary eyes scanned the murky forest, on guard against any lurking hostiles. Worn, threadbare camo fatigues, badly in need of replacement, testified to a long, grueling campaign. Dark camouflage paint obscured their features, masking their individuality. Battered Kevlar helmets bore a variety of scrawled labels and slogans:

MONKEY KILLER

BEDTIME FOR BONZO

ENDANGERED SPECIES

MONKEY SEE, MONKEY DIE

Uniting the troop was a common insignia, AΩ. Some wore the Greek letters hand-drawn on their clothing, others had tattooed them onto their bare arms and skin, but they all bore the emblem proudly. To do otherwise would have been traitorous, not just to their own unit, but to the entire human race. The insignia was a constant reminder of just how much was at stake—and the unthinkable consequences of failure.

An advance scout, taking point, halted abruptly. He whispered urgently to his commander, who was only a few paces behind him.

"Captain—!"

Captain Rod Wilson, late of the U.S. Army, held up his hand, signaling the rest of the unit to stop. He was a rugged combat veteran who had never expected his tour of duty to extend beyond the end of the world. Wondering what the scout had spotted, he hurried forward to join the soldier, who pointed up the slope straight ahead. Wilson raised his M16 assault rifle to peer through its gunsight and was rewarded with a glimpse of the enemy.

Three apes—chimpanzees, to be exact—occupied a ridge roughly one hundred yards away. Two of the chimps stood guard, while the third watered their horses at a trickling stream. One of the guards clutched a stone-tipped wooden spear, the other toted a Remington semi-automatic rifle.

Wilson scowled. By now, the sight of apes employing firearms and horses no longer provoked shock, but Wilson still found it disturbing nonetheless. He was old enough to remember when apes were just *animals*, confined to circuses and zoos and laboratories. Caged like the beasts they were. Before everything changed, before the virus…

Apes were not native to North America. There had been a time when *Homo sapiens* had been the only primate living free on the continent, when no chimps or orangutans or bonobos or gorillas had inhabited these woods. Bile rose at the back of Wilson's throat as he contemplated the unnatural creatures on the ridge.

They didn't belong here. They were *wrong*.

And they couldn't be allowed to exist.

He lined up the gun-toting ape in the crosshairs of his gunsight. His finger tensed on the trigger. The humans had the advantage of surprise only until the first gunshot, so he intended to make that shot count.

Say your prayers, monkey, he thought. *If monkeys pray.*

A hand fell on his shoulder before he could squeeze the trigger.

A furry, thickly knuckled hand.

The hand of an ape.

Momentarily startled, Wilson turned to see a large male gorilla looming directly behind him. The ape's army helmet matched those of the human soldiers, marking him as part of the captain's unit. A heavy rucksack, stuffed with weapons and gear, hung upon the ape's hairy back. Wilson recognized this particular ape, which went by the name of "Red" because his thick black fur had a slightly reddish tinge. Red was an ugly bastard, but clever enough to know his place—and to come in handy sometimes.

What? Wilson asked silently, interrogating the gorilla with his eyes.

Red pointed up.

Craning his neck back, Wilson peered at the verdant canopy overhead, where another helmeted ape crouched furtively in the branches, looking very much at home high above the ground. Not for the first time, Wilson envied the apes' natural gift for climbing, and resented them for it.

Evolution made humans soft. We're paying for that now.

He made eye contact with the chimp in the tree, who pointed at the ridge where the three apes were loitering. Looking back at the ridge, Wilson wasn't sure at first what the chimp was seeing from his elevated vantage point. Just the three hostiles they had already spotted, or something else?

What am I not seeing?

It took him a moment but then he spotted it: a long, low trench wall made up of heavy logs and stones, artfully concealed by overlapping layers of leaves and branches that put the soldiers' own crude attempts at camouflage to shame. The leafy cover blended smoothly with the surrounding wilderness, hiding the wall from view unless you were actively looking for it.

Well, I'll be damned, Wilson thought. *Those sneaky kongs.*

Heaven only knew how many more hostiles might be hiding behind the concealed fortifications. The sharp-eyed chimp in the tree had definitely earned his rations for the day; Wilson and his soldiers had practically walked right up to the wall without seeing it. That could have been a fatal mistake.

Good thing our own monkeys were on the ball.

Wilson nodded at Red, acknowledging the timely alert, before deciding that he ought to notify the Colonel of their discovery. A wireless communications headset was affixed to the captain's helmet; he clicked it on and whispered into the mike.

"Echo two-six to command. Colonel, we have eyes on three kongs in the north woods. A couple of our donkeys think there are others here, too." He kept his voice cool and controlled, despite his growing excitement. "Maybe this is it, maybe the base is near."

Two years, he thought. *Two years we've been slogging through the woods, trying to track these damn dirty apes to their lair. Have we finally got a bead on them?*

The Colonel's voice replied via the headset, speaking too softly to be heard by anyone else, including Red, who remained close at hand. Wilson listened attentively.

"Yes, sir," he responded. "Copy that. Over."

Clicking off, he waved up more soldiers from the rear. They reacted with admirable speed and efficiency, fishing additional arms and ammo from the bulging rucksacks carried by Red and two other apes, who obediently accepted their role as pack mules. Chimpanzees were known to be seven times stronger than the average human, which made them useful as porters as well as scouts.

Too bad they stink like hell, Wilson thought.

"You!" he said to one of the apes in a low voice. "Over here."

The chimp loped over to the captain on all fours, walking on his knuckles as well as his bare feet. Wilson frankly preferred to see apes moving like quadrupeds instead of walking on two legs like humans; they were less creepy that way. He extracted an M79 grenade launcher from the ape's pack. The "bloop gun" resembled a stubby, sawed-off shotgun. He swept his gaze over the troops under his command, picking out one of his best marksmen.

"Preacher," he said.

A young soldier crept forward to join the captain, tightly gripping a loaded military crossbow. Preacher was a fresh-faced Latino youth still in his teens; Wilson wondered how much Preacher even remembered of what life used to be like, back when humanity ruled supreme over the planet. Like so many young men and women these days, he had come of age in a world turned upside-down. In a reality that still worked the way it was supposed to, he'd be worrying about prom and graduation now, not hunting upstart monkeys who thought the future belonged to them. The apes—and the Flu—had robbed Preacher of the life he should have lived. And not only him, but an entire generation of men and women.

Time for payback. Wilson indicated the three apes on the ridge. "The one with the gun," he specified.

Preacher nodded and readied his weapon. The captain did the same, aiming the loaded grenade launcher at the hidden trench wall. Behind them, the rest of the unit prepared themselves for combat. Gleaming bayonet blades, thirsty for simian blood, were affixed to rifles. Safeties were unlocked.

Wilson steeled his features, betraying no sign of fear or trepidation. His jaw was set in determination, the better to inspire the brave men and women under his command. All eyes were on the captain as he silently counted down with his fingers.

Three… two… one!

Preacher fired his crossbow. A twenty-inch carbon bolt struck the armed chimpanzee in the chest, killing him instantly. He toppled over into the trench behind the wall, much to the shock of his two companions, who barely had time to react before Wilson fired his own weapon. A pair of 40 mm grenades screamed across the woods and slammed into the apes' fortifications, exploding on contact.

A fiery orange and yellow detonation blew the wall apart, sending chunks of rock and timber flying, along with the bodies of the closest apes. Scores of stunned and injured apes also spilled from the open trench behind the breached wall. Gorillas, orangutans, bonobos, and chimpanzees, many of them bleeding and broken, tumbled down the slope onto the smoking rubble, while losing their grip on their weapons. Guns, spears, bows, and arrows were strewn about like fallen leaves and branches, of little use to the embattled apes. Crackling flames and acrid white fumes added to the chaos. The echoes of the explosions rang in Wilson's ears. Wounded apes screamed in fear and agony.

You had it coming, the captain thought.

The other soldiers opened fire on the apes before the animals had a chance to regroup or retaliate. A deadly hail of bullets tore into hairy hides. Arrows struck home in target after target. A fat-faced male orangutan, his shaggy orange coat now streaked with bright wet splashes of red, staggered to his feet, only to be brought down by another bolt from Preacher's crossbow. More grenades arced through the air and into the exposed trench. Deafening explosions rocked the hillside, and frantic birds and small animals fled in terror. The wind carried the unmistakable odor of war back toward Wilson and his troops. He breathed it in deeply.

You smell that, monkeys? That's the smell of mankind taking back our future.

Further up the ridge, above the trench, the two surviving chimps overcame their shock. They leaped back onto their horses and wheeled them about, attempting to escape up the wooded slope behind them, but a sniper nailed one of them in the head. The ape, which had been watering the horses only moments ago, fell from his horse and crashed to the ground, leaving only a single chimp on horseback: the sentry with the spear. Digging his heels into his mount's side, he galloped up the hillside, screeching in warning. Rising smoke aided his escape as he disappeared into the trees and the distance. Wilson frowned, but consoled himself that one lone chimp didn't matter in the long run.

Let him run, he thought. *The rest of these monkeys won't be so lucky.*

"Come on!" he shouted to his troops over the din of battle. After slinking covertly through the woods for hours, afraid to even breathe too loudly, it felt good to give voice to their righteous fury at last. Eager to press their advantage, he led the charge up the hill toward the stricken enemy. Whooping and shooting, his soldiers chased after him, hyped up on adrenaline and the promise of victory. They fired at will at the shell-shocked apes. Caught off-guard and off-balance, the besieged animals didn't stand a chance.

Serves them right, Wilson thought, *for thinking these woods belong to them.*

"Let 'em have it!" he shouted. "No prisoners!"

2

Spear was not just the chimpanzee's weapon of choice; it was his name. Even as a child, almost as soon as he could climb, he had fearlessly hurled himself through the air from branch to branch and tree to tree, so the name "Spear" had found him as surely as a javelin striking its target. Now he wished he could truly fly like a spear instead of merely pushing his horse to gallop more swiftly than it ever had before.

Faster, he urged the horse. *Faster!*

The horse raced through the woods, its hooves pounding against the forest floor and tearing up great clods of earth in its headlong flight from the screams and gunshots and explosions behind them. It wove expertly between the trees and leapt over rotting logs and brambles. Riding bareback, holding on tightly to the horse's reins, Spear spurred his steed on although this was hardly necessary; the horse wanted to escape the slaughter just as much as its rider did. Spear screeched at the top of his lungs, desperate to sound a warning. He couldn't believe how quickly the humans had come upon them. One minute he had been standing guard with his companions, not truly anticipating any danger; the next, his friends were dead, the wall was breached, and all was blood and flame and smoke and death.

The tribe needed to be warned. *Caesar* needed to be warned.

More gunshots echoed through the forest behind him. Spear prayed that his fellow apes had rallied and were returning fire at least. It seemed to him that the noise of the battle was following him instead of receding as he galloped away from the fighting; could that mean that a retreat was underway, with any surviving apes shooting back at the humans' relentless onslaught as they attempted to escape?

Spear wanted to think so.

His frantic screeches warred with the pounding of the horse's hooves. Spear feared that none would hear him in time, but then his desperate shrieks were answered by a rising chorus of simian screeches and hoots coming from up ahead and growing louder by the moment.

Yes!

Hope flared in his chest. Pulling back on the reins, he brought his horse to a sudden stop. Lather dripped down the horse's heaving sides. It strained at its bit, desperate to keep running from the massacre and rearing up on its hind legs. Spear tightened his grip on the reins and clung to the horse with his legs to avoid being thrown.

No, he thought. *Wait… wait!*

He peered through the trees ahead. His spirits soared as, heralded by the thunder of hooves, an entire company of mounted ape soldiers came riding toward him, armed for combat. The charging cavalry was composed of every species of great ape, united to defend their endangered colony, and seemed almost as numerous as the trees they rode out of. Spear was impressed at how quickly the cavalry had mobilized in response to his cries. Caesar had trained his forces well.

And with good reason.

Spear grinned at the reinforcements. Thick black hairs bristled along his back and shoulders in an aggressive display, making him appear even bigger and more intimidating than he actually was. He bared his canines. *No more retreating*, he vowed. *No more running from the humans.* The teachings of Caesar filled him with pride and courage.

Apes together strong.

Screeching in fury, he turned his horse back the way it had come. He raised his spear high and pointed it toward those he had left behind to face the guns and malice of the enemy. More apes on horseback poured out of the hills and joined in behind him, charging down the wooded slope toward their implacable foes.

Humans had begun this attack, but apes would end it.

The battle of the hill raged on as Preacher fought alongside his unit against the retreating apes, who were not going down as easily as he had hoped. Preacher had seen combat before, but nothing this fierce. Enemy fire targeted the humans as they chased after the apes, intent on wiping out every last one of the monkeys despite the bullets and spears and arrows flying every which way. Bodies, both human and simian, littered the forest floor, while the moans and whimpers of the wounded were disturbingly hard to tell apart. Panic nibbled at Preacher's resolve, but he was no deserter. Taking shelter behind the trunk of a massive redwood, he fired shot after shot from his crossbow, drawing fresh bolts from the quiver at his hip. His shots hit more often than they missed, bringing down one ape after another. Frantically reaching for another bolt, he was dismayed to find his quiver empty.

How had he gone through his supply so fast?

His eyes searched anxiously for Red, who, along with the other donkeys, had fallen back to keep out of the line of fire. Preacher shouted at the gorilla.

"Reload!"

Red hurried toward him on all fours, bearing his heavy pack of gear. Preacher hurriedly retrieved a fully loaded quiver from the rucksack and discarded the empty one. Grateful for the gorilla's prompt response, he nodded at Red, only to see that the ape was looking past him at the front lines of battle, where the retreating apes were being cut down by the soldiers' guns and arrows. Gorillas just like Red were dead and dying upon the hillside, bleeding out onto the greenery. Red watched the slaughter with cold brown eyes and a stony expression that offered no hint of what was going through that clever monkey brain of his.

How does he feel about this? Preacher wondered. *Guilty about betraying his own kind? Or is he just glad to be on the winning side?*

If the bloodshed troubled Red, his face held no evidence of it.

Preacher strapped on the fresh quiver and cautiously stepped out from behind the tree trunk, ready to rejoin the fray. Red tagged along with him, but they only got a few steps before a startling sight drew their gazes upward.

Two—no, three—trails of spiraling white smoke hissed through the air high above their heads. The vaporous streamers arced through the cold gray sky before smacking to earth and rolling across the ground toward Preacher and his comrades, spewing thick, billowing fumes everywhere. The young soldier gasped out loud, uncertain what was happening but knowing already that it wasn't anything good. He shared a confused look with Red, who appeared to be just as surprised and disoriented by the smoke.

What the hell?

His crossbow armed and ready, Preacher looked around fearfully, but dense, opaque smoke had hidden his sight lines, taking away his targets. He couldn't fire his weapon for fear of hitting a human instead of an ape.

And then he heard it: the thunderous pounding of hooves.

Many, many hooves.

Oh crap. Preacher's mouth suddenly went as dry as the Mojave as he remembered the chimp that had gotten away on horseback earlier.

That's not just one monkey on a horse.

The ape cavalry thundered down the slope, charging from the woods above the breached fortifications. Riders with slings hurled another volley of crude smoke bombs over the heads of the retreating apes, causing a second wave of fuming missiles to smack down amidst the human invaders, fomenting confusion. At the forefront of the cavalry, Spear relished the soldiers' obvious surprise and disarray. It was not enough to make up for all the death and carnage the humans had brought to the forest, but it was a good start. The faces of his murdered friends were still fresh in Spear's memory and his hackles bristled in rage.

We've only begun to make them pay, he thought. *If they thought they feared apes before...*

The riders met the tide of fleeing apes, who were in woeful shape. Spear was shocked and angered by how severely the survivors' ranks had been thinned, and by the number and extent of their injuries. Maimed and bleeding apes, many who would bear the scars of the humans' sneak attack for the rest of their days, scrambled madly away from the massacre. A wounded chimpanzee clung to the back of a limping gorilla, who sported ugly burns and cuts of his own. Another ape cradled a broken arm against his chest as he was forced to flee on only three limbs, and an orangutan winced in pain with a crossbow bolt wedged in his side; one of his bulging cheek flaps was shredded to ribbons. More able-bodied apes took to the trees, firing back at the humans with guns and bows. Spear admired their valor, even as he thanked providence that he and the cavalry had arrived before it was too late.

We will save our brothers, he thought, *and avenge the fallen!*

He screeched loudly to break through the clamor. Raising his spear high, he watched with pride as the panicked apes halted their retreat. Fear faded from their faces as they spied the cavalry and realized that they were no longer outnumbered. Panic gave way to fury as all that were able turned back toward the humans and bared their teeth. Simian war cries rose in savage chorus.

Spear's heart swelled. Lowering his spear, he spurred his steed forward, leading the charge. Enraged apes ran back toward the smoke-filled battlefield, alongside the charging cavalry.

The humans would wish they had stayed far away from these hills.

We're screwed, Preacher thought. *Big time.*

Along with the rest of his unit, he stumbled blindly through the smoke, unable to see more than a foot in front of him. The harsh fumes stung his eyes and invaded his throat and lungs, leaving him coughing and gasping for breath. Clutching his crossbow, he turned in circles, unsure from which direction danger might be coming. Watery eyes searched in vain for targets to shoot at. Angry shouts and curses filled the woods as he heard the other soldiers raging against the smoke, bumping into trees and each other. Red and the other donkeys screeched and jabbered in alarm. Preacher wondered if they regretted switching sides.

I would if I were them.

The thunder of hooves grew louder and more frightening. A sudden whistling noise drew his gaze upward in time to see a torrent of wooden spears and arrows raining down on them. Screams erupted all around him. Dimly glimpsed figures, barely more than vague silhouettes in the smoke, hit the ground and didn't get back up again. And still the lethal missiles kept plummeting from the sky, claiming new victims. A stone-tipped spear struck the earth right at his feet, causing him to jump backwards into the hard, unyielding tree. The back of his helmet smacked into the trunk hard enough to hurt, but Preacher barely noticed the impact. He felt like he was trapped in some hellish limbo where death struck at random and without warning. He couldn't believe how quickly the tide of battle had turned against them.

We were winning, damn it! We had them on the run...!

Another scream came from only a few yards away. An agonized voice cried out hoarsely.

"RETREAT!"

Preacher had no idea who had issued the order, but he didn't have to be told twice. Ducking low to present a smaller target, and half-expecting to be skewered at any moment, he ran for his life. A moss-covered log blocked his escape and he dived over it, seeking cover, only to find himself tumbling headfirst down a steep slope into a ditch. He landed hard, the breath knocked out of him, blurry eyes peering up at the trees towering high above him. Part of him wanted to just keep lying there, to close his eyes and hope the battle moved on without him, but the terrifying prospect of being left behind in the ape-infested woods was enough to convince him that he needed to keep moving. He lifted his head to orient himself.

Dead eyes looked back at him.

Preacher bit back a scream as he found himself face to face with the captain's lifeless body, just one of several dead soldiers lying in the ditch, which now resembled a mass grave. Preacher recognized all of the corpses: Ward, Chambers, Chavez, Robbins, Shimoda. An arrow pierced the captain's throat. Glassy eyes stared blankly into oblivion.

The apes had killed him. The apes had killed all of them.

Preacher feared that he was as good as dead, too. Down in the grave with his fallen comrades, he could hear the apes drawing nearer. They screeched and hooted at each other like the animals they were. Agitated horses neighed and whinnied. Gunshots sounded far too close by, a sign that the battle was still underway, or were the apes simply picking off the last few humans? Preacher wondered briefly if Red and the other "good" apes had gotten away, then wondered why he cared.

For all Preacher knew, he was the only human soldier left.

He groped about for his crossbow, which he'd lost rolling down the hill, but couldn't find it. Most of the bolts had fallen out of the quiver as well, leaving him more or less unarmed. He didn't want to die like this, alone in the woods with no one but the dead to share his final moments. Fear threatened to override his training, but he tried to hold himself together even though he was shaking like a leaf. He reached out trembling hands and pried the captain's headset from the corpse, which was still warm to the touch. The dead man's blood stained his fingers.

Sorry, Captain, he thought. *I need this more than you do now.*

He hoped to God that the equipment was still working.

Grimacing, he put on the headset and powered it up.

"Colonel? Colonel, do you copy?"

Static crackled in his ears, crushing his hopes. An endless, excruciating moment passed before a calm, authoritative voice responded. Preacher gasped in relief as he recognized the familiar cadences of his commanding officer.

"Who is this?" the Colonel asked.

Preacher's mouth was dry. He somehow worked up enough spit to speak.

"Preacher... it's Preacher, sir."

He had no idea if the Colonel knew him by name. He was nobody important, just another grunt in the war.

"Where are you, soldier? I need your position."

"I don't know!"

The Colonel's voice remained steady, reassuring. *"What do you see?"*

Preacher wasn't about to lift his head out of the ditch just to report that he saw some trees and bushes. His own voice quavered, nearly cracking under the pressure. What if the apes heard him, too?

"I can't see anything! We lost a lot of men, sir. The captain is dead!"

The Colonel seemed to take a moment to process that intel. *"You're in command now."*

"Command, sir?" Preacher tried to make the Colonel understand. "I think it's just me by myself now!"

The apes were definitely closer. He could hear them stomping through the brush toward him. Preacher peered up, waiting tensely for an ape to come into view. He knew his time was almost done.

"Sir, I don't think I'm gonna make it." His throat tightened, overcome with emotion. Bad enough to die young fighting a winning battle, but to go down in defeat at the hands of an ape, without even accomplishing the mission… "I'm sorry, sir. I'm so sorry!"

The Colonel answered gravely:

"I understand, soldier. Just kill as many of them as you can."

But it was already too late for that. Searching fruitlessly for his crossbow amidst the dead bodies, Preacher heard a hostile grunt from above. He froze as he looked up to see several apes glaring down at him with murder in their eyes. Spears and rifles were aimed at him, even though any one of the apes could probably tear him limb from limb with its bare hands. No mercy showed on their simian features, nor did Preacher expect it to. Humans and apes had been mortal enemies for most of his life, which was apparently now at its end. Preacher swallowed hard and braced himself for whatever came next. He was already in a grave. The rest was just a formality.

Go ahead, he thought. *Get it over with.*

3

Caesar contemplated the grisly aftermath of the battle. Apes scavenged for weapons, stripping guns and ammunition from the bodies of dead human soldiers; a necessary task, but a distasteful one. The ape leader—still in his prime—turned away from the looting and slowly made his way toward the exposed trench, whose camouflage and defenses had failed to spare it from the humans' assault. The shattered remains of the wall were strewn across the landscape, testifying to the force of the enemy's explosives. Charred timbers still reeked of smoke and scattered brush fires needed to be put out.

He watched grimly as ape bodies, not all of them intact, were lifted out of the blasted depths of the trench. He did not try to count the dead; there would be time enough later to tally their losses. For now it was more important that the scores of wounded apes were attended to; he feared that, despite the best efforts of their healers, many more of his people would succumb to their injuries in the hours and days to come. The apes' "victory" had been a costly one.

The battle is over, he thought, *but the mourning has just begun.*

Sentries posted in the trees kept careful watch just in case there were more humans afoot. Caesar trusted them to sound the alarm if necessary as he descended into what was left of the trench. Gorillas, chimpanzees, orangutans, and bonobos, injured or otherwise, looked up to gaze upon their imposing leader with awe and reverence. His very presence provoked a reaction from all present; wide-eyed apes nudged each other, alerting their fellows to his arrival. Even the wounded roused themselves and raised their heads at his approach.

Caesar was used to this response. He was their leader after all… and their liberator. It was he who had unleashed the virus that had elevated their intelligences, and who had freed them from captivity in labs and zoos more than a decade ago.

Now pushing twenty years old, Caesar had some gray around his muzzle, but his authority remained unquestioned. Conscious of his people's regard, he projected strength and fortitude. His hard, stoic expression displayed no sign of fear or weakness. Only the pain in his distinctive green eyes betrayed how much the suffering of his people affected him.

Will the bloodshed never end? he thought. *Will the humans never leave us in peace?*

A pair of gorillas flanked Caesar on either side. Luca was a grizzled silverback who had been one of Caesar's most trusted lieutenants for many years. After being liberated from the San Francisco Zoo, he had fought beside Caesar upon the Golden Gate Bridge in the early days of their freedom and had eventually become the chief of the gorilla guard and an integral part of Caesar's inner circle, remaining loyal even during the dark days of Koba's short-lived coup two years ago. At least twice Caesar's size by weight and a head taller to boot, he was formidable even by gorilla standards. Dark brown eyes peered out from beneath his prominent brow ridge.

Luca was accompanied by Winter, a young albino gorilla whose white fur and pink eyes stood out amidst the blackened, shadowy depths of the trench. Less inured to the ravages of war, he looked upon the bloody wreckage with obvious distress. He bent low, automatically assuming a defensive posture. A low whimper escaped his lips.

Caesar wished he could have spared Winter this horrific spectacle, but the times would not allow such mercies. Winter was a promising young ape, quick of mind and strong of limb, whom Luca thought highly of, but Winter could not defend their people, let alone help to lead the colony in the future, if he was shielded from the harsh realities of the world as it was. He needed to know what the humans were capable of at their worst, to appreciate the danger that the apes had faced ever since they had first risen from captivity, before Winter was even born.

A cruel lesson, Caesar thought, *but a vital one.*

Descending deeper into the trench, beneath a concealing cover of earth, Caesar found himself facing another unpleasant reality—and a dilemma.

A handful of human prisoners awaited his judgment. The captive humans were down on their knees, their hands bound behind their backs. Lowered helmets concealed their faces as they stared bleakly at the packed-earth floor of the trench. A party of guards, led by a stalwart chimpanzee named Spear, stood watch over the prisoners. Caesar understood that it was Spear who had sounded the alarm about the attack, alerting the cavalry in time to halt the humans' advance and prevent them from inflicting even greater harm on his people. As grievous as the day's losses had been, Caesar was all too aware that matters could have gone much worse.

If the humans had managed to locate the fortress...

Spear came forward and offered up his open palm in supplication. Caesar brushed his own fingers lightly across the other chimpanzee's palm, acknowledging the tribute, before turning his attention to the prisoners. Spear and the other guards stepped aside to let him draw nearer to the bedraggled humans, who looked up fearfully at his approach. A young Latino soldier gulped.

Do they know who I am, Caesar wondered, *or are all apes the same to them?*

His unforgiving gaze swept over the prisoners. He noted that one soldier, crouching behind the others, still had his head down, hiding his face beneath his helmet. The soldier's body was largely concealed behind the other prisoners, but Caesar could tell that he was large for a human. A sudden suspicion deepened the scowl on Caesar's face. Sniffing the air, he caught a distinct whiff of treachery.

Not human.

He nodded at Spear, who roughly yanked the helmet off the prisoner, revealing the distinctly simian features of a gorilla.

And a traitor.

The gorilla defiantly refused to look at Caesar, who was sickened but not surprised by the turncoat's presence among the soldiers. He had heard reports of renegade apes siding against their own kind. He squinted at the traitor's face.

I know you, Caesar thought.

More than two years had passed since the vengeful chimpanzee named Koba had attempted to overthrow Caesar and launch an all-out war against the humans, but the memory of that bitter betrayal still pained Caesar. Koba had been his friend and ally once, but his hatred of humanity had won out over his loyalty to Caesar, whose quixotic pursuit of peace had damned him in the eyes of Koba and his followers. Koba was dead now, by Caesar's hand, but the damage he had done to ape unity lived on in disgruntled outcasts like the one at his mercy now.

Red. Caesar knew this ape well. He had once followed Koba.

Spear tossed the ape's helmet to Caesar for his inspection. It appeared to be a standard-issue army helmet, designed to protect the fragile skulls of humans, yet Caesar was puzzled to see an unfamiliar insignia crudely scrawled on the helmet:

$A\Omega$

Looking more closely at the prisoners, he observed that they all sported the same insignia somewhere on their clothes or bodies. He saw it tattooed on arms and necks and drawn with markers on their torn and bloody uniforms. He recognized the letters as belonging to an ancient human alphabet, but their meaning eluded him. Although he'd spent years contending with various remnants of the United States military, the letters belonged to no branch of the armed forces known to him.

A new enemy?

He cast a quizzical look at the young Latino soldier, whose helmet bore the same insignia. A tag on his uniform identified him as "Preacher," although Caesar was unclear as to whether that was his name or his vocation. The trembling human was smart enough to grasp what Caesar wished to know.

"It's... it's Alpha Omega."

That meant nothing to Caesar, who kept his gaze fixed on Preacher, demanding more of an explanation. Knowing your enemy was vital to anticipating their actions.

"Means we're the beginning and the end," a dark-haired female soldier volunteered. She had $A\Omega$ inked on her neck. Her voice held an unmistakable note of defiance, despite her precarious situation. "Humanity's survival depends on us."

Caesar wanted to know what exactly she meant by that. Before he could learn more, however, he saw the guards and prisoners turning their attention to something behind him. Slow, waddling footsteps announced the arrival of a newcomer to the scene. Recognizing the familiar gait of an old friend, Caesar went to greet him.

Maurice was a mature orangutan and one of Caesar's senior advisors. A former circus ape, he had befriended Caesar back when they were both confined to a prison-like "primate shelter" in San Francisco, before Caesar had masterminded their escape from captivity. As wise as he was compassionate, Maurice was more of a teacher than a warrior, but he had stood with Caesar through numerous trials, including their battles against both the humans and Koba's rebels. Caesar trusted him with his life and often relied on the orangutan's thoughtful nature and sage advice. A shaggy orange coat covered his bulky frame. Long arms and short legs spoke to his species' arboreal roots, while bulging cheek flaps attested to his seniority.

Like most apes, Maurice preferred sign language to human speech, for which simian vocal cords were ill-suited. His eloquent hands and fingers brought grave tidings.

Twenty-two dead, the orangutan signed. *Many more injured*.

The news fanned the anger burning in Caesar's heart. Turning back toward the prisoners, he glowered at the humans who had wrought such death and havoc on his people. His lips peeled back, exposing his teeth and gums.

Preacher's eyes widened.

"You're him," he blurted. "You're Caesar."

Caesar was startled to hear his name on the human's lips. It seemed his reputation did indeed precede him. He wasn't entirely sure how he felt about that. Being feared as the leader of apes also made him a target.

"We've been looking for you for so long," Preacher confessed. Now that he had found the nerve to speak, he seemed unable to contain himself. "We heard you had a hidden command base, but we could never find it. Some of us were starting to think you might be dead, but the Colonel said no, you were out here somewhere—"

The Colonel. Caesar didn't have a face to go with that label, but he knew well that this "Colonel" was the human truly responsible for today's carnage. He glared at the prisoners. Their lives were in his hands now.

"Just kill us already," said another soldier, who was tagged as "Travis." His face was pale and sweaty beneath the camo paint smeared across his face. Fraying nerves strained his voice.

"Shut up, man!" the woman snapped at him. "Lang" appeared to be her name. "You trying to get us all killed?"

"What?" Travis objected. "They're animals. He's going to slaughter us—"

Caesar had heard enough. He stepped slowly toward Travis, whose angry words evaporated as the ape's shadow fell over him. He swallowed hard and shrank from Caesar, who loomed above him on two legs. The other soldiers looked afraid as well, although Lang was doing her best to hide it behind a defiant façade. Caesar could practically smell the fear wafting from them. He gave them a moment to fully appreciate just how close to death they were.

Then he spoke:

"I… did not start this war."

His deep, gravelly voice was hoarse and halting, issuing from a throat that nature had never intended for human speech, and held an edge sharp enough to cut through flesh and bone. The humans gaped at him.

Good. They need to listen closely to what I have to say.

"The ape who did… is dead. His name was Koba. I killed him."

He let that sink in before continuing. His voice took on an even harder edge, the better to impress his words upon the prisoners.

"I only fight now… to protect apes."

"Yeah?" Travis glanced over at Red. "What about him? And we got ten more just like him."

Caesar was saddened to hear that Koba's departed followers had turned against their own kind. He looked sternly at Red, who finally met his eyes, staring back at Caesar with undisguised hate.

"I know these apes. They followed Koba. They tried to kill me. They fear what I will do to them. They believe that I cannot forgive."

In truth, those fears were not entirely unfounded. Caesar had once believed that apes were inherently better than humans, more honorable and trustworthy.

He knew better now, thanks to Koba.

"So now they serve you… just to survive."

"I no *fear* you!" Red snarled. His gruff voice and crude command of English sounded even less natural than Caesar's, but his fierce words were clear enough. "*You* must fear! How long you think woods can protect you?" The gorilla scoffed out loud at the notion. "Humans *destroy you*. Their *Kerna*," he said, mangling the pronunciation of *colonel*, "has no mercy. Humans follow *all* he say. To them, he *more* than just human. He *everything*."

Spittle flew from the turncoat's muzzle. Vengeful eyes blazed beneath heavy brows as he glared at each of his captors one after another. Even Caesar felt a chill run down his spine, while Winter was visibly unnerved by the other ape's threats. The young gorilla took an involuntary step backward, provoking a frown from Luca, even as Red kept railing at them:

"He says: first Caesar die... then you *all* die."

Spear erupted in fury, seizing the renegade ape by the shoulders and hurling him violently to the ground. He looked prepared to do more, but Caesar held up his hand and shook his head. Still seething, Spear brought himself under control and reluctantly backed away from Red, while shooting figurative spears at the traitor with his eyes.

Caesar knew exactly how Spear felt.

Get him out of here, he signed to Luca.

The mighty silverback passed the command on to Winter, giving the younger gorilla an opportunity to conquer his fear. Despite his obvious qualms, Winter pulled himself together and stepped forward to take custody of the turncoat, who resisted violently even with his arms bound behind his back. He roared and snapped at Winter, but was in no position to resist the other gorilla, who dragged him away by his ankle.

Caesar was glad to be rid of him.

That left only the human prisoners to be dealt with. Shocked into silence by the vicious confrontation between the apes, they waited anxiously, perhaps expecting to be dragged away to their doom at any minute. Sweat drenched their faces, smearing their war paint. A whiff of urine indicated that at least one of the humans had pissed themselves in fright. Caesar guessed it was Travis.

Luca sighed heavily, his hairless black chest rising and falling. He signed to Caesar:

What should we do with them?

* * *

Ape hands cinched a knot tight, binding the prisoners' hands to the reins of one of two horses that had been drafted to carry them back to wherever they'd come from. The humans sat astride the horses, sharing the two mounts. Ape guards surrounded them, ensuring the humans' cooperation, as Caesar and his advisors observed the preparations. Preacher stared at Caesar in confusion, as though he couldn't really believe what was happening.

"You're letting us live?"

Caesar couldn't blame the soldier for being baffled by their restraint considering all the innocent apes he and his comrades had killed or maimed in their unprovoked attack. Few would argue that death would not be a fitting punishment for their crimes, but Caesar wanted more than just an eye for an eye. He had a larger purpose. Justice was a luxury his people could ill afford.

"Tell your Colonel… you have seen me now. And I have a message for him: this fighting can stop. Leave us the woods… and no more humans will die."

His declaration drew mixed expressions from the humans. Some looked skeptical, some hostile, and others simply looked relieved to be alive. Only the one called Preacher appeared at all grateful for the mercy being shown them, or so Caesar judged. He nodded at Luca, who gave the horses' hindquarters a resounding swat, sending them on their way. Nimble guards darted out of the way as the horses bolted away from the trench, taking the humans with them. The freed soldiers peered back over their shoulders at the apes until they finally vanished from view. Their stunned faces suggested the suspicion among some of the humans that the apes' show of mercy had just been a trick all along, that they had never truly believed that Caesar would set them free…

How little they understand us, he thought. *They cannot*

see past their fear to realize that apes only want peace.

Most apes at least.

Caesar wondered if he had erred in letting the soldiers live. This was hardly the first time that he had spared human lives as a show of good faith, but such gestures had yielded little in return. Was he foolish to keep striving for peace? The humans had shown no mercy to the apes they had slaughtered. Perhaps he *should* have executed the prisoners. That's what Koba would have done.

Which was perhaps reason enough *not* to do so...

He listened as the fading hoof beats of the horses were swallowed up by the forest. Maurice came up behind him, joining Caesar and Luca. He signed to Caesar:

Do you really think they'll give him the message?

"They *are* the message," Caesar replied. "I showed them mercy. He will see we are not savages." He spoke to convince himself as much as the others. "Let us hope this works. They are getting closer..."

Today's raid was the closest the humans had yet come to reaching the apes' hidden sanctuary. Caesar shuddered to think how far they might have gotten had Spear not managed to alert the cavalry in time. Only the guards at the wall had faced the invaders today, not their families and children. But how far would the humans get next time?

If there was a next time.

A sudden commotion, coming from the trenches, disturbed his reverie. Upset apes, shrieking and barking in alarm, swarmed toward him, but Caesar could not immediately determine what the trouble was—until Winter staggered out of the crowd, clutching his head. Blood streamed from a vicious gash on his brow, staining his snow-white pelt. Caesar noted with alarm that Winter's prisoner, the turncoat ape Red, was nowhere to be seen.

It was not hard to guess who had spilled Winter's blood.

Luca grunted in concern and loped to meet the other gorilla. A shaken Winter looked up at Luca, visibly distraught and humiliated.

Red attacked me, Winter signed. *He got away!*

Ashamed, the young gorilla looked toward Caesar. He lowered his eyes, unable to meet his leader's gaze.

I'm sorry, Winter signed. *Forgive me.*

Caesar said nothing, disturbed by the news. Red's escape spared him the necessity of deciding the fate of the turncoat ape, but it was troubling to know that Red and his fellow outcasts were still out there, collaborating with the humans hunting their own people. The very idea of apes siding with humans against apes was an affront to everything Caesar had fought and worked for all these many years.

At least, he thought, *they do not know where to find us.*

Yet.

4

Caesar led a somber procession through the forest, as the sun began to dip toward the west. He sat astride a horse, while behind him able-bodied apes assisted their injured brothers and sisters. The bodies of those lost in battle were draped over the backs of horses. The bodies of the humans had been left behind as a warning.

The ape leader was glad to leave the blood-soaked hillside behind, although the loss of life—and the constant threat posed by the relentless humans—weighed heavily on him. Red's vile threats echoed at the back of his mind, promising more trials to come. He was eager for this long day to be over.

His spirits lifted somewhat as he heard a low roar up ahead, coming from beyond the nearest trees. The roar grew steadily louder as an imposing waterfall came into view. White water cascaded down a sheer rock face nestled deep in the primeval wilderness, falling hundreds of feet to a wide mountain river below. Mist rose above the churning froth at the base of the cliff, and sunlight reflected off the rippling surface of the river.

A faint smile lifted the corners of Caesar's lips.

They were almost home.

The procession paused at the shore of the river to take advantage of the cool, clear water. The apes slaked their thirst and watered their horses. Wounds were washed to stave off infection. Weary legs took a break from marching.

Dismounting from his horse, Caesar found a private spot to rest and watch over the proceedings. He sat apart from the others, save for Maurice, who joined him by the river. Caesar welcomed his friend's company. Glancing over at Maurice, he saw a troubled look come over the orangutan's face as he gazed upon a cluster of apes a few yards away, who were taking stock of the guns and ammunition they had pillaged from the humans. Firearms were inspected and bartered. A gorilla tested the gunsight of an automatic rifle, taking aim at imaginary targets.

Maurice shook his head mournfully. *Look what we've become*, he signed.

Caesar envied his friend's gentle nature. He, too, would have preferred a world where apes had not been forced to adopt the weapons and warlike ways of humans, although chimpanzees had always been less averse to conflict than orangutans even before their respective intelligences had been heightened. He offered Maurice a reassuring smile.

We'll get through this, my friend, he signed.

Maurice appeared to take comfort from his leader's assurances. He nodded and started to reply, only to be interrupted by a high-pitched trumpeting sounding out over the placid scene. Caesar sprang to his feet and looked to the densely wooded slopes overlooking the river, where a multitude of apes broke from cover—after keeping watch over the returning warriors all this time.

Reacting to the alarm, hundreds of apes burst from camouflaged lookout posts hidden in the trees and along the edges of the cliff. High above the falls, a lone chimpanzee blew into a hollowed-out ram's horn, warning that trespassers were approaching. More apes answered the call.

Caesar shared a worried look with Maurice.

Had they been followed back to the falls—by humans?

The apes on the shore, who had been relaxing from their journey only moments before, took up their weapons and peered tensely back the way they had come. They formed living shields around the injured apes to protect them from whatever or whoever was coming. Newly acquired crossbows and rifles were turned toward the woods. Caesar braced himself for combat.

Perhaps the earlier raid had been merely the precursor to a larger assault?

The tension grew more unbearable with every heartbeat. Caesar held his breath as a small party of newcomers emerged on horseback from the woods. His nerves were stretched taut until the fading sunlight fell upon the faces and form of the riders—and Caesar's fears were instantly washed away by a sudden rush of happiness and relief.

Four apes sat atop horses draped with saddlebags, slumping wearily after riding for days. Dust caked their hairy bodies. They were no strangers to Caesar.

Far from it.

His heart swelling, Caesar and the others bounded toward the new arrivals, calling out to them as they dismounted. A strapping young chimpanzee with striking blue eyes approached Caesar, who waited expectantly. Old scars streaked the younger ape's chest and right shoulder. Maurice and the others backed away to give the two chimps more space. They stared intensely at each other, overcome with emotion, before Blue Eyes finally gestured to Caesar.

Hello, Father, he signed.

A broad smile broke out across Caesar's face as he joyfully embraced his eldest son. The crowd gibbered happily, celebrating the reunion, and joined in greeting Blue Eyes and his companions, who had been gone for months.

The return of his son, safe and apparently unharmed, was just what Caesar needed after the horrors of the day. He hugged Blue Eyes and patted his back affectionately before finally turning to the other travelers, whom he was also greatly pleased to see again. He grinned at Rocket, a nearly hairless chimpanzee who was roughly the same age as Caesar. Rocket had also been a prisoner at that forlorn primate shelter, along with Maurice, before Caesar had led the captive apes to freedom. Although he and Caesar had once been rivals and adversaries, those days were long behind them. Rocket had proven himself a staunch friend and ally time and again.

Welcome home, Caesar signed. *You look tired.*

Rocket shrugged and signed back. *It was a long journey.*

Father, Blue Eyes signed excitedly. *We found something!*

Caesar could tell from his son's eager expression that he bore glad tidings. He was eager to hear more, but perhaps in a more secure setting. The false alarm of moments ago reminded him just how exposed his forces were out in the open like this. In addition, he was certain that he was not the only ape who was more than ready for the comforts of home and hearth. And Blue Eyes' mother would be anxious to see her son as well.

Let's go inside, he signed. *You can tell me all about it.*

He led the assembled apes toward the outer edges of the falls, where they passed through high curtains of cascading water to enter the cavernous sanctuary beyond. A vast fortress hid behind the falls and the surrounding slopes, sheltering Caesar's people. Moss carpeted the rough stone floors and walls of the cavern. Shallow puddles gleamed like reflecting pools, while stacked tiers of rock created multiple levels for the apes to gather on, and the misty spray from the falls cooled the cave. Ape children hurried forward to greet the returning warriors, while their mothers chased after them, struggling with varying degrees of success to keep their excitable offspring under control. Males embraced their wives and sweethearts. Adults were swarmed by their younger siblings and cousins. Tears flowed also, as the friends and family of the fallen learned of their losses. Loved ones fretted over the injured. Healers were summoned to attend to the wounded.

Amidst the tumult, Caesar spied his wife, Cornelia, pushing her way toward him and Blue Eyes, her face beaming with excitement. Joy gleamed in her beautiful chestnut eyes. A crown of brightly colored vines and seed pods adorned her head. Blue Eyes' own face lit up as he spotted her as well.

Mother, he signed.

Reaching him, she embraced Blue Eyes, who hugged her back just as vigorously. A tentative yelp signaled the presence of a small chimpanzee, no more than two years old, who shyly hid behind Cornelia's legs.

Smiling, she coaxed the bashful toddler out of hiding.

Cornelius, she signed, *don't you recognize your brother?*

Blue Eyes crouched to stroke the little chimp's head. Cornelius relaxed, basking in his older brother's attention. Lifting her eyes from the touching scene, Cornelia grinned mischievously as she looked past Blue Eyes at an approaching ape.

Someone else has missed you too, she teased her eldest.

Rising to his feet, Blue Eyes turned to discover a lovely female chimpanzee standing right behind him. Lake was the same age as Blue Eyes and their mutual attraction was no secret to anyone who knew them. Caesar was amused by the rapt expression on his son's face as he gazed once

43

more upon his sweetheart, who smiled coyly back at him. Leaning toward each other, they tenderly pressed their brows together.

Caesar shared a knowing look with his wife, recalling the early days of their own courtship. He looked forward to becoming a grandfather someday.

Provided they found a way to stay safe from the humans.

The apes' council room was a cavern deep within the fortress. Mounted torches illuminated the grotto, throwing flickering shadows onto the rough-hewn walls. Caesar's symbol—a stylized diamond enclosed in a circle—was carved into the granite floor of the chamber. Only his closest confidants knew of the origin of the symbol, which was patterned after an attic window that once, many years ago, had been Caesar's only window on the world, back when he was an innocent young ape being raised by a loving human father. His world had grown immeasurably since those carefree days, but the symbol served to remind him where he had begun—and how far he'd come.

Caesar and his council—including Cornelia, Maurice, Luca, Winter, and Lake—had convened to hear what Blue Eyes and his expedition had discovered. Conscious of the never-ending threat posed by the increasingly aggressive humans, Caesar had dispatched his son and a few other trusted lieutenants to discover what lay beyond the besieged forest. Now the apes gathered in a circle as Blue Eyes and Rocket laid out a map upon the floor using colored stones and pebbles. Caesar did not recognize the terrain indicated by the stones, which was presumably located far beyond the territory his people had previously explored. Blue Eyes, the dust of the road now brushed from his fur, pointed enthusiastically at one spot in particular.

This place, he signed. *It's beautiful.*

Luca pondered the map. *And you're sure there are no humans anywhere near it?*

None, Rocket insisted.

Blue Eyes looked at Caesar. *This is it, Father. We can start over. A new home for our people.*

Caesar was encouraged by his son's report, but was careful not to raise his hopes too high or too soon. Age had taught him caution, and the danger of jumping to conclusions too soon. Acting without thinking too often led to disaster. Caesar had learned that many years ago when he had angrily lashed out at a human for the first time—and found himself confined to a cage as a result.

An elderly orangutan, christened Percy, leaned forward to inspect the map. He gestured at a row of large, jagged stones.

What is beyond these mountains?

Blue Eyes lifted a small leather pouch from the floor and thrust his hand inside. Extracting a handful of golden sand, he spilled it dramatically onto the map between the mountains and their proposed new home.

A desert, he signed. *We had to cross it, too. The journey is long, but that is why the humans will not find us.*

He wiped the last traces of sand from his hands and looked around expectantly at the faces of the council members. He was obviously thrilled by his discovery. That Rocket vouched for his glowing description of this distant paradise carried much weight with Caesar as well. Not that Caesar didn't trust his son's judgment. There had been a time, some five winters ago, when Blue Eyes had been rash and rebellious, straining the relations between father and son. The jagged scars on Blue Eyes' chest and shoulder, left behind by the claws of an angry grizzly bear that had taken him by surprise during a hunt, were a lasting reminder of how careless and impulsive the young chimp had once been, but Blue Eyes had grown and matured since then, having learned many hard lessons during Koba's brief reign of terror. Caesar was proud of the ape his son had become, and took his counsel seriously. He raised his hand to convey as much, when Winter leapt to his feet and signed his opinion.

We should leave tonight!

Tonight? Lake protested from her place by Blue Eyes' side. *Are you crazy?*

How much longer can we wait? Winter signed. *The humans are getting closer. They won't stop until they kill us all!*

It was obvious that the day's atrocities—and Red's venomous words—had shaken the young gorilla even more than Caesar had realized. Blue Eyes reached out to reassure the other ape, placing a comforting hand upon his arm.

Winter, he began.

The gorilla pulled away from Blue Eyes, rejecting the overture. Luca growled angrily at his protégé, who was embarrassing him before the council. Blue Eyes was Caesar's son and heir. He was not to be disrespected in this manner.

But Winter could not contain himself.

He's been gone, he signed, indicating Blue Eyes. *He doesn't know how hard it's been!*

Caesar frowned. Blue Eyes had proven himself in combat against both the humans and Koba's revolutionaries; Caesar knew his son fully appreciated the danger posed by the humans. He held his tongue, however, not wanting to fight Blue Eyes' battles for him. His son deserved the chance to respond to Winter's challenge on his own.

I know you are scared, Blue Eyes signed. *We all are, but this will take planning—*

"*If* we go," Caesar said aloud.

All eyes turned toward him. Blue Eyes was clearly taken aback by his father's terse interruption. Disappointment showed upon his face. Caesar was pained by his reaction, but had felt compelled to speak before matters went too far. He respected his son's advice and passion, but this was not a decision to be made lightly... and, ultimately, it was his decision to make.

There might come a day when Blue Eyes would succeed him as leader of the apes.

But not today.

"There were only four of you, son," he attempted to explain. "There are hundreds of us."

You said it was dangerous, Maurice added. *Especially getting past the humans, out of the woods.*

The prospect of leading a vast exodus of apes, including females and children and the old and infirm, out of the safety of the forest was a daunting one, even with the promise of a safer haven somewhere at the end of the journey.

"Father, trust me." Blue Eyes' voice rang out with passion. "This is a risk worth taking."

Perhaps, Caesar thought. Certainly, staying put posed a risk as well.

Blue Eyes appealed to Cornelia, who sat at her husband's side.

"Mother...? What do you think?"

If you believe in this place, she signed, *so do I. But your father is right. We must consider carefully.*

To his credit, Blue Eyes nodded in agreement, accepting her views without protest; Caesar took this as further proof of how greatly his son had matured over the years.

He softened his expression as he addressed the council.

"We have been through much. But today... my son brings us hope."

He ambled forward and laid his hand upon Blue Eyes' head, smiling fondly. He had no intention of letting this dispute come between them, or cast a shadow over his son's long-awaited homecoming.

"It is so good to see you." His throat tightened as strong emotion thickened his voice. "I am very proud of you."

He hoped Blue Eyes would never doubt that.

5

Drums pounded rhythmically above the roar of the waterfall as twilight fell over the forest, streaking the horizon with vivid shades of purple and crimson. The entire population of the fortress, young and old alike, had gathered on the banks of the river to bid farewell to those slain by the humans. Drummers slapped their instruments with their hands and feet, as though beating for hearts that were now forever still. Mourners chanted along with the drums. Wildflowers adorned the bodies of the fallen, which were laid out on large unlit wooden pyres. Chimps, gorillas, orangutans, and bonobos rested together, just as they had lived together in life.

Unlike humans, the apes had yet to segregate themselves by breed, or pit one class of ape against another. Caesar wondered if perhaps that was because they remained united against a common enemy. He prayed his people would never divide themselves by species, even if the human threat someday passed away.

Apes together strong.

Accompanied by his friends and family, Caesar watched solemnly as the torch bearers approached the pyres, which were much larger than he would have wished. Over a score of apes waited to be consumed by the coming blaze. The tragic waste of simian life sickened Caesar.

The pain in his green eyes was not lost on Maurice.

You feel responsible, the orangutan signed.

"I am responsible," Caesar said softly. "Our youngest have known only bloodshed."

Koba *started this war*, Maurice signed. *He is to blame.*

"No." Caesar shook his head. "I should have seen… that he could not forget what the humans did to him. That he would seek revenge. But I was blind."

A former lab animal who had been subjected to cruel tests and tortures before Caesar liberated him, Koba had learned only hate from humanity. In the end, that hate had driven him to choose war over peace, and rebellion over his loyalty to Caesar. Both apes and humans were still paying for Koba's vengeance, even though that tormented, treacherous ape had died years ago.

"He was my friend," Caesar said. "And his blood is on my hands too."

The torch bearers lit the pyres. Sticky sap crackled and bubbled, causing the flames to spread quickly until the bodies of the dead were all but lost in a rising orange and yellow blaze. Caesar could feel the heat of the conflagrations against his face and fur. Nestled securely in his mother's arms, little Cornelius whimpered in fright at the tremendous fires. Cornelia stroked the child's head to calm him. Her eyes were wet with grief.

No one could have known how much darkness was living inside him, Maurice insisted.

Caesar wished he could believe that.

Sparks and flames and smoke drifted upwards from the pyres, along with, perhaps, the souls of the martyred apes. The humans had believed in an afterlife, Caesar knew, where the living would someday be reunited with the dead. Caesar had no way of knowing if this was true for apes as well, or even if he wanted it to be.

Because that might mean he would meet Koba again.

Caesar held Koba's life in his hand. The renegade ape dangled high above the gutted remains of an unfinished human skyscraper in the ruins of San Francisco. Smoke and flames and red-hot embers rose from the building's sub-basements, where an explosion had just brought down large portions of the structure, injuring several apes and nearly killing both Caesar and Koba as they battled for primacy. Caesar, wounded and bleeding, stood upon an unstable steel girder as he held onto Koba's forearm with one hand. Only Caesar's own waning strength kept Koba from falling hundreds of feet to his death.

Koba glared up at Caesar with his one good eye; the other had been blinded by the humans long before the two apes had first met. Old scars bore witness to his brutal treatment at the hands of his human captors so many years ago, but could that possibly excuse Koba's own crimes? He had plotted against Caesar, attempted to assassinate him, and launched an all-out assault on a human colony that had all but extinguished any hope of peace between humans and apes. If any ape deserved to die, it was Koba.

Caesar wrestled with his conscience. Ape shall not kill ape *was the first law he had taught his people after raising their intelligences. He believed in that law with all his heart.*

But Koba no longer deserved to be treated like an ape.

Caesar let go of Koba's arm and watched his old friend fall. Screaming in fear, Koba plummeted toward his death, falling endlessly toward the raging fire far below, which blazed like a funeral pyre...

"Koba!" Caesar cried out as he woke from the nightmare. Green eyes snapped open even as his heart pounded like the drums that had sent the dead on their way mere hours ago.

Escaping the burning tower of his dreams, he found himself in his private dwelling in the fortress: a small cave in the upper levels of the cliff face, hidden behind cascading sheets of water that formed the far wall of the chamber, across from the comfortable bed Caesar had built with his own hands when the apes had first sought shelter in the caverns behind the falls. Cornelia and their youngest slumbered peacefully beside him, their dreams untroubled by past betrayals. Blue Eyes rested nearby in his own bed, sleeping soundly after his epic journey. Caesar suspected that Blue Eyes would soon seek new lodgings to share with Lake, but for now he savored having his family all in one place.

The memory of Koba's death receded back into the past as Caesar seized on the here and now, the better to put the nightmare behind him. He breathed deeply to calm himself. His racing heart slowed to a more moderate pace. Moonlight filtered through the falling water, casting a subdued blue radiance upon the floor of the cave. Not for the first time, the sight and sound of the falling water soothed Caesar's spirits. He still missed their former city in the trees, where the apes had lived and thrived before Koba's war, but he was growing used to their new residence in the fortress, which had so far proven much more secure and harder to find as far as the humans were concerned. If that soldier, Preacher, were to be believed, the humans were still searching in vain for the concealed fortress.

And now Blue Eyes wanted Caesar to move their people again?

His family at peace around him, Caesar contemplated

the moonlit waters falling ceaselessly before his sleepless gaze. There was a rugged beauty to the falls that he would surely miss should he indeed decide to—

Three dark shapes, veiled by the falling water, descended past the opening, quickly dropping out of sight.

Caesar blinked in confusion, not entirely sure what he had just seen. The blurry, indistinct forms had vanished just as quickly as they appeared, before he'd truly had a chance to register their existence. Had it just been a trick of the light and foaming water? Rising warily from the bed without disturbing Cornelia and their child, he slowly approached the wall of water, which appeared normal once again. Caesar briefly dared to hope that his weary eyes had deceived him, but then he spotted something peculiar: a strange thin line hanging down the side of the falls, being whipped about by the cascading water.

That had never been there before.

Mystified, Caesar reached uncertainly for the line, then threw caution to the wind and plunged his arm into the icy water and grasped for it. Determined fingers closed on the line and yanked it toward him, away from the cascade. His anxious gaze fell upon a taut length of red nylon rope.

A climbing rope.

Understanding dawned, bringing a sudden jolt of fear that chased away the last of his late-night grogginess. Instantly alert, he turned toward his family and saw Blue Eyes stirring. Sitting up, the sleepy chimp peered at his father with bleary eyes. Confusion was written on his face.

Stay here, Caesar signed urgently. *Protect your mother and brother.*

Blue Eyes immediately grasped that the situation was deadly serious. He nodded grimly, even without understanding the nature of the emergency. Caesar regretted that there was no time to explain, but knew that he was needed elsewhere.

The humans have found us at last. No ape is safe.

Three silent figures moved briskly and efficiently through an unlit corridor in the hidden fortress. The roaring falls, which had helped conceal the apes' sanctuary for so long, now served to muffle the stealthy tread of the strike force. Their leader smirked in the darkness, appreciating the irony.

Human see, human do.

Emerald beams from their rifles' laser sights swept the mossy granite catacombs before them as the soldiers advanced, seeking their primary target. Encountering no opposition, they came to a fork in the corridor.

The leader did not hesitate. Undaunted by the dilemma, he signaled the other two soldiers to go left, while he struck out toward the right on his own.

Eenie, meenie, he thought.

Caesar crept cautiously through the sleeping halls of the fortress, making his way down a narrow, winding passage. He was torn between sounding a general alarm, which might provoke the invaders to abandon stealth and open fire indiscriminately, and trying to ambush the humans before they even knew that their incursion had been detected. At the moment Caesar held the advantage of surprise in that the intruders were unaware that he was hunting them. Perhaps there was still a chance to end the attack before it even commenced?

Or was he just fooling himself?

Rounding a corner, he came upon a huge hulking figure. Startled, he jumped backwards in alarm, only to hear a deep, familiar grunt. Luca was standing guard in the corridor, cradling a rifle in his large, meaty arms. The vigilant gorilla peered at Caesar in surprise, no doubt wondering what his leader was doing prowling the fortress at this late hour. His eyes widened beneath his bony brow.

Caesar! he signed. *Is everything all right?*

Caesar shook his head. *How many others on patrol? Five?* The gorilla held up his fingers. *Six—?*

Get them! Caesar ordered. *Rocket, too!*

Cornelia crouched behind several large, mossy rock formations in their family dwelling, her youngest son clinging to her back. Ordinarily, the rocks served as furniture—seats, tables, shelves—but now they shielded her and her sons from whatever menace stalked the sleeping fortress. Straining her ears, she heard no shouting and fighting, but she knew that Caesar would not have instructed Blue Eyes to protect her and little Cornelius unless the danger was both real and serious, which meant only one thing:

Humans.

Blue Eyes gestured for Cornelia and the toddler to stay behind him. He clutched a sharp wooden spear as he stood watch over the shadowy cavern, which was lit only by the moonlight coming through the falls—and a bright green beam shining into the dwelling from the corridor outside. Cornelia knew enough of human tools and weapons to recognize the unnatural beam of light and know what it was called.

A laser.

The emerald beam was proof that the enemy had penetrated the fortress and was drawing nearer. Crouching between her and the invader, Blue Eyes stared intently at the laser light. His body tensed, coiled to pounce as the eerie green glow spilled into the dwelling, sweeping its interior coldly and methodically. Cornelia's keen ears picked up low, furtive breathing and footsteps just outside the cave, drawing ever closer and closer...

For a moment, her memory flashed back to being imprisoned in a human lab many years ago, cowering in her cage, waiting for the scientists to come and conduct their cruel "experiments" on her. She felt just as trapped and frightened now—except that now she had to fear for her children's safety as well.

Both my sons are in danger.

Blue Eyes sprang forward as a shadowy figure violated the sanctity of their home. Cornelia reached back and covered Cornelius's eyes as a brief, violent scuffle played out in the murky cave, silhouetted against the moonlit falls. The green light darted chaotically across the walls, threatening to blind her if it came her way. Inarticulate grunts and groans disturbed the nocturnal stillness. Her nose wrinkled at the stink of freshly spilled blood.

Human blood.

Blue Eyes stood, panting, over the body of his victim: a dark-haired human female wearing a damp military uniform. Smeared camo makeup hid her face. AΩ was tattooed on her hairless neck. An automatic rifle lay upon the floor of the cavern, just beyond reach of her limp, unmoving fingers. Bright arterial blood seeped from a deep wound above her heart—and dripped from the point of Blue Eyes' spear.

One human dead, Cornelia thought, *but how many more are there?*

She was appalled by the violence, but relieved that it was Blue Eyes who was standing over the dead human and not the other way around. Grateful for his protection, she looked proudly upon her firstborn—even as another green laser beam targeted the back of his head.

No! she opened her mouth to scream. *Not my child!*

The soldier stalked the dark, narrow corridor, the beam from his laser sight lighting his way through the pitch-black tunnel. Glancing about apprehensively, he whispered into his headset:

"Nothing down here, Colonel. Any sign of him?"

In the darkened passage, it was almost impossible for him to see what was right ahead or might be coming up behind him. Waiting anxiously for an update from his commander, the soldier failed to notice a wiry gray shape emerge from the deep shadows behind him and creep toward the unsuspecting human.

"Colonel—?"

Powerful hands, many times stronger than any human's, grabbed the soldier from behind and smashed him into a granite wall as easily as if he were a rag doll. Flesh and bone crunched against the unyielding stone. Silenced muzzle flashes strobed the corridor as his finger involuntarily pulled the trigger in a terminal spasm. The rifle flared only briefly before darkness reclaimed the passageway, even as the lifeless soldier landed in a heap upon the floor. Blood stained the wall where his head had collided with solid rock.

Flickering torchlight entered the hall, falling upon Rocket as the triumphant chimpanzee reached down to retrieve the dead soldier's rifle. He looked up at Caesar and Luca as they arrived. The gorilla walked behind Caesar, bearing the torch. Caesar was impressed and relieved by how quickly Rocket had dispatched that soldier, but his friend looked more worried than excited about his kill.

I heard him talking, Rocket signed and pointed to the body. *The Colonel… he's here!*

Caesar's eyes went wide. Taking the torch from Luca, he came forward to take a closer look at the dead human. The light from the torch revealed that the body belonged to Travis, one of the soldiers whose lives Caesar had spared before. He was the agitated, excitable one, Caesar remembered, although the man's lifeless face no longer displayed any feelings at all. Caesar frowned, realizing that his moment of mercy had only granted Travis a few more hours of life—and possibly endangered them all.

How did they find us? Caesar wondered. *I was certain we weren't followed.*

Static crackled and a gruff voice escaped the dead man's headset:

"I got him, soldier—"

Caesar snatched the dislodged headset and held it to his ear.

"I got him," the voice repeated. "Let's go."

Caesar listened to the transmission with mounting horror. He knew that there could be only one "him" that the soldiers were after.

Me, he realized. *They came for me.*

But if they "got" another ape by mistake, that could only mean…

My family!

Panicked, Caesar let go of the torch and bounded through the fortress, practically bouncing off the walls, leaving Rocket and Luca behind in his desperate haste to get back to his cave even as he feared that he was already too late.

I should have never left them alone!

He burst into his dwelling just in time to see a solitary figure fish the red nylon rope from the waterfall and start to clip it to an anchor on his belt. Silhouetted against the moonlit cascade, he turned toward Caesar at the sound of the ape's approach. For the first time, Caesar laid eyes upon the humans' infamous leader.

The Colonel.

He presented a nightmarish figure in the underlit gloom of the violated dwelling. Shocks of greasy camo paint darkened his features, beneath a shaved skull that was even balder than Rocket's. A sandy-brown beard made up for his hairless head, while pitiless azure eyes were ringed by painted black shadows. His military fatigues were still damp from his climb down by the waterfall earlier. A rifle was slung over his shoulder.

The man's eyes widened at the sight of Caesar, and his gaze darted away from Caesar to something on the floor. The ape tracked his gaze to discover—

Blue Eyes sprawled lifelessly, a bullet wound in the back of his skull, not far from the body of a dead human soldier. Cornelia lay beside him, a bright red circle between her eyes. That both were beyond saving was painfully, horribly obvious.

His wife… his son… were gone.

Time froze for a moment as Caesar's entire world came crashing down on top of him. He reeled unsteadily, every muscle going weak, until he lifted his eyes to see the Colonel still standing there, only a few yards away from his victims.

Fury gripped Caesar. Baring his fangs, he growled at the murderer, who hastily swung his gun off his shoulder. Self-preservation drove Caesar to dive for cover behind the nearest large rocks just as the Colonel opened fire. The rifle's muzzle flared brightly and bullets chipped away at the stones protecting Caesar, who feared that it wouldn't be long before his shelter gave out.

But the furious roar of many apes rushing toward the dwelling convinced the Colonel that a strategic retreat was in order. Backing toward the falls, he shouted into his headset.

"Get me out! Now!"

Turning away from Caesar, the Colonel leapt straight through the waterfall into the open air beyond. Daring to lift his head above the rocks, Caesar spied the human dangling on the other side of the falls, barely discernible through the frothing cascade of water. He watched in dismay as the Colonel held on tightly to the nylon rope as he was pulled upward away from the cave opening.

No!

Caesar sprang from cover to charge after the Colonel, as apes poured into the dwelling, too late. He barreled past the other apes, including Rocket and Luca, who watched in shock as Caesar flung himself into the falls after the Colonel.

You can't escape me! I won't allow it!

Intent on revenge, he barely noticed the cold water striking him as he plunged through the falls, hundreds of feet above the churning river far below. His flailing hands grabbed onto the rope, which swung wildly beneath his weight. Holding onto the cable for dear life, he peered up at the Colonel, who was already high above him as he ascended toward the top of the falls. The sudden jerking of the rope alerted the Colonel, who looked down to see Caesar furiously climbing toward him.

You murdered my family! Your life is over!

Seemingly unfazed by the alarming sight of a vengeful ape coming at him, the Colonel drew a carbon-steel combat knife from his boot and scowled at Caesar, who scrambled up the rope as only an ape could until he was almost within reach of the human. He bared his teeth and gums, wanting nothing more than to tear the Colonel apart with his bare hands.

He never got the chance, however, as the Colonel's knife sliced through the shrinking length of rope between them, cutting Caesar loose. He plummeted toward the water far below, reaching fruitlessly for his enemy even as he fell.

He hit the water hard, the impact knocking the breath from him, and sank below the foam into the river. The sudden immersion came as a jolt and he kicked and splashed frantically back toward the surface. Gasping for breath, his head broke through the surface of the water as he frantically searched for the murderer. Despair and frustration clawed at his heart as, through the cold, clammy mist, he spied the Colonel disappearing over the top of the cliff, hundreds of feet beyond Caesar's reach.

The killer had escaped.

For now, Caesar thought bitterly. *Only for now.*

6

Caesar watched in silence as the bodies of Cornelia and Blue Eyes were lifted from the blood-stained stone floor, along with the body of the dead human female, whose remains were treated with considerably less reverence. Still soaked from the plunge into the river, he sat motionless, sinking into a whirlpool of grief and rage, as his murdered wife and firstborn were carted away by hushed, attentive apes. His closest friends—Luca, Rocket, and Maurice— stood beside him in this time of tragedy, but Caesar was too overcome by emotion to even acknowledge their presence. Only the volcanic intensity of his gaze hinted at the all-consuming fury growing inside him. His heart felt as hard and deadly as the bullets that had killed his loved ones.

How did they find us? Rocket signed to Luca. *How did they know where Caesar slept?*

Luca shook his head in bewilderment as he replied. *Only apes knew.*

Two young gorillas entered the dwelling and reported to Luca, who as leader of the gorilla guards was in charge of the fortress's security. The apes shot worried glances at

Caesar as they delivered ominous tidings.

Winter was not at his post, one of them signed. *We can't find him anywhere.*

Caesar followed the discussion intently but remained as still as stone. Luca and Maurice exchanged worried looks as an unthinkable possibility was forced upon them.

Could he have turned against us? Maurice signed.

Caesar recalled the white gorilla's obvious fear and distress earlier, when faced with the possibility of being hunted down by the Colonel and his soldiers. It was possible, he supposed, that Winter was merely a deserter, fleeing the fortress to seek safety elsewhere, but then how did the humans find the apes' hidden fortress—and know where to look for Caesar? As Luca had just observed, only an ape could have given away that secret.

And Winter was missing.

Suspicion hardened into certainty as Caesar found yet another target for his wrath. Luca must have arrived at the same conclusion, for he turned to Caesar with a look of profound remorse upon his broad, heavy countenance.

I'm sorry, Caesar, he signed. *Winter was in my command.*

Caesar said nothing, but did not blame Luca for Winter's apparent perfidy. He knew what it was like to be betrayed by an ape you trusted. He had not seen Koba's treachery coming, despite too many warning signs.

"My youngest," Caesar asked finally. "Where is he?"

He dreaded hearing that Cornelius had perished as well, although it was hard to imagine that the toddler had survived where his mother and older brother had not. Then again, the Colonel had been after a full-grown chimpanzee, not a toddler. Was it possible that Cornelius had been overlooked by the assassin?

They're still looking for him, Luca signed.

THE OFFICIAL MOVIE NOVELIZATION

For him or for his body? Caesar thought. He looked away from Luca, not wanting to know what the mournful silverback meant. He wasn't sure he could bear losing his other son as well.

Let's help them look, Maurice suggested to the others.

Caesar assumed the orangutan wanted to give him a chance to grieve for his loved ones in privacy. He appreciated the gesture as Maurice herded the others out of the cave, leaving Caesar alone with his sorrow.

And his anger.

Caesar waited for tears to come, but his desire for revenge burned too hot to allow for weeping. His seething gaze traveled to the spot where he had found Blue Eyes and Cornelia lying dead upon the rough, cold floor. Their spilled blood had seeped into the porous stone, leaving the stain of murder upon it. Blue Eyes' spear still lay upon the floor not far from where his body had rested. Its bloody tip declared that Blue Eyes had died trying to protect his family, but this was cold comfort to his father. Stirring at last, Caesar found himself drawn to the site. He staggered toward it as though in a trance.

Two brass bullet casings gleamed in the moonlight. Caesar crouched to inspect them, unable to look away from the evidence. The shells were physical proof of what had happened, forcing him to face the fact that this was not merely another nightmare from which he would soon wake to find his family still alive and intact. Cornelia and Blue Eyes were not just sleeping while he darkly dreamed of war and betrayal; they were truly gone for good.

But... only *two* shell casings?

He reached for the shells, but was startled by a faint sound behind him. Snarling, he snatched the fallen spear from the floor and whirled about to confront whoever dared to invade his home. So intense was his rage, his seething need to avenge his family, that it took him a moment to realize that the noise was coming not from some lurking human assassin but from his own terrified child, who was peeking out fearfully from a shadowy crevice in the rocks. Eyes wide, Cornelius shrunk from the intimidating sight of Caesar brandishing the bloody spear, his fur bristling aggressively.

Cornelius!

Shocked back to his senses, Caesar was stricken by the frightened look on his little son's face. Lowering the spear, he softened his expression and knelt down before the petrified child. He held out his hand, but Cornelius remained reluctant to emerge from the cleft. Caesar realized that his son had been cowering in the rocks all this time, afraid to show his face amidst all the commotion. He couldn't blame Cornelius for being scared; the toddler had just seen his mother and brother brutally executed right before his eyes.

And his father wasn't there to protect him, Caesar thought. *To protect any of them.*

Forcing a gentle smile to his lips, Caesar beckoned to his only surviving son, but Cornelius's traumatized eyes stayed fixed on the spear in his father's hand. Caesar was ashamed to realize that he was still holding onto the weapon. Moving slowly, so as not to alarm Cornelius, he gently placed the spear down onto the floor and held out his arms.

Come to me, son, Caesar thought. *Don't be afraid.*

Sobbing, the little chimp crept cautiously out into the open and over to his father. Caesar pulled him into a tight embrace, his heart aching as he felt Cornelius's small body trembling against his. His throat tightened, so that he couldn't have spoken even if he'd tried.

Cornelius's survival seemed like a miracle.

But Caesar would have his revenge, no matter what.

* * *

The armory was kept off-limits to most apes, Caesar having learned a brutal lesson from Koba that not all apes could be trusted with guns. Rows of scavenged weapons, taken from the humans after various skirmishes, lined the grim stone walls of the cavern, along with a generous supply of ammunition. Alone in the armory, Caesar picked up a military assault rifle to inspect it.

Maurice appeared in the chamber's one and only entrance. Caesar glanced back and saw a troubled look in the orangutan's gentle brown eyes. He looked away from Maurice, returning his attention to the armory's store of weapons. He put down the rifle and examined another, but Maurice would not be ignored. He grunted to get Caesar's attention.

We need to think about what to do next, he signed. *The humans know where we are now. They will be back.*

Caesar nodded, still hefting the rifle.

"Tell everyone... to prepare for the journey... to our new home."

Just like Winter had wanted, Caesar recalled, *before he betrayed us.* The bitter irony was not lost on Caesar. If he had listened to Winter's terror-stricken plea and ordered an immediate evacuation, would Cornelia and Blue Eyes still be alive? Could they have escaped before the humans attacked?

It's the wisest decision, Maurice said, visibly relieved. He offered Caesar a sad smile. *And what better way to honor your son's memory.*

Caesar appreciated the thought, but he wasn't ready to wax sentimental, not while his family had yet to be avenged—and the Colonel still lived. He kept on inspecting the guns, searching to find the one in the best condition. He could take no chances when it came to the urgent task ahead.

Maurice lingered in the armory, waiting for Caesar. He shifted his weight, eying Caesar uneasily as the chimpanzee remained preoccupied with picking out a weapon. Maurice grunted softly.

Caesar looked up at him, annoyed at the interruption, even though he knew Maurice was only thinking of the welfare of their people. Male orangutans were solitary creatures by nature, so Maurice had no family to speak of, but he had always been devoted to the ape community.

When should we leave? he asked.

Caesar selected a gun, testing its weight. "I'm not coming with you."

Dismay appeared upon Maurice's face. He stared at Caesar in shock, even as he belatedly grasped his friend's intentions.

You're not going after them…?

Caesar didn't see how he had a choice. Gripping the gun, he stared fiercely into space, wishing he had the Colonel in his sights at this very minute.

"Not them. *Him.*"

By morning, preparations for the exodus were already underway. The entire population had spilled out of the fortress onto the riverbank as apes of every species hurriedly loaded up a caravan of horses with whatever provisions and possessions they could take with them. It was an ambitious undertaking, but none questioned its necessity; last night's invasion—and the deaths of Caesar's wife and heir—had been more than enough to convince the apes that the fortress was no longer safe. Worried eyes kept watching the trees, half-expecting the humans to return in force at any moment. Armed apes stood watch as the assembly made ready to set forth in search of a new home that only a handful of them had ever seen. Of the four apes who knew the way to their destination, only three were still alive.

Heads turned as Caesar made his way through the teeming crowd, holding onto Cornelius's small hand. Busy apes paused in their hasty labors to cast pitying looks at their grieving leader, mourning the tragedies that had befallen him. Hushed whispers and somber gazes followed Caesar, who kept his gaze fixed directly ahead of him, ignoring the sympathy and condolences offered him by his people. There would be time enough for mourning later, perhaps. For now, his mind was set on one task and one task alone.

Once he made sure his only living child was safe.

He found his inner circle waiting for him further down the river, away from the falls. Maurice, Luca, and Rocket were gathered along the shore, sadly watching him approach with little Cornelius. Lake in particular gazed down at the child, who was understandably apprehensive and subdued, and tried to give Cornelius a reassuring smile. She looked up at Caesar.

"You loved my son," he said to her. "Look after his brother... until I return."

His voice was gruff, his expression stoic. Only his eyes betrayed how hard this was for him—and the anguish he carried.

Lake's own eyes welled with tears. She nodded gravely and signed.

You have my word.

That was good enough for Caesar, but Maurice waddled forward. It seemed that he was still not entirely reconciled to what was happening. He shook his great head from side to side, regarding Caesar with a dubious expression.

And if you don't return? he asked.

Caesar paused only a moment before answering. "Then please make sure he knows who his father was."

Lake crouched before Cornelius and held out her hand, smiling warmly, but the toddler only tightened his grip on Caesar's hand. He peered anxiously up at Caesar, as though fearful of losing his father as well. The thought of abandoning his child at this juncture broke what was left of Caesar's heart, but his resolve to revenge himself upon the Colonel remained undimmed. He guided Cornelius toward Lake, even as Maurice still attempted to turn him from his course.

Caesar, your son needs you, the orangutan signed. *We need you. We trust you to lead us.*

There was wisdom in Maurice's words, Caesar knew, but his friend failed to realize just how furiously the rage within him burned. There was nothing left inside him except the need for vengeance. He could be no father to his son, no leader to his people, as long as thoughts of revenge consumed his every waking moment. He looked down at Cornelius, remembering how close he had come to spearing his own son only hours ago. The fear on the toddler's face as he'd stared in horror at his father's wrath was seared into Caesar's memory.

"I no longer trust myself," he confessed.

A crestfallen look came over Maurice's face and he fell silent, apparently at a loss as to how to respond. The melancholy interlude was interrupted by the arrival of Spear, flanked by two chimpanzee lieutenants. Caesar had summoned Spear for a reason, impressed by how the valiant ape had handled himself during yesterday's raid on the wall. Spear's bravery and quick thinking had saved many lives.

"Apes… are in your care now," Caesar said.

He had asked Luca to lead their people in his place,

but the gorilla had declined, perhaps still blaming himself for Winter's apparent treachery. Rocket had not wanted the position either, for reasons Caesar didn't entirely understand. Perhaps he didn't fully trust himself as well? They had all suffered much in recent years. Rocket had lost his own son, Ash, to Koba's madness only a few years ago. No doubt Blue Eyes' death had hit Rocket hard as well. Ash and Blue Eyes had been best friends, growing up together, and now both of them were gone.

Let Spear take charge then, Caesar thought. *A new leader to take our people to a new home.*

Spear accepted the responsibility without protest. He nodded solemnly.

How long until you rejoin us? he asked.

"I don't know." Caesar mustered a smile he didn't feel. "Very soon, I hope. Be careful."

Spear knelt and held out an open palm in supplication. Caesar gave the young ape his blessing, while privately wondering if he would ever personally look upon the supposed haven Blue Eyes had found. In truth, Caesar had no way of knowing if he would survive the mission before him. It might well be that killing the Colonel would cost him his own life.

He would consider that a fair exchange.

Spear rose and set off to carry out Caesar's decree. Within hours, before the morning sun had even reached its zenith, the caravan was ready to depart. Spear rode ahead and barked out commands to the assemblage. Apes mounted horses, assisting the young and the elderly as needed, and fell into line with Spear and the vanguard of the procession, which consisted of hundreds of apes, their steeds, and their supplies. Caesar took a moment to survey the impressive sight of his people on the move, and wished them well in their travels, before turning his back on the caravan and walking off in the opposite direction. His solitary figure moved against the flow of the crowd until he reached his own horse and climbed onto it. His heels dug into the horse's side, urging it on.

He left his friends—and his son—behind him on the shore. He could feel their eyes upon him as he rode away.

But he did not turn back.

7

Caesar rode alone through the forest, a rifle slung across his back. For a time, he could still hear the massive exodus setting off back at the falls, but the noise gradually subsided as he headed down an old man-made road through the woods. Foliage encroached on the cracked and pitted asphalt, which was still divided by a painted yellow strip. An abandoned truck sporting the faded logo of a forgotten soft-drink company rusted nearby. It seemed as though Caesar had the forest to himself until a sudden rustling behind him sent him on his guard. Turning his horse around, he peered warily at the shadowy woods, ready to flee or defend himself if necessary. He cradled the rifle in his arms and released the safety. He and his people had been caught by surprise before.

Never again, he vowed.

The steady clip-clopping of hooves reached his ears, preceding the arrival of three apes riding out of the trees. Maurice, Rocket, and Luca trotted toward him on horseback, openly defying his decision to embark on this quest alone. The riders came to a halt only a few yards in front of him, braving Caesar's scowl and smoldering glare. He was not happy to see them.

This was his risk to take, not theirs.

The human base camp is always moving, Luca signed. *But my scouts think they know where it is. Let me take you.*

Rocket held up a rifle of his own. *You'll need me to back you up.*

Caesar was unmoved by their arguments.

"No," he said firmly.

Please, Rocket signed. *I know what it's like to lose a son.*

His heartfelt plea gave Caesar pause. Ash had died at Koba's hands, hurled from a great height when the young chimp had refused a command to execute defenseless humans. Caesar had not personally witnessed Ash's murder, but Blue Eyes had... and Caesar *had* seen how much the loss of Ash had pained Rocket, who had never had the opportunity to avenge his son because Caesar had killed Koba instead.

I killed Ash's killer, Caesar reflected. *Can I now deny Rocket a chance to help me avenge my own son? And Luca an opportunity to make right what Winter may have done?*

That hardly seemed fair.

I might not make it back, he signed.

That's why I'm coming, Maurice insisted. *To make sure you do.*

Caesar realized that his friends would not be dissuaded any more than he would in their place. Bowing to the inevitable, while hoping that he was not leading them to their deaths, he nodded and turned his horse back the way he'd been going before. The other apes fell in behind him.

It's the four of us then, Caesar thought, *against the Colonel and his soldiers. But I'll take four apes against any number of humans...*

The hunting party rode in silence for a time, not

wasting breath on conversation, as they gradually made their way north along the coast until they came within sight of a small bay directly ahead. A cold wind blew off the water, salting the air. Gulls squawked in the distance. Caesar briefly halted and pointed to a thin black tendril of smoke rising up through the gray overcast sky many miles ahead. The apes slowed and exchanged quizzical looks.

The humans' camp?

Luca frowned, clearly troubled at the prospect of what they might find there. Such as, perhaps, a turncoat white gorilla?

We shall see, Caesar thought.

They rode toward the distant smoke, heading further down toward the shore, and gradually came upon what appeared to be an abandoned oyster farm on and about the bluffs overlooking the mud flats at the edge of the water. Dilapidated shacks, docks, and boathouses had lost most of their peeling paint to the elements, and were overgrown with seaside shrubs and grasses. An overturned barge lay half-buried on the beach, its rotting keel encrusted with barnacles. Derelict cars and trucks, along with pieces of rusty machinery, were being steadily reclaimed by nature. At least one building had apparently caught fire at some point, whether intentionally or by accident it was impossible to tell. A wooden sign, welcoming visitors, dangled on a chain beneath a weathered wooden gateway at the entrance to the oyster farm. Caesar assumed that the place had been sitting empty ever since the virus wiped out most of humanity over a decade ago.

The one exception, and the only sign of life, was in a rundown shack that appeared to be slightly better maintained than the surrounding ruins. Smoke billowed from its chimney. Caesar sniffed the air, but the smoky aroma overpowered any other odors. There was no way to tell how many humans might be in the vicinity.

Peering out at the moribund farm through a stand of cypresses, the apes tethered their horses and crept toward the shack on foot, their rifles at the ready. They moved cautiously along the dirt road leading through the farm, uncertain as to what exactly they had stumbled onto. Broken oyster shells littered the ground, making stealth difficult, as the apes had to step carefully to avoid slicing their feet.

Could this be the soldiers' base camp? Caesar found it unlikely that the Colonel and his troops could all be crowded into a single shack, but decided that the site required further investigation, just in case it was being used as a temporary refuge by the strike force that had invaded the fortress. He looked about warily, but detected no guards posted along the perimeter of the campsite.

Caesar doubted the Colonel would be so careless...

A lone human emerged from around the corner of a collapsed boathouse, bearing an armload of driftwood. Dirty and unshaven, his tattered clothing just as grimy as the rest of him, he didn't have the look or bearing of a soldier; more likely he was just a random, ragged survivor who had somehow managed to outlive the bulk of humanity. Beneath the whiskers and grime, he appeared to be in his forties, old enough to remember when his kind had still dominated the planet. Those were often the angriest humans, Caesar had learned, and the most dangerous.

Spotting the apes, he froze in his tracks, while they stared back at him in silence. Rocket glanced at Caesar, awaiting his cue, but Caesar simply watched the human carefully, curious to see what the man would do next. Unlike some apes, Caesar did not assume that all humans were enemies. He had known a few decent ones in his time.

Like Will... and Malcolm... and Ellie...

"I'm just gonna put this down," the man said, indicating the load of firewood in his arms. Very slowly, he began to lower his burden.

Caesar permitted this.

The man abruptly dropped the wood, whipped around the hunting rifle Caesar now saw was strapped to his shoulder, and fired wildly at the apes. The sharp report of the gunshot violated the sepulchral atmosphere of the farm. Maurice started as the bullet whizzed past him, missing his head by inches.

A second shot rang out—and the man fell backward onto the ground.

Caesar clutched his own smoking rifle as the other apes turned toward him in shock, stunned by how rapidly Caesar had dispatched the human. Caesar's own face was impassive, betraying neither anger nor remorse. He had killed before, but never this dispassionately. Caesar realized that the slaughter of his family had broken something inside him, and it might well be that he would never be truly whole again. The Colonel was not the only one without mercy anymore.

I gave the human one chance to prove he was not a killer, Caesar thought grimly. *But only one.*

Lowering his weapon, he walked past his friends without a word toward the lifeless body of the human he had just killed. The others joined him as he stooped to examine the corpse.

Upon closer inspection, the man's ragged clothing was only barely recognizable as military fatigues. Caesar's eyes narrowed as he saw AΩ crudely tattooed on the man's right forearm.

So he *was* one of the Colonel's soldiers—or had been.

Luca glanced around, but there was no indication that there were other humans about. No lurking soldiers appeared to avenge their brother-in-arms. Luca signed in confusion:

What's he doing out here alone?

Rocket shrugged and signed, *Maybe he's a deserter?*

Possible, Caesar thought. He regretted that the soldier had not kept himself alive long enough to be questioned. He wanted the Colonel dead at his feet, not some lone straggler. This was just a waste of time and ammunition.

A muffled crash, coming from the shack, jolted the apes to action. Caesar nodded at Luca, who lumbered over to the ramshackle abode and took hold of the door handle. Caesar and the other apes covered Luca with their rifles as the gorilla ripped the pitted wooden door off its hinges and flung it aside. Sunlight invaded the murky interior of the shack, but its inhabitant could not be seen through the doorway. Everyone looked to Caesar for guidance.

Caesar briefly considered moving on and leaving the shack and whomever it was hiding in peace, but decided against it. He still needed information regarding the Colonel's whereabouts and plans, and could not risk giving the shack-dweller an opportunity to warn the soldiers of the apes' approach. They might even have a radio in there.

He signaled the other apes to follow him.

Guns drawn, they cautiously entered the shack, on guard against sneak attacks. Lit only by the sunshine glinting in behind the apes, the inside of the shack was narrow and cramped, even more so than the tunnels and corridors back at the fortress. Rotting wood paneling was peeling off the walls and cobwebs hung from the ceiling. Mold encroached on nearly every surface, offending Caesar's acute sense of smell. Boxes and bags of supplies: canned food, bags of beans and flour, batteries, and duct tape were stacked haphazardly throughout the shack, making it feel even more claustrophobic. The smoke turned out to be coming from a compact propane heater venting out through the chimney. The place felt more like an above-ground bunker barely fit for human habitation, but it was obviously home to someone.

Or someones.

Caesar scanned the shadows as the apes stalked through the shack without encountering any opposition. His eyes searched every nook and cranny where a vengeful human might be hiding, but found them empty of threats. His concentrated gaze zeroed in on a closed door at the rear of the shack. He held up a hand to silently signal the other apes as he tightened his grip on his rifle, rested his finger on the trigger, took a deep breath, and threw his shoulder against the door. The flimsy construction was no match for the strength of a determined chimpanzee, and he burst into the cramped bedroom beyond and swept the muzzle of his gun before him, prepared to open fire at whatever human might be waiting in ambush. His heart pounded, pumping adrenaline through his veins, as his eyes blazed ferociously. He had already shot one human today; he would not balk at killing another at the first sign of danger.

Show yourself, if you want to live!

But instead of a soldier, poised to attack, he found...

A little girl?

A small blonde-haired waif, no more than eight or nine years old, cowered like a frightened animal in the bottom half of a bunk bed, a moth-eaten blanket pulled up to her chin. She was backed up against the wall as far as she could, staring up at Caesar with large, frightened eyes. For an instant, Caesar flashed back to Cornelius looking at him with the same fearful expression when Caesar had lunged at him with the spear last night, and he felt a twinge of guilt for scaring the defenseless child, but then he remembered what the humans had done to Cornelius's mother and brother and his heart hardened. He regarded the human child stonily, keeping his gun pointed at her. His heart, his blood, remained primed for mortal combat.

A shaggy orange hand reached out and rested upon the barrel of the rifle, gently forcing it down so that it was aimed at the floor instead. Caesar allowed Maurice the liberty, but he said nothing as he slowly assumed a less aggressive posture. Caesar breathed deeply to settle his bellicose emotions and scale down from his heightened state of battle-readiness.

He did not need to kill again… or at least not yet.

Caesar coldly turned away from the girl, ignoring the worried looks upon the faces of the other apes, and gestured at the contents of the shack.

"Look around. Take what we can use."

He could tell that his newfound ruthlessness and seeming lack of emotion concerned them, but that couldn't be helped. The more tender portions of his being had died with his family. Revenge was all that drove him now. There was no room in his heart for sentiment or distractions.

8

Rocket and Luca followed Caesar back into the cluttered heart of the shack, to sort through the provisions piled there, leaving Maurice alone with the human girl. The orangutan observed her with both curiosity and pity. Her long, sun-bleached hair was matted and badly in need of grooming. Grime coated her face, hiding it almost as effectively as the dark camo paint employed by the soldiers. Her feet, poking out from beneath the blanket, were bare, the nails untrimmed. He'd seen baby apes, back at the primate shelter, that had looked better cared for. Threadbare clothing, fraying at the edges, struck Maurice as a poor substitute for an ape's hairy coat.

Squeezing further into the cramped room, he glimpsed something lying on the floor by the bed. He stepped forward to take a closer look, alarming the girl, who shrank into a corner as though trying to curl herself up into a ball. Her obvious terror tugged at Maurice's gentle heart. He tried to comfort her as he would an ape child, by cooing and panting softly at her. Reaching down, he retrieved the item on the floor, which turned out to be a crude rag doll, fashioned to resemble a human female.

Maybe this will calm her, he thought.

Taking care not to make any sudden movements, he held out the doll to the girl. She eyed it longingly, hesitating, before darting out from behind the blanket. She snatched the toy from his hands, then retreated back to her corner. She hugged the doll close to her while watching Maurice warily. He wanted to think that she appeared *slightly* less frightened now, but perhaps that was just wishful thinking on his part.

He wondered as to her relationship to the dead man lying in the dirt outside the shack. Had the nameless soldier been her father or just her caretaker? How had they found each other in the ruins of the humans' world, and how long might the girl have been living in the derelict oyster farm?

Perhaps she can answer such questions, Maurice thought, *if we can earn her trust?*

He slowly reached out his arms to her. She froze, anxious blue eyes tracking the movement of his large simian hand, which was many times the size of hers. Maurice tried to assume a non-menacing expression, even though he was all too aware of how large and intimidating he must seem to the tiny child. He stretched out a single finger and gently stroked the doll's head.

The girl blinked in surprise. Looking up at Maurice, she studied him intently, concentrating with all her strength. Gradually, as she realized that he was not going to eat her or her doll, her fear appeared to ebb. Her eyes lost their panicked look and her small body grew less taut. It occurred to Maurice, belatedly, that the girl had yet to utter a sound, not even to scream or cry. Had she been scared speechless so far? He wondered what it would take to coax her into talking.

He was reluctant to address her using human speech. In his experience, most humans still found talking apes upsetting, and he preferred sign language in any case. He hooted softly at her again, trying to get her to say something.

Her mouth opened in response, but no words emerged. Only a low, inarticulate whimper.

Rooting through the shack's contents proved worth the effort. Luca claimed a dusty metal compass from a battered lockbox he found in a cupboard, which also held a pair of binoculars and a couple of working flashlights. Grunting, he showed off his haul to Caesar and Rocket.

Caesar was glad of the equipment, which might prove useful later on, but was growing impatient to get back on the Colonel's trail. Every moment they delayed meant that the murderer might be getting farther away; this detour was costing them valuable time.

He glanced back at the bedroom in the rear. He was just wondering what was keeping Maurice when the orangutan appeared in the doorway. Caesar saw to his surprise that the human girl was tagging after Maurice, peering out curiously from behind the ape's large, shaggy form. A beaten-up rag doll dangled from her grip.

Something wrong with her, Maurice signed. *I don't think she can speak.*

That was the least of Caesar's concerns at the moment. He glanced coldly at the child, then back at Maurice.

"We must go," he said.

To his frustration it was already late afternoon by the time they left the shack and commenced to get underway again. Caesar and Rocket mounted their horses, which they had retrieved from the trees, as Luca guided the remaining two steeds into the campground. Maurice approached his horse, about to climb onto it, but paused and looked back at the shack.

Caesar saw that the girl had followed them out into the open. She wandered over to the body of the dead soldier, which was still lying on the ground beside his gun. Despite his impatience, Caesar was struck by the child's odd reaction to the corpse. He had anticipated tears and hysterics, but if anything she appeared strangely fascinated by the lifeless remains, as though she didn't entirely grasp what she was seeing.

Caesar did not have a lot of experience with human children, but he doubted this was normal. Had she been so badly traumatized by the horrors of the last few years that she was damaged somehow?

Maurice turned to Caesar. *She'll die out here alone*, he signed.

A flicker of sympathy passed through Caesar; this helpless child was not his enemy and bore no blame for his family's death. But he had a blood debt to settle and babysitting a stray human orphan played no part in that. The girl would only slow them down and get in the way of his vengeance. Maurice had to know that. This was no errand of mercy they were on.

"We cannot take her," Caesar said firmly.

Maurice listened thoughtfully, nodding.

I understand, he signed. *But I cannot leave her.*

Frustrated, Caesar glared at the stubborn orangutan.

Dusk had fallen as the party, now larger by one, continued along the shore, trusting in those old reports from Luca's scouts. The girl rode behind Maurice, clinging to his back as an ape child might, her dirty face pressed against his shaggy coat.

Caesar scowled at the sight, shooting his friend a hard look. For better or for worse, Maurice had always followed his conscience, no matter how inconvenient or dangerous, so Caesar had known there would be no arguing with the orangutan on this point. He found himself wondering, however, if it had been a mistake to let Maurice and the others accompany him after all.

Maurice acknowledged Caesar's stern glare with a conciliatory nod, as though to assure Caesar that the girl would be no trouble.

Caesar was unconvinced.

A grunt from Luca interrupted their silent exchange. Looking ahead, Caesar saw rows of crudely constructed crosses posted along the edge of the tidal flats, where the beach surrendered to marsh and brush. Made of driftwood, bound together by tape or twine, the crosses were staked into the ground at the heads of fresh mounds of dirt and looked of much more recent vintage than the overgrown wreckage back at the oyster farm.

Investigating, the apes discovered that beyond the tall grasses, a grove of cypresses was filled with row after row of crosses, each accompanied by a corresponding mound of earth. The apes looked about them, unnerved by the ominous tableau.

Must be where they bury their dead, Maurice signed.

Caesar contemplated the crosses. Although the symbol meant nothing to apes, he knew that humans often used crosses to mark their burial places. Riding through the primitive cemetery, he was surprised to see that the trunks of nearby cypress trees were riddled with bullet holes. Squinting at the ground, despite the fading daylight, he saw brass bullet casings strewn across the floor of the clearing. He winced at the sight, recalling the empty shells on the floor of his former dwelling place, before forcing himself to focus on the mystery at hand.

"Looks like some were killed *here*," Caesar said.

This was no mass grave left over from the Flu pandemic of several years ago, he deduced. As he understood it, the only humans still alive were those with a natural immunity to the virus, making any new outbreaks unlikely. Judging from the bullet holes and casing, humans had not just been buried here.

They had been executed.

Grunting, Luca called them over to another discovery. Just beyond the graves, lying in a heap in a small clearing, were the charred remains of a bonfire, in which a large number of human artifacts had been all but incinerated. Blackened eyeglasses, belt buckles, medals, and military dog tags could be seen among the ashes.

They burned their things too, Luca signed.

That some recent atrocity had transpired here seemed evident, even if the motives behind the massacre remained unclear. Maurice gazed at the pile of charred personal effects in bewilderment.

Why would they kill their own people? the orangutan signed.

Caesar wished he knew. There was a puzzle here that he couldn't quite make out the shape of yet. He had always been good at puzzles, even as a small child growing up in Will's house in the city, but he felt like he was missing a few vital pieces of this one. Caesar frowned; he didn't like being in the dark when it came to what the humans were up to these days.

A shame that lone soldier forced me to kill him.

He was still mulling over the mystery when Luca called out to him from the opposite end of the graveyard. Crossing the cemetery, he joined Luca, who pointed through the trees at the distant pinpricks of light in the distance. Squinting in the twilight, Caesar made out faraway campfires and the vague silhouettes of tents. His eyes widened.

The humans' base camp, Caesar realized. *We found it.*

His lips peeled backwards in savage anticipation, baring his teeth and gums. A low growl escaped him.

Now I just need to find the Colonel…

9

A field of khaki tents was spread out in the twilight. Crouching in the brush, Caesar used the binoculars they had scavenged from the looted shack to survey the humans' camp from a safe distance. Luca and Rocket flanked Caesar as he checked out the camp.

$A\Omega$ was painted on the side of the tent immediately in view. Moving beyond the symbol, Caesar was disturbed to see various slogans painted here and there throughout the camp:

THOSE WHO FORGET THE PAST ARE DOOMED TO REPEAT IT.

THE ONLY GOOD KONG IS A DEAD KONG.

REMEMBER THE GOLDEN GATE.

The hostile graffiti chilled Caesar's blood. He remembered the female soldier from the raid, the one Blue Eyes had killed later on, declaring she and her fellow soldiers represented "the beginning and the end." There was a ring of fanaticism to that language that worried Caesar, as had Red's insistence that the human soldiers were utterly devoted to their murderous leader.

"*To them, he more than just human,*" the renegade ape had declared. "*He everything.*"

All the more reason to remove the Colonel from the world.

As Caesar continued to search the camp via the binoculars, a pair of apes briefly passed through his view. He tracked them to an open area between the tents where large groups of human soldiers were warming themselves around the camp fires. In the dim lighting, it was difficult to make out who the apes were, but Caesar's nose wrinkled in disgust at the sight of the turncoat apes attending to the humans by filling their cups. He wasn't sure what appalled him more, that the apes were traitors or that they were serving as slaves.

One of the apes turned toward Caesar and Red's detested features came into view. *I should have known,* Caesar thought, *that he would go running back to the Colonel.*

Then the other ape stepped into the light of a campfire. Fury replaced disgust on Caesar's face. He lowered the binoculars, unable to look upon the scene for a moment longer.

Luca noted the change in Caesar's expression. *Did you find the Colonel?* he signed.

Caesar did not trust himself to speak. Instead he simply handed the binoculars to Luca, who raised them to his own eyes. Caesar knew what he was seeing: the snow-white fur of a rare albino gorilla, one very well known to them both.

"Winter," he snarled.

The sun had set and Red was tired and hungry. He had endured much over the last day or so, both before and after his escape from Caesar's forces, and wanted nothing more than to rest.

But first the human soldiers had to be fed.

He and Winter moved among the humans, bearing buckets of chipmunk stew which they ladled out to the impatient soldiers as the humans sat around their fires. Winter, who was new to this, was visibly fearful and hesitant; Red guessed that the white gorilla had never been this close to so many armed humans in his life.

He'd better get used to it, Red thought, *if he wants to live.*

"Donkey," a soldier snarled at Winter. "Over here."

Red watched worriedly. All the humans were on edge after their losses against Caesar and his apes, and this particular soldier, Boyle, was volatile at the best of times. A pale-skinned human with short yellow hair and perpetually angry eyes, Boyle was like a defective grenade; you never knew when he might go off.

Winter cringed, flustered by Boyle's hostile tone. Red loped over to intercede, hoping to head off any trouble.

"Okay, okay," Red said, trying to placate Boyle. "He come…"

Red nodded at Winter, urging him to hurry up. The gorilla approached nervously and Boyle held out a tarnished metal bowl. Winter took the bowl and filled it hastily… too hastily. A dollop of lukewarm stew spilled onto the soldier's boot.

"Hey! Hey!" Boyle sprang to his feet, rage contorting his ugly human face. "You stupid—!"

He kicked the bucket out of Winter's hand, sending stew flying. Acting on instinct, the gorilla snarled at the human, who drew his gun and aimed it straight at the ape's face. Winter froze in alarm, realizing he had crossed a line.

Idiot gorilla, Red thought, backing away. He wasn't going to risk his life to save Winter's. *I tried to teach him…*

"Come on, Boyle," a human voice protested.

Preacher rose from a log to try to calm Boyle. Red knew Preacher to be less of a bully than many of the other humans; Red hadn't decided yet if the immature young human was friendly to apes or just weak. He recalled that Preacher was one of the soldiers whose lives Caesar had spared.

"Shut up, Preacher!" Boyle snapped. "What're you, a donkey lover now? I think you're going soft 'cause that kong let you go."

Around the campfire, some of the other soldiers snickered. Preacher backed down, his cheeks blushing in humiliation and anger. Red recognized that the human had been shamed before his tribe, like a chimpanzee forced to submit to a dominant male. All that was missing was a ritual supplication.

Boyle kept his gun pointed at Winter's face.

"Get me a new bowl," he growled at the gorilla.

Winter looked anxiously at Red, who soberly indicated that he should comply with the soldier's orders. That Boyle had not already put a bullet in Winter's brain was a good sign.

Perhaps the white gorilla was going to live through the night after all.

A mobile kitchen had been set up in one of the larger tents. The cooks had departed now that the stew had been prepared, so there was no one to help Winter as he rummaged under a supply table for a fresh bowl to replace the one that had landed in the dirt. His heart was still pounding from his close brush with death at the angry human's hands. Not for the first time, he wondered if he had made a terrible mistake by surrendering to the humans.

Perhaps it wasn't too late to slip away into the forest and strike out on his own?

Finding a clean bowl at last, he stood up in the dimly lit tent, trying to work up the nerve to escape or to return to the campfires. A grimy mirror over a wash basin captured his reflection and he gazed morosely at the image, barely recognizing himself. Less than two sunrises ago, he had been a respected member of the apes' guard, trusted by both Luca and Caesar himself. Now he was a traitor and a slave, who had just come close to being executed for spilling a drop of soup.

What has become of me? he thought. *What have I become?*

He could never return to the fortress, he knew that. Even if he hadn't already told the Colonel where it was, Caesar and the other apes would never forgive him for that betrayal. He could only stay with the humans, and hope that Red could help him stay alive, or he could risk deserting the camp, becoming an outcast and fugitive to both sides.

Neither prospect held any hope for his future.

Unable to look at himself any longer, he started to turn away from the mirror—just as another face appeared beside his.

Spinning around, he found Caesar standing behind him, staring at him with cold, merciless eyes. His icy silence was more terrifying than any accusing words or growls would have been.

No, Winter thought frantically. *You can't be here!*

Panicked, he turned toward the exit, only to find Luca blocking the way. The looming silverback glowered at Winter in a manner that promised no forgiveness. Winter spun toward the opposite end of the tent, where Rocket waited.

He was surrounded.

Winter retreated back against the wash basin as Caesar slowly moved toward him.

"Where is the Colonel?" he demanded.

Even though the young gorilla was larger and stronger than Caesar, he wilted before the chimpanzee's forbidding gaze and tone. He swallowed hard before signing in reply.

He's gone.

Caesar eyed him skeptically, advancing even closer. "Gone?"

Glancing around anxiously, Winter saw the other apes closing in on him, too. His hopes sank as he tried to convince Caesar that he was telling the truth.

This morning, he signed. *He took many soldiers with him.*

Luca and Rocket exchanged worried looks, clearly troubled by the news, but Caesar merely kept his baleful eyes fixed on the trembling gorilla, who tried to appease Caesar by revealing everything he had overheard from the humans.

Men are coming down here, he signed, *from their base in the north. The Colonel and his soldiers are going to meet them at the border.*

"What border?" Caesar asked. "*Why?*"

I don't know, Winter signed. *But more of us are leaving to join them in the morning.* He flinched as he realized that he had just referred to the Colonel's forces as "us," including himself in their ranks. *Red thinks they'll all be coming back here... to help the Colonel finish off the apes for good.*

Caesar came to a halt only inches away from Winter.

Please, the gorilla signed. *I know I betrayed you, but can't you see? We'll never beat them. I was just trying to survive. Red told me the humans promised to spare us if we helped them.*

He relived that moment back at the trenches, when Red had convinced him to switch sides while there was still a chance. Shaken by the sight of dozens of dead and maimed apes, and their defensive wall blown to pieces by the humans' explosives, Winter had made his choice, which he now regretted with all his heart.

I beg you, he signed. *Forgive me!*

Caesar appeared unmoved by his pleas. His voice, as it escaped his lips, was taut with barely contained fury.

"My son... my wife... are dead."

Guilt mixed with fear in the Winter's soul. He had known that apes would die, of course, when he'd told the Colonel where to find the fortress behind the falls, but putting names and faces to the dead hurt even worse than Winter had feared. He knew now that Caesar could never forgive him.

The raucous laughter of humans, strolling by outside, offered him one last desperate chance at rescue. The shadows of the passing soldiers could be seen through the mesh windows of the tent. Winter opened his mouth to shriek for help, but Caesar's hand clamped down over his mouth, silencing him. His other hand seized the gorilla's throat in an iron grip that surprised Winter with its strength. He wrestled Winter to the ground, even as Luca and Rocket rushed in to help him subdue the thrashing gorilla, who found himself outnumbered three to one. He struggled violently to free himself, to call out to the humans before it was too late. He knew his life depended on it.

Ape shall not kill ape, Caesar had taught.

But that had not spared Koba...

Holding Winter down, determined to keep him from crying out, Caesar spared a glance in the direction of the human soldiers outside, who were visible only as dim silhouettes through the walls of the tent. He saw with dismay that some of the shadows had turned toward the tent, as though attracted by the muffled noise of the scuffle. Their harsh laughter subsided to a worrying degree.

Quiet! Caesar thought. *Not another sound!*

He tightened his grip on Winter's throat, but the frantic ape would not stop struggling. Although held down by the three older apes, the white gorilla fought desperately to break free and sound an alarm. Pink eyes stared wildly at the shadows of the soldiers, who were his only hope. Caesar squeezed Winter's throat with all his strength, choking him harder and harder, until the flailing ape finally fell still. Caesar tensely watched the shadows, holding his breath, and bit back a gasp of relief as the soldiers turned away from the now-silent tent and continued on by. He waited, frozen in place upon his foe, as the shadows gradually receded from view.

He exhaled slowly, as did Luca and Rocket. His friends nodded at Caesar before staring grimly down at the unmoving form of Winter. They cautiously released their grip on the traitor ape, but he remained where he lay, no longer fighting for his life. Caesar took his hand away from the gorilla's mouth, from which no breath emerged. Bloodshot eyes stared blankly at the wall of the tent.

Winter was dead—at Caesar's hands.

The realization stunned the ape leader, even though he knew that Winter had brought this fate on himself. Luca and Rocket lowered their eyes, unable to meet his, as Caesar let go of the dead ape's throat, grappling with what he had just done. Even with Koba, he had merely let his enemy fall to his doom. Caesar had never actually killed another ape with his bare hands.

Until now.

10

Safely distant from the humans' tents, the apes sat glumly around a campfire of their own. Winter's death cast a pall over the gathering as his former friends and mentors stared bleakly into the fire, each coping with the gorilla's ugly fate in their own way, or so Caesar assumed.

He had it coming, Rocket signed at last.

Maurice nodded, but his somber visage belied his response. The orangutan had not taken part in the violence at the camp, having stayed behind to watch over the horses and the human girl, but he was surely affected by Winter's demise as well. Maurice had taught Caesar's laws to a generation of ape children. Winter had once been one of his students, too.

This is war, Luca insisted, as though trying to convince himself. Winter had been the silverback's protégé before he'd turned his back on his own kind. Now Luca had to live with Winter's death as well as his betrayal.

Caesar said nothing, lost in his own thoughts. He sipped absently from a canteen fashioned from a hollowed-out gourd before noticing that the girl child had sat down beside him at some point. She peered up at him guilelessly with placid blue eyes. She alone, Caesar reflected, was untroubled by the night's disturbing events.

He considered the girl, momentarily grateful for the distraction, and handed her the drinking gourd, which she guzzled from thirstily, the cool water streaming down her chin. He started to wonder what her story was, then spied something out of the corner of his eye that drove all thought of the child from his mind. His eyes widened in shock as he realized that there was now a dark figure sitting before the campfire, directly across from him.

Peering across the flames, Caesar saw an unknown ape squatting on the opposite side of the fire, seemingly unnoticed by Maurice and the others. Rising sparks and smoke danced between Caesar and the new arrival, whose head was lowered ominously. Alarmed and bewildered, Caesar gaped at the nameless ape, who slowly lifted his head to reveal a scarred, familiar face and only one good eye. Koba grinned at Caesar across the rippling hot air dividing them. A hoarse voice spoke from beyond the grave.

"Ape... not kill ape."

Caesar awoke with a start to find himself lying on the ground near a dead fire, the morning sun shining down through the treetops. Disoriented, he lifted his head to discover Maurice standing over him.

The humans, the orangutan signed urgently. *They're moving out.*

The news helped dispel the lingering echoes of the nightmare from Caesar's mind. Scrambling to his feet, he sighted Rocket and Luca several yards away, crouching tensely behind the tree as they spied on the humans' camp. He heard the rumbling thunder of men and horses on the move. Caesar recalled Winter saying that the soldiers would be heading north in the morning to meet up with the Colonel and rendezvous with even more troops coming their way. Apparently he had been telling the truth.

Before I killed him, Caesar thought.

His own course was clear. If the soldiers were leaving to join the Colonel, then so was he. Winter may have paid for his treason, but the Colonel was still alive. They would follow the soldiers for as long as it took.

To the ends of the earth, if necessary.

The apes rode after the Colonel's troops, maintaining a discreet distance, as a small army of mounted human soldiers headed east, leaving the coast behind in favor of the wooded valleys and canyons beyond. Fog helped conceal Caesar and his comrades as they trailed the convoy across miles of rugged, overgrown plains and marshes. Eerie souvenirs of mankind's fallen civilization were scattered along the route, including the mammoth steel carcass of a downed 747 passenger jet which lay incongruously in a field of high grasses and wildflowers. Traveling further, the apes passed by a long strip of deserted highway, populated only by the rusting husks of abandoned cars, trucks, and trailers. Weeds sprouted through the cracked concrete. The collapsing roofs and spires of forgotten ghost towns could also be glimpsed along the way, so that at times it felt to Caesar as though they were pilgrims on some endless funeral procession, marked by the crumbling monuments of a bygone world that had died choking on its own blood.

Because of the virus, he thought. *The same virus that elevated the apes.*

Was it any wonder that so many humans blamed the apes for mankind's downfall, even though the virus had been birthed by a human scientist in a human lab?

In time, the snow-capped peaks of the towering Sierra Nevada mountains loomed before them. Abandoning the plains and valleys, they ascended into the rugged peaks, where the climate grew colder and snowier and less hospitable, until at last they found themselves climbing a steep trail while thick white flakes blew against their faces, making it difficult to even see where they were going. Hairy coats provided a degree of protection against the cold, as they had during chilly winters back in the redwood forest, but the harsh weather was a brutal reminder that apes had evolved to thrive in tropical climates, not this frigid wilderness. Caesar had not worn clothing since turning his back on human ways many years ago, but he envied the human soldiers whatever winter gear and garments they possessed. Only by keeping moving could he and the others combat the cold. He shivered atop his horse, blowing upon his fingers to keep them from going numb.

But if the humans can cross these mountains, so can we.

His green eyes squinted into the blowing snow, trying to find the trail ahead. Concerned for the others, he glanced back over his shoulder to see how they were faring. He glimpsed Maurice on his own horse, sheltering the human girl with his shaggy body. The mute child clung to her massive guardian, seeking the warmth of his body. Snow dusted the orangutan's orange fur, making him look prematurely ancient. Caesar peered past Maurice, hoping to check on Luca and Rocket. The balding chimpanzee had little fur left on his body these days. Caesar hoped that Rocket was not suffering too severely from the—

The crack of a distant gunshot rang out, echoing down the hills.

The horses bucked fearfully. Caesar took firm hold of the reins, while raising his free hand to signal the others to halt. The apes dismounted hurriedly, taking cover in the tall evergreens alongside the trail. Maurice pulled the girl more closely against him, wrapping his huge arms around her protectively. Caesar peered from behind a frost-covered oak tree, trying to figure out what was happening.

Who was shooting at whom?

Two more gunshots could be heard over the wind. The other apes huddled among the trees, looking to Caesar for direction. He gestured for them to stay where they were. As nearly as he could tell in the middle of a full-fledged snowstorm, no one was shooting at them yet. Caution dictated that they wait this out, even as the delay chafed at his temper.

None of this was getting him any closer to the Colonel—or his revenge.

Caesar lost track of time as they hunkered down in the woods. The blizzard gradually subsided, making it easier to see and hear, but Caesar didn't hear any more gunshots. The apes cautiously emerged from hiding, scanning the trail for hostile human soldiers. Fresh snow crunched beneath their feet, but the noise attracted no gunfire.

Whatever they had heard, it appeared to be over.

Climbing back onto their horses, the apes rode on through the mountains. Caesar watched their surroundings carefully, on guard against an ambush, but all he spotted up ahead was another crude wooden cross, like the ones they'd found before, staked into the snow on the side of the trail. Made from what appeared to be freshly broken tree branches, the cross looked brand new, as though it had been erected just a short time before.

While we were hiding in the trees?

Caesar called another halt, and the apes dismounted to investigate. Luca looked about warily and signed to Caesar:

Where did they go?

Caesar shook his head, not having any answers. Here was another piece of the puzzle, but he still couldn't make out the big picture. Approaching the cross, he made a grisly discovery. Three bodies were lying there, face down, already being buried by the snow. Maurice tucked the girl behind him to spare her from the sight, while Caesar crouched down to brush the snow from the bodies, exposing the lifeless forms of three human soldiers, all sporting the now-familiar AΩ insignia somewhere on their uniforms or flesh. Hoods had been pulled over their heads, execution-style. Bloody bullet wounds in their backs made it clear how they had died, even if the why remained a mystery.

Three gunshots, Caesar noted. *Three bodies.*

Caesar tugged one of the hoods off and rolled the body over. The corpse belonged to a female soldier. Her frozen eyes glittered like glass. Dried blood was caked beneath her nose.

Rocket unmasked another body, which turned out to be that of a lanky young male. His eyes were mercifully shut, but he also had caked blood around his nostrils. Rocket bent over to take a closer look—and the soldier's eyes snapped open.

The human, who had apparently been left for dead, gasped at the sight of the apes, who were just as startled by his unexpected resurrection. Panicked, he started to scramble away, but, reacting quickly, Caesar hurried over and grabbed the soldier's leg before he could flee. He had no intention of letting the wounded human loose until he had some answers.

"Why... did they shoot you?"

But the human just stared back at him with frightened eyes. He blinked in confusion as though he couldn't even comprehend what Caesar was saying. His frantic eyes locked on the little girl, who peered at him from behind Maurice. Their gazes met but failed to communicate; they simply gaped at each other in bewilderment. The man opened his mouth as though to speak, but all that emerged were incoherent gasps and grunts.

Maurice's eyes widened in surprise. *He cannot speak either...?*

Caesar tried to make sense of this new mystery. He turned to Rocket for assistance.

"Help me get him up."

The other chimp reached down toward the soldier, but with an unexpected burst of strength, considering the bullet in his back, he yanked his leg free from Caesar's grasp and scrambled backward across the snow, desperate to get away from the apes. Wild eyes darted back and forth, seeing escape, as Caesar moved toward him cautiously, trying not to spook him.

But it was no use. Rolling onto his knees, the man sprang to his feet and sprinted into the snowy woods. Caesar considered chasing after him, but what would be the point? The mute human obviously held no answers.

Only more questions.

The apes watched as the human vanished into the trees, where he would no doubt succumb to the gunshot wound before long. Maurice's puzzled gaze drifted from the girl to the woods and back again. He signed in confusion:

What is wrong with them?

"I don't know," Caesar admitted.

11

Afternoon found all four apes high in treetops, trying to pick up the soldiers' trail. Each of them had climbed a different tree in hopes of spotting the convoy. The lofty vantage point offered Caesar an impressive view of the colossal mountain range stretching out endlessly around them, but the trail had gone cold in more ways than one.

Where could they have gone? Maurice signed.

"Winter said they were heading to a border," Caesar said.

Yes, Luca signed, *but which way is that?*

Caesar wished he knew.

Far below the girl sat atop Maurice's horse, craning her neck all the way back to see the apes in their perches. Growing bored, she looked down to play with her doll, rocking it back and forth in her tiny arms.

Neither she nor Caesar noticed as a furtive figure crept from the woods behind the girl. A well-worn green parka, complete with a fur-lined hood, concealed the figure's identity. Scuffed snow boots made little sound as the figure snuck up behind one of the unattended horses and quietly rummaged through a saddlebag. His breath misted before his lips as he fumbled to extract a flashlight from the bag, only to clumsily drop it into the snow at his feet.

He froze, looking around to see if anyone had heard the flashlight hit the snow, but the girl on the other horse remained focused on her doll, oblivious to the stranger's presence. Growing bolder, he dug deeper into the bag and was rewarded by the discovery of a shotgun. He grabbed the barrel of the gun, but his greedy haste provoked the horse, who snorted loudly in protest, alerting Caesar, who looked down to see the stranger rooting through the apes' supplies.

Who?

Caesar hooted to inform the others, and Luca, seeing the intruder, let out a spine-chilling roar. Startled, the girl finally looked up from her doll, as the figure, realizing he'd been seen, leapt onto the back of the surprised horse and galloped away with their supplies.

After him, Caesar signed, but his companions needed no urging. The apes scrambled down from the trees, swinging from branch to branch, until they reached the remaining horses, which they hurriedly mounted, with Rocket forced to share Luca's steed. Wasting no time, they set out in pursuit of the stranger in the green parka, who veered from the trail into the snowy woods, his horse's hooves throwing up clouds of white powder.

No, Caesar thought. *You're not getting away that easily.*

Caesar and his posse chased after him, weaving through the tall evergreens and leaping over ravines and logs while striving to keep their elusive quarry in sight, even as he darted in and out of view. Caesar knew that if they lost sight of Green Coat, as he'd started thinking of the nameless thief, for more than a minute or so, they'd never be able to find him again. The High Sierras offered many places to hide.

The apes began to gain on Green Coat, despite his headlong flight. Breaking from the woods, he rode at full tilt up a vast snow-covered slope that stretched high into the mountains. The apes burst from the forest after him, charging up a stark white incline that dwarfed them all. Toppled cables and half-buried metal gondolas informed Caesar that humans had once skied upon this slope; he'd never witnessed that peculiar pastime with his own eyes, but had learned of it while being raised by humans back in the city.

Leading the chase, Caesar pressed his horse to greater speed as the gap between the apes and Green Coat steadily closed. Frustrated by the chase, Caesar hoped that they could at least pry some valuable information from the thief to make up for their trouble. Or would this human prove just as incommunicative as every other human they'd encountered on this quest so far?

He'd better be able to speak, Caesar thought, *for his sake.*

A flash of gunfire sparked from the fugitive's shotgun, alerting Caesar and the others to danger. They ducked, but the blast missed them by a wide margin, ricocheting instead off one of the fallen gondolas with a metallic *ching*.

Two more shots rang out, both going wildly astray. Clouds of snow and ice erupted where the blasts hit the slope, nowhere near the apes or the horses. Either the thief was just trying to scare them or he was a truly terrible marksman.

Caesar decided he could live with either explanation, even as Green Coat disappeared over the crest of the slope. Staying in pursuit, the apes followed him to the top of the slope, where they came upon an unexpected sight.

A large, rambling ski lodge was built into the rocky mountainside. Time, neglect, and the elements had taken their toll on the looming multi-story structure, but it had clearly been quite impressive in its day, when there were still humans enough to seek winter sports and diversions. Sturdy timber walls, reinforced with stone and mortar, still stood, more or less. Assorted outbuildings surrounded the central lodge, while a skeletal ski-lift tower could be glimpsed a short distance away. An intact flight of steps led up to the lodge's wide front porch. Tall frosted windows concealed what lay beyond the front door. A faded sign in front of the structure identified it as "The Inn at Deer Creek," a name that meant nothing to Caesar. The stolen horse, now riderless, wandered idly through the pristine white grounds before the once-majestic hotel, which was clearly yet another decrepit relic of the past.

Caesar signaled the others to proceed cautiously as the apes dismounted and approached the buildings, their rifles drawn. They had only taken a few steps, however, before Green Coat bolted from behind one of the adjacent outbuildings and dashed through the front entrance of the central lodge. An ornate glass door, which had somehow survived the collapse of civilization, slammed behind him.

The other apes looked to Caesar. He nodded silently and raised his rifle higher as he led Rocket and Luca up the front steps and through the front door, while Maurice and the girl waited outside, pressing their faces against the frosty door pane. They had come this far already, Caesar decided, and he had no desire to leave an armed stalker unaccounted for; they needed to find out who this was— and what must be done about him.

Entering the hotel, the armed apes gaped at the resort's once-opulent lobby, which time and the elements had transformed. Every inch of the cavernous space, from the sweeping staircases to the tattered furnishings, had been glazed by crystalline layers of ice. Snow swirled in the air, drifting down through a large gap in the ceiling.

Icicles hung like stalactites from the broken rafters and landings, as well as from a rustic chandelier constructed from antlers. Plunging sheets of ice, resembling frozen waterfalls, reminded Caesar of his former fortress. His breath misted before him as he contemplated the frozen lobby, which was eerily beautiful in a way, despite the heaps of fallen timbers and debris scattered everywhere.

He spotted boot prints on the floor. Signaling his companions to stay back, he followed the tracks across the lobby to the shadowy depths of a large stone fireplace built into one wall, beneath an immense stone chimney. He silently pointed out the prints to the other apes, as the party converged on the empty hearth, which was deep and dark enough to conceal whoever might be hiding inside it.

They paused before the opening. Canned food, firewood, and other supplies were heaped to one side of the hearth, while a thick layer of ash suggested that the fireplace had recently been used. Caesar cocked his rifle loudly and leveled it at the fireplace. Rocket and Luca did the same. Still aiming to avoid killing the thief if possible, Caesar hoped that Green Coat got the message.

You have one chance to cooperate, he thought. *Choose wisely.*

The stolen shotgun was tossed out of the hearth, landing with a thud at the ape's feet. Caesar nodded with satisfaction; perhaps Green Coat—whoever he was—was not suicidal after all.

Then a pilfered pair of binoculars came sliding out of the hearth as well, along with Luca's compass. The startled apes exchanged looks; who knew the thief's greedy fingers had been so busy?

Rocket swiftly retrieved the shotgun, and the apes waited expectantly, their weapons raised, as Green Coat slowly emerged from the hearth, making no sudden or aggressive moves. His head hung remorsefully, still hidden by the hood of the parka. Raising his gloved hands in surrender, he looked up at his captors, revealing the nervous, apologetic face of... an ape.

An adult male chimpanzee, in fact, although Caesar saw at once that Green Coat was not exactly an impressive specimen of their breed. Small and timid-looking, he was at least a foot shorter than either Caesar or Rocket. His small, rounded head boasted more skin than hair, with only a pitiful scruff of beard, while his ears were oversized even by chimp standards. His scrawny frame was practically lost in the battered parka, which appeared to be a few sizes too large for him.

He grinned sheepishly at the other apes and pointed to his chest.

"Bad ape," he grunted haltingly. "Bad ape."

Caesar was not entirely sure what to make of the odd little chimp, whom he didn't recognize as one of the apes he had liberated from the city years ago, but it was hard to regard him as a threat. Rocket slowly lowered his gun.

Who are you? he signed.

The ape tilted his head in confusion, as though he didn't comprehend the question. He did not reply.

Where are you from? Luca asked.

The chimp peered at the gorilla's gestures with a baffled expression.

I don't think he understands, Luca signed to the others.

Caesar was getting that impression, which flummoxed him to a degree. He had grown so accustomed to all apes knowing sign language that it felt strange to encounter one who did not.

I don't recognize him, Rocket signed, confirming Caesar's own conclusion. *He's not one of us.*

So where had he come from, if not from the ape colony

in the redwoods? Caesar examined the chimp for a moment before speaking to him.

"Are you... alone here?"

The chimp looked uneasily from face to face, so that it was unclear at first if he understood Caesar's words any better than he had the signing, but then he looked back at Caesar and nodded.

A solitary ape, living alone in the mountains? Caesar was trying to imagine how that could have come to pass when a creaking noise behind him caused all heads to turn toward the lobby's main entrance, where Maurice and the girl could be seen standing in the open doorway. They peered uncertainly at Caesar, his companions, and their peculiar new acquaintance. The girl, Caesar observed, was shivering badly from the cold. Her threadbare clothing was ill-suited to this altitude and climate. It bothered him, vaguely, that he had not given this much thought until now.

Green Coat noticed the girl, too. He started to lower his hands, causing Rocket to raise his rifle suspiciously, but the "bad ape" simply removed his parka and held it out before him as he called to the girl.

"Cold...?"

Caesar watched with interest, along with the other apes. When the girl did not respond to the chimp's invitation, remaining huddled against Maurice, Bad Ape looked to Caesar instead. Holding out the ratty coat, he pointed at the trembling human child.

"Cold."

Caesar could not deny that. After a moment's hesitation, he accepted the parka on the girl's behalf.

12

A toasty fire crackled in the hearth, combating the cold invading the lobby from outside. Accepting the hospitality of the Bad Ape, who seemed to have no other name, Caesar and his party warmed themselves before the flames. The chimp's parka now enveloped the girl, who was no longer shivering. Her wide eyes took in an impressive hoard of scavenged supplies lying in heaps around the fireplace. Dry goods, canned foods, and a treasure trove of miscellaneous tools and relics suggested how the ape had managed to survive on his own for so long.

Bad Ape beamed as he stoked the fire for his new guests.

"I see girl," he explained. "Think you… human. But you… *apes*. Like me!"

Understandably excited to be in the company of his own kind, he grinned at Caesar and the others, until he noticed the girl picking up a shiny silver trinket from his hoard. Looking on, Caesar identified the item as an old car emblem. Polished silver chrome spelled out the name of a forgotten automobile brand:

Nova.

Bad Ape gently retrieved the emblem from the girl,

kindly shaking his head as he returned it to the pile. Caesar glanced around at the frozen remains of the ski lodge. The dilapidated ruins looked barely habitable, at least by human standards. Apes, on the other hand, were less spoiled by the creature comforts humans had grown dependent on.

"You... live here?" he asked.

Bad Ape nodded rapidly. "Long time. Long, long time."

A thought seemed to strike him and he scurried away from the fire to rummage through a nest of old blankets and cushions nearby. He returned bearing a small stuffed animal fashioned to resemble a scaly green crocodile. He handed the plush toy to Caesar and sighed wistfully.

"Home. Old home."

Puzzled, Caesar inspected the toy. Turning it over, he found a partial answer embroidered on the belly of the crocodile:

World Famous Sierra Zoo.

He looked up at Bad Ape. "Are there more like you? More apes... from zoo?"

Many of his own people had come from the San Francisco Zoo, where Caesar had liberated them in the early hours of his revolution against the humans. He had always known that there must have been other zoos throughout the world, but there had been no way to know what had become of the apes in those zoos. He and his followers had been too busy struggling to survive and stay safe from the humans.

"Dead," Bad Ape answered, shaking his head. "All dead. Long time."

As in twelve years, Caesar guessed.

"Humans get sick," Bad Ape continued solemnly. "Apes get smart."

Caesar nodded in understanding. He feared he knew what had happened next.

"Then humans kill apes. But not me…" His grin returned as he boasted of his survival. "Not me. I run."

Caesar's estimation of the other chimp rose. To have escaped the vengeful humans, and to have survived so long on his own, was an impressive accomplishment that suggested that there was more to Bad Ape than met the eye.

"You learned to *speak*…?"

"Listened to humans." His face contorted with mock fury as he mimicked an angry human, shaking his finger at empty air. "'Bad ape! Bad ape!'"

His act broke off as he noticed that the girl had reclaimed the gleaming Chevy Nova emblem from his junk pile. He reached out and took it from her again.

"No… no touch."

The girl gazed longingly at the precious trinket as he set it down. He watched over it for a moment, then seemed to remember something else and rushed away without explanation, leaving Caesar and the other apes bemused and perplexed by their excitable host.

Amazing, Maurice signed. *Always thought we were the only ones. Wonder if there are others out there somewhere? Others like us?*

Caesar had deliberately exposed the apes in his colony to the virus that elevated their intelligence, but perhaps the virus, spreading through the human population, had affected other apes as well? It was a staggering idea to contemplate. For all Caesar knew, there could be intelligent apes all over the planet by now.

"Here! Eat! Eat!" Bad Ape came bounding back into their midst, energetically handing out brown plastic packages that Caesar recognized as vacuum-packed military food rations. "New friends! Special day!"

He tore the top off one of the scavenged packs and started gobbling down the dehydrated meal inside. He gestured eagerly for the other apes to do the same.

Caesar looked over the pack in his hand. Human soldiers called them MREs, he knew, short for Meals, Ready to Eat; he and his apes had confiscated similar packages over the years, although they generally preferred to hunt and forage for their own food in the forest. This particular pack supposedly contained a "bean and rice burrito" and bore an official military seal:

U.S. GOVERNMENT PROPERTY: CA STATE BORDER
QUARANTINE DETENTION AND RELOCATION CENTER.

The word "border" leaped out at him.

"Where did you get this?" he asked.

Bad Ape glanced at him in confusion. Caesar held up the package and indicated the label. The other chimp looked away, made uneasy by the query.

"Bad place," he said in a hushed tone. "*Very* bad. I find… long time ago. After zoo. Looking for food. Find *human* zoo. Zoo for *sick*."

Quarantine, Caesar realized, engrossed in the ape's tale. It was a detention center for those infected with the virus.

"Big walls," Bad Ape said. "Big walls. Sick humans try climb. Bad humans kill. Then get sick too. All dead now." The chimp shuddered at the memory. "All dead."

By now, Maurice and the other apes were also listening intently to Bad Ape's haunting story. Caesar's imagination all too readily filled in the blanks.

"Bad humans?" he echoed. "Soldiers?"

Bad Ape nodded, clearly recognizing the word. "Soldiers."

The possible significance of the chimp's tale was apparent to Caesar and his companions. They exchanged meaningful looks as they absorbed what they had just heard. Rocket signed to the others:

An old, deserted military camp on the border?

Luca picked up the thread. *Maybe this is where the Colonel and the troops from the north are going to meet?*

Caesar thought it worth investigating.

"Is it far?" he asked Bad Ape. "Can you take us?"

"Human zoo?" The chimp reacted with alarm to the very idea. "No… no go back there. Everyone dead." He shook his head emphatically. "I come here. Safe here. Never go back!"

Caesar sympathized with the ape's distress, but needed Bad Ape's help if they were going to catch up with the Colonel. He placed his hand on the other chimp's shoulder.

"Please. You must take us."

"No! Can not take! Can not take!"

Scared, he shoved Caesar's hand away too aggressively to suit Rocket, who lunged at him in anger, roughly grabbing hold of him, but Caesar moved to restrain Rocket before the loyal ape dealt too harshly with Bad Ape, whom they could not afford to agitate further. He shook his head at Rocket, urging patience.

We need to win his trust, Caesar thought. *Not treat him like an enemy.*

"Look!" Bad Ape pointed frantically at a small window along the nearest wall. His voice quavered as Rocket continued to hold onto him. "More snow! Can not go, must stay here!" He kept pointing insistently. "Look, look!"

Glancing at a larger window by the front entrance, Caesar saw that the scared chimp spoke the truth. It was indeed snowing heavily outside.

He nodded at Rocket, who grudgingly released Bad Ape, eliciting a sigh of relief from the other chimpanzee, who acted as though he had just received a stay of execution. He grinned happily at the falling snow, which he seemed to think had come to his rescue.

"You stay here. Eat. Rest." He beamed at the other apes,

the first he had seen since the early days of the plague. "With me."

Caesar stared grimly at the snow, which gave no evidence of letting up anytime soon. Bad Ape was right to a degree; they could not set off for the camp on the border for the time being. There was nothing to do but wait, and enjoy the meager comforts of the lodge and the fire.

Relaxing, Bad Ape noticed that the girl was still eying the silver Nova emblem. He sighed, as though surrendering to the inevitable, and handed it to her.

"Here. You keep."

Eyes bright, the girl eagerly took possession of the trinket. Bad Ape looked at Caesar and the other apes, obviously hoping that his generosity had won their approval. Caesar couldn't help sympathizing with the lonely ape, who had lived in solitude for so long. Twelve years was a long time to go without seeing another of your own kind. Caesar could only imagine what it must mean to Bad Ape to spend time with other apes again.

Now if they only could persuade him to lead them to the border...

13

Caesar couldn't sleep.

The fire in the hearth had died down to a few fading embers, while swirling snow still invaded the lobby through the gap in the ceiling. As nearly as Caesar could tell, the others were all fast asleep, exhausted by the day's exertions, but his own restless mind refused to shut down. Second guesses tortured him as he imagined countless choices or scenarios that might have saved his family from the Colonel, who was getting further and further away even as Caesar tossed and turned, snowbound within the melancholy ice palace. Abandoning any hope of sleep for the moment, he sighed and sat up quietly.

His envious gaze fell upon the human girl, who was curled up peacefully against Maurice's belly, hugging her doll. The shiny car emblem—her gift from Bad Ape—remained clutched between her tiny fingers. Maurice's arm shielded the girl, as though she was his own child.

An ape child.

A pang jabbed Caesar's heart. His eyes grew moist. He remembered sleeping with Cornelius that way... and Blue Eyes...

"Who is… child?" a soft voice asked.

Startled, Caesar turned to see that Bad Ape was awake as well. He cast a questioning look at the girl.

"I don't know," Caesar admitted.

"But… she with you?" Bad Ape asked, understandably confused.

I suppose she is, Caesar thought, nodding. "She has no one else."

Bad Ape gazed at the girl in pity. "I see you look at her… just now." He turned toward Caesar. "Look sad."

Caesar did not know how to respond. His pain ran too deep to face, let alone speak of to a stranger. He held on to it in silence.

Bad Ape studied him, mulling things over before venturing a guess.

"You… have child?"

He smiled sweetly at Caesar, blithely unaware that he was treading on dangerous ground, until Caesar shot him a withering look. Bad Ape's face fell and he clapped his hands over his mouth. Looking away from the chastened ape, Caesar felt a twinge of guilt; Bad Ape had not known of the fresh wounds his innocent query had reopened. Sighing, Caesar broke his silence.

"He was killed," he said gruffly. "By humans."

Understanding—and sympathy—dawned on Bad Ape's face.

"Oh… soldier?"

Caesar nodded, staring at the dying fire. His throat tightened, making speech even more difficult than usual. A pensive look came over Bad Ape's usually comical countenance as he processed what Caesar had told him.

"I had child," Bad Ape confessed.

Caesar turned to him in surprise. He did not need to ask what had become of the child; the solitary chimpanzee had already revealed the fate of his fellow apes years ago. Humans had killed them.

Old memories, long buried, haunted the other ape's eyes. He looked at Caesar.

"You think… you will find him… at human zoo? Soldier?"

Caesar peered grimly at the fading embers in the fireplace.

"I don't know. Maybe."

Bad Ape thought this over.

"Then… maybe I take you."

Along with Rocket, Luca guided the four horses toward the front porch of the ski lodge. The sun had risen and the snow had finally abated, so Caesar was anxious to get off to an early start. Luca was not entirely sure what had prompted Bad Ape's change of heart, but he wasn't going to—what was the human expression again—look a horse's gift in the mouth? Mounted upon his own horse, the gorilla hoped they were doing the right thing chasing after the Colonel. He understood why Caesar was hunting the Colonel, and he blamed himself for not seeing the danger posed by Winter's cowardice, but he worried about the apes they had left behind. Would Spear be able to lead them to safety on his own? Without Caesar to guide them?

Caesar needs revenge, he thought, *but our people need Caesar.*

He saw the girl standing alone on the front porch, hugging herself against the cold despite the oversized parka Bad Ape had generously given her. Icicles hung from the eaves of the porch roof, which sagged beneath the accumulated snow piled on it. She was staring up at the bright pink flowers of a dogwood tree poking up through the snow. The rosy blossoms provided the only trace of color in the stark white landscape, so it was perhaps no surprise that the girl was captivated by the flowers, which were out of reach of her small arms.

But they were not beyond Luca's reach. The gorilla rode forward and plucked a small branch off the tree. Bending down toward the girl, who was practically level with the mounted gorilla as she stood on the porch, he gently slipped the flowers behind her ear, and was rewarded with an incandescent smile. He gazed down on the child kindly, until he heard the front door opening.

The silverback hastily straightened and assumed a more imposing posture as Caesar and Maurice exited the lodge. Slightly embarrassed by his moment of sentiment, he hoped that Caesar had not seen him toying with flowers. Theirs was a serious mission after all, dealing with matters of life and death and justice. It would not do for him to look weak or softhearted.

Maurice crouched next to the girl, and she hopped onto his back exactly as an ape child would. Satisfied that she was secure, the orangutan left the porch and climbed onto his horse. Caesar mounted his steed as well, ready to resume their quest, assuming their new guide had not changed his mind again. Luca wondered briefly if the sad, silly little chimp had given them the slip, but then the lodge's door swung open once more, and Bad Ape hurried out to join them.

The strange little chimp had dressed for the trip, in a manner of speaking. Ill-fitting snow boots covered his feet, a moth-eaten blanket was draped over his scrawny frame, while a striped wool cap rested on his balding pate.

Luca resisted the urge to laugh while his companions stared blankly at Bad Ape, who was clearly unaware of how ridiculous he appeared, as he looked speculatively from horse to horse, wondering who he was to partner with.

Thinking quickly, Luca grunted and pointed at Rocket's horse. Grinning, Bad Ape made for the horse before the other chimpanzee could protest. Rocket shot Luca a dirty look, appearing utterly crestfallen, as Bad Ape clumsily struggled to climb up behind him. Luca chuckled under his breath.

That had been a close call!

Freshly fallen snow crunched beneath the horses' hooves as the party made their way through the wintry woods, leaving the derelict ski lodge behind. Maurice glanced down at the girl, who was tucked in front of him atop their horse, and saw that she was staring at Caesar, who was riding beside them, sipping from a drinking gourd. She licked her lips.

Ever a teacher, the orangutan saw an opportunity to try teaching her sign language. Grunting softly to get her attention, he pointed at Caesar, then made the appropriate sign by sliding a finger along his neck:

Thirsty.

He repeated the gesture.

Thirsty.

The girl stared at him blankly, but Maurice did not give up. Experience had taught him that some children needed more instruction than others. Taking her small hand in his, he demonstrated how to sign the word, while noting that Caesar was looking on with interest. The apes' brooding leader appeared intrigued despite his recent sorrows.

Maurice shaped the girl's fingers to form the sign again, but, to his disappointment, she showed no interest in the lesson. Instead she looked over at Caesar, who met her curious gaze. His expression softened somewhat, for perhaps the first time since the tragedy back at the fortress.

Concerned about his friend's state of mind, Maurice chose to take this as a good omen, even as he worried about the girl's seeming inability to communicate. Granted, he had never tried to teach a human sign language before, but, coupled with her apparent muteness, he had to wonder if there was something truly wrong with her...

14

Sunlight spilled through the trees marking the end of the woods. The apes had been traveling for hours through the dense, snowbound wilderness, having left anything resembling a trail early on. Bad Ape fidgeted restlessly on Rocket's horse, growing visibly more anxious by the moment, which told Caesar that they must be nearing their destination. It was late afternoon, but, with any luck, they would arrive at his human zoo before nightfall.

"There," Bad Ape said fearfully, pointing toward the light.

Caesar raised a hand to call a halt. According to Bad Ape, the camp was now just a graveyard, but Caesar suspected that might no longer be the case. He both hoped and worried that they were closing in on the Colonel and his troops, which meant that they had to proceed cautiously. Leaving their horses behind, the apes crept to the very edge of the forest, where they took cover behind the last few trees. Squinting into the sinking sun, Caesar got his first look at what he hoped would be the final station on this pilgrimage of revenge.

An enormous canyon lay before them. Steep, snow-covered cliffs descended in rocky shelves toward the vast unseen expanse at the bottom of the gorge. The peak of a prison-style warden's tower rose from the depths, confirming that they had indeed reached the human zoo Bad Ape so dreaded. A faded California state flag, bearing a portrait of a grizzly bear, hung from a pole sticking out the tower; Caesar winced, recalling the claw marks that had scarred Blue Eyes' chest. The rest of the camp remained out of sight.

Caesar held out his hand and Luca gave him the binoculars, allowing Caesar to look more closely at the watchtower. The intimidating cement-and-steel structure had seen better days; corrosion pitted and stained its walls, causing the light to glint off it. Cracked glass windows offered a glimpse into the interior of the tower, which appeared to be deserted at the moment, much to Caesar's disappointment. He had hoped to spot the Colonel in his lair.

He started to lower the glasses, then noticed something peculiar about the ragged flag. Using the binoculars, he realized that the flap was hanging upside-down—and that AΩ was painted in black across it.

I was right, he thought. *This is it. The camp by the border.*

Where I'll find the Colonel.

A hint of movement, further down the side of the canyon, caught his eye. Shifting the glasses, he spied small silhouetted figures far below, barely visible along the edge of the lowest granite ledge he could see from this vantage point. Even with the binoculars, he could barely make them out. He assumed they were human, but they could also have been apes for all he could tell.

Soldiers? Sentries?

Lowering the binoculars, he signed to his lieutenants: *Luca, let's take a closer look.*

He nodded at Rocket, then looked back at the others. *Stay here. Keep them safe.*

He and the gorilla furtively exited the safety of the woods. Keeping low, they slowly made their way down the slope toward the jutting granite shelf where the figures had been seen. Their cautious pace, and the thick snow, meant that it was sunset by the time Caesar managed to get a better view through the binoculars while lying in the snow, peering out over the top of a frosted ridge at the snow-covered shelf jutting out hundreds of feet below. The dimming light was a mixed blessing. On the one hand, it helped conceal the skulking apes; on the other, it made it harder for Caesar to discern what he was seeing.

The figures on the ledge were erecting a row of tall, X-shaped wooden structures along the edge of the cliff. Caesar counted roughly a dozen crosses, but could not figure out what purpose they served.

Perhaps some kind of perimeter defense?

Or scarecrows?

He put down the binoculars, confused. Lying beside him on the ridge, Luca signed in curiosity.

What are they doing?

Caesar shook his head. "I don't know."

Resorting to the binoculars once more, he attempted to make sense of the baffling activity. Luca grunted urgently, in a way that demanded Caesar's attention. He looked over at the gorilla, who pointed down past the crest of the ridge.

What's that? Luca signed. *A patrol?*

Caesar turned the binoculars toward a smaller, higher ledge just below the ridge, where a pair of horses were tethered. Caesar's pulse sped up at the sight and at its ominous implications.

Don't see any riders, he began.

A blurry shape suddenly rose into view, charging up

the other side of the ridge from the ledge just beneath it. Caesar dropped the glasses to discover a human soldier looming above him, his raised rifle pointed directly at the vulnerable ape, who realized that he was only a heartbeat away from joining his murdered wife and son. The soldier pulled the trigger without hesitation.

Click.

The gun jammed, shocking Caesar and the soldier both. The human's expression went from anger to fear in an instant as he reared backwards and attempted to lunge at Caesar with his rifle's bayonet. The chimpanzee expected to be skewered upon the point of the weapon, but—

Luca dived in front of Caesar, shielding his leader, and the blade plunged into the gorilla's gut, even as he grabbed the human with both hands and yanked him to the ground, where he fell upon the man and wrestled with him as they rolled across the frozen ridge. Massive fists pummeled the human with bone-breaking force, until the gorilla collapsed on top of the human, pinning him to the snow, not far from where the bloody bayonet had landed, staining the snow red. Both human and ape lay still, no longer fighting.

Luca!

Scrambling to his feet, Caesar rushed toward his friend, hoping there was still time to save him, but another soldier appeared from further along the ridge and took aim at Caesar, who found himself on the wrong end of a rifle barrel for the second time in as many minutes.

It seemed Luca's sacrifice had been in vain.

A loud whack, instead of a bang, came from the soldier, who crumpled onto the ice and snow, revealing Rocket right behind him. The other chimp gripped the rifle he had just clubbed the human with, saving Caesar's life. The butt of the rifle waited above the head of the downed soldier, just in case he tried to get up again.

He didn't.

Rocket panted, out of breath from rushing to the rescue. He signed apologetically at Caesar, as though embarrassed to have disobeyed his leader's orders to stay with the others.

I saw them from up there. He gestured at the top of the canyon. *Coming for you...*

Caesar was grateful for his friend's timely appearance, but what about Luca? Taking only a moment to verify that there were no more soldiers assailing them, the apes hurried to check on the wounded gorilla. Luca rolled painfully off the battered remains of the human soldier, who had clearly not survived the ape's ferocious attack.

Gasping, Luca clutched his punctured gut. Blood seeped past his fingers.

Too much blood.

Sheltered in the woods, Maurice waited with Bad Ape and the girl. His worried eyes searched the twilight for their absent friends, concerned for their safety. Dusk had deepened the shadows under the trees since Rocket had rushed to aid Caesar and Luca after spotting a human patrol heading their way. Maurice had not heard any gunshots, which was encouraging, but it was also possible that the other apes had been taken prisoner at gunpoint by now.

And that more soldiers would be coming for the rest of them.

The girl clung to Maurice's shaggy back, peering over his shoulder. He was just starting to wonder how long they should wait before investigating when Rocket returned, climbing the hillside toward them with a grim expression on his face. He carried a rifle equipped with a lethal-looking bayonet that Maurice did not recall seeing before.

The orangutan knew at once that things had gone badly, even before Caesar came into view, carrying Luca across his back. The gorilla outweighed Caesar by nearly two hundred pounds, and was dead weight, but Caesar shouldered the burden, following right after Rocket. The gorilla moaned softly, obviously too injured to walk.

But how badly?

Retreating further into the safety of the woods, Caesar gently lowered Luca to the ground, while Maurice and the others gathered around them. A deep gash in Luca's abdomen explained the ape's distress—and offered little hope of survival. Maurice stared aghast at the wound; it required no enhanced intelligence to connect the gash with the bayonet Rocket now toted.

The humans were dealt with, Maurice deduced, *but at what cost?*

As Maurice looked on, Caesar knelt beside the dying gorilla. His eyes were dry but filled with emotion as he gazed down on Luca, who smiled weakly up at him. Fading fast, Luca nonetheless managed to raise a hand and hold it out to Caesar, who grasped it firmly. Luca signed to him with his other hand.

At least this time... I was able to protect you...

Caesar held Luca's gaze in silence until Luca's hand finally released his grip on Caesar's and drifted slowly onto the snow. Maurice felt his own heart breaking; he and Caesar and Rocket and Luca had been through much together over the last years. Bad Ape, who had barely had an opportunity to get to know the heroic gorilla, proved smart enough to maintain a respectful silence.

The girl, who had been mutely observing the poignant scene, surprised Maurice by clambering down from his back and stepping onto the ground. He watched in wonder, transfixed along with the other apes, as the child bravely approached Luca and climbed onto his chest. She stared intently at Luca, her little face only inches from his much larger one, as her moist eyes displayed more genuine emotion than Maurice had ever seen there before. Certainly, she seemed much more affected by the gorilla's final moments than she had been by the man Caesar had shot back at the oyster farm.

She is a riddle, he noted, *but a riddle with a heart*.

Maurice wondered what Luca had done to touch that heart as the gorilla, still clinging to life, if only for a few more heartbeats, gazed at the human child as she removed a flowery twig from behind her ear... and gently tucked it behind his. A faint smile briefly showed upon his face, belying his intimidating features, before the light faded from his eyes and the smile departed along with his life.

Luca, their great friend and ally, was dead.

Caesar remained beside the ape's lifeless body, staring silently. A complicated mix of rage and guilt could be seen in his eyes. Rocket and Bad Ape kept their distance, letting Caesar be alone with his grief, but Maurice felt moved to speak. He grunted softly to get Caesar's eye.

I know how much you have lost, the orangutan signed. *But now we have lost another. And no matter what we do, our revenge will never bring your family back*.

Caesar merely stared back at him, his face a stoic mask.

Please, Maurice urged him. *It's not too late to leave this place. To join the others*.

Rocket objected vehemently to Maurice's suggestion. *Luca gave his life!* he signed. *We cannot turn back!*

Maurice understood Rocket's emotional desire to carry on the mission in Luca's honor, but it was Caesar that Maurice had to make see reason. Luca's sacrifice, as tragic as it was, should not inspire them to get more apes and humans killed.

Caesar, he pleaded with his hands.

But Caesar turned away from him, not wanting to hear. He shook his head gravely before speaking at last.

"They must pay…"

His vengeful words filled Maurice with despair—and disappointment. Caesar was their great leader and liberator, who had raised apes from ignorance and savagery and single-handedly guided them to freedom. He had fought and planned and sacrificed for his people for twelve winters, against often overwhelming odds. He was the greatest ape Maurice had ever known and would surely be the greatest ape he would ever know. Maurice owed him everything, including the sharpness of his wits.

But, for the first time, Maurice looked on Caesar and found him wanting.

Now you sound like Koba, he signed.

Caesar turned and glared at Maurice, visibly stung by the accusation and by its source. His expression darkened as he glowered at his oldest friend, who had been staunchly at his side since they had first met in the primate shelter so many years ago. Rocket looked on in shock and disbelief, having never seen Caesar and Maurice at odds before. Bad Ape just looked confused.

A tense moment, pregnant with the possibility of violence, ensued before Caesar spoke again. Rage, tightly controlled, simmered in every syllable.

"It was a mistake to bring you all. This is *my* fight. I will finish this alone." He swept his fierce gaze over the other apes. "If I am not back by morning… go. Join the others."

He rose at last from Luca's side and took the bayonetted rifle from Rocket. Without another word, he turned and set off back toward the canyon, where the humans and the Colonel no doubt waited.

Maurice wondered if he would ever see his friend again.

15

Night cloaked Caesar's descent as he covertly made his way down the steep, snow-packed wall of the canyon to reach the broad ledge he had been spying on before. A crescent moon gave him just enough light to see by even as he kept to the shadows, watching out for any further soldiers on patrol. Caesar wondered if the two men from the ridge had been reported missing yet. If so, it might well be that the camp's security had been tightened and that the Colonel was on guard.

Only one way to find out, he thought.

The foreboding watchtower loomed beyond the ledge, rising up from the floor of the canyon, which remained out of view. Searchlights mounted somewhere below swept the lower slopes of the mountain, forcing Caesar to time his approaches carefully to avoid being exposed by the luminous beams. Breathing hard, Caesar slowed as he approached the enigmatic X-shaped structures at the edge of the cliff; the figures who had erected the crosses had left when the sun had, but the crosses remained. Caesar's eyes widened as he began to make out shadowy figures roped to the crosses, struggling weakly against their bonds.

What is this...?

Confusion turned to horror as he drew nearer and saw that the pitiful figures were apes, twelve in all, barely conscious and struggling to breathe while bound to the X's by their hands and feet. Aghast, Caesar looked from ape to ape, his mind reeling at the awful spectacle before him. Not even back in the old days, when apes had been treated like animals by humans, had he seen anything this barbaric or pointlessly sadistic. Caesar had seen war, and the horrors of war, but... never anything like this.

He staggered toward the crucified apes but was distracted by a disturbing murmur rising from the canyon that hinted at something even more terrible than the tormented apes before him. The unnerving sound echoed the plaintive groans and whimpers of the suffering apes, only magnified many times over. His heart pounding, he turned away from the crosses and rushed to the brink of the ledge, where his anguished eyes saw his worst fears confirmed.

My people!

Hundreds of apes were crowded into outdoor holding pens in the middle of a sprawling prison camp nestled at the base of the mountains, some three stories below the ledge Caesar stood upon. The noise that had drawn him was the collective moans and cries and anxious chattering of the imprisoned apes, who, in their numbers, could only be his apes. These were not a few stray zoo escapees like Bad Ape; this was an entire community of apes locked up like animals.

The exodus, Caesar realized. *They've been captured. All of them.*

Guilt shocked him like the electric cattle prods the ape handlers had used back at the primate shelter years ago. He had let his people go on without him and now...

He stumbled back from the edge, overwhelmed. Desperately seeking answers, he looked again at the

134

crucified apes—and finally recognized one of them as Spear, the valiant young chimpanzee he had placed in charge of the exodus. Caesar hurried over to Spear, who seemed too weak to even notice his leader's arrival.

Caesar was stunned by the other ape's appearance. Spear barely resembled the vigorous chimp who had ridden to battle against the human raiders not too long ago. His head sagged forward, his chin resting upon his chest. His dark fur had lost its healthy luster, ribs protruded through his flesh, as though he had been starved. Painful breaths wheezed from his lungs. He was haggard and trembling, looking near death.

What have they done to you? Caesar thought. *What have they done to all of you?*

Caesar reached forward and gently lifted Spear's face with both hands. The tortured ape's eyes flickered open, unfocused at first, then filled with wonder as he finally recognized Caesar. He gaped at his leader, unable to believe what he was seeing.

Yes, Caesar thought. *I'm here.*

Unfastening the bayonet from his rifle, he used the blade to slice through the ropes binding Spear to the X. The other chimp slumped to the snowy floor of the ledge, tottering unsteadily upon his knees. Caesar crouched to steady him and felt Spear's abused body shaking. No words escaped the ape's cracked and bleeding lips. Instead he struggled to sign to Caesar:

You came... Some of us were starting to think you'd abandoned us for good... but I knew you'd come...

The ape's constant faith in him tore at Caesar's heart. He wasn't sure he deserved it.

"What happened?"

When we got into the mountains, Spear signed, *we heard horses. I thought it was you, that you'd finally come back...*

The words were like a knife twisting in Caesar's gut.

They came out of nowhere, attacked us. Spear shook his head, his face twisting in shame. *I don't know how they found us...*

Caesar knew. "They... were on their way here."

He cursed the cruel fate that had sent his people fleeing across the state and into these mountains at the same time that the Colonel and his soldiers had headed this way as well, to make his rendezvous with the troops coming from further north. The apes had marched right toward the very menace they'd been trying so desperately to escape.

They must have spotted us, Spear signed. *Tracked us... waited for the right moment.* He shuddered at the memory. *It was over so quickly. Many died, the rest of us were taken prisoner.*

Caesar recalled the countless apes trapped in the holding pens below. *Apes in cages... just like it used to be.*

We were sure they would kill us, Spear signed. *But the Colonel stopped them...*

Caesar blinked in surprise. Had he understood correctly?

There was madness in his eyes, Spear tried to explain. *He said they could use us, before we died. And they brought us all here.*

Caesar remembered the Colonel's icy blue eyes, staring back at him from behind the mask of camo paint, just before the killer had escaped through the falls. But he didn't understand. Why would the Colonel herd Caesar's people to this remote, forgotten camp? Why hadn't he just slaughtered the defeated apes, the same way he had murdered Cornelia and Blue Eyes?

"*Use* you?" he echoed.

Spear started to reply, but the last vestiges of his strength ran out. Collapsing, he fell forward onto the snow, revealing long ugly welts across his back. Swollen red stripes crisscrossed the chimpanzee's flesh, visible even through his fur. Appalled, Caesar instantly recognized the welts for what they were.

The marks of a lash.

He tenderly lifted Spear from the snow, cradling the injured ape in his arms. Despite his debilitated state, the loyal chimp tried to tell Caesar what he needed to know.

They've been forcing us to work, he signed feebly. *They beat us, strung us up here, to make the others work harder.*

Caesar's need to destroy the Colonel grew stronger. "What... kind of work?"

Spear wanted to answer, but he was near his limit. His eyes fluttered, closing, but he forced them open long enough to sign haltingly, only a few words at a time.

Your... little son... is here.

The words struck Caesar like a blow. *Cornelius!*

He didn't know whether to be relieved that his child had survived the massacre—or terrified that Cornelius had fallen into the hands of the Colonel and his bloodthirsty soldiers. Rendered speechless by the news, it took him a moment to find his voice again.

"Try to hold on, please!" he urged Spear. "I will get you out of here! All of you!"

But it was obviously too late for Spear; he had been abused too badly for too long. His life visibly slipping away, he gazed up at Caesar with bleary, bloodshot eyes that were rapidly losing their light. A hoarse, agonized whisper escaped his lips.

"Caesar..."

The ape leader peered into Spear's eyes as the dying chimpanzee uttered his final words.

"We... needed... you..."

Guilt crashed down on Caesar as Spear passed away in his arms, the victim of both the humans' cruelty and

Caesar's failure to protect his people.

I should have been there, he thought bleakly. *I should have never left them.*

He heard the groans of the other apes hanging on their crosses and feared he was also too late to save them. Still holding onto Spear's lifeless remains, he was about to see to them when, without warning, a hairy foot stepped into view. Startled, he looked up to see Red standing over him, holding a rifle.

You! Caesar thought. *Traitor!*

The butt of the rifle slammed into him.

16

Water dripped somewhere in the darkness as Caesar slowly, painfully regained consciousness. His skull throbbed and his face was pressed against a rough, icy surface. Wincing, he opened his eyes, which were immediately assailed by a harsh yellow light shining down from above. Freezing water splattered all around him.

Where...?

Lifting his head, Caesar attempted to get his bearings, even as his vision shifted in and out of focus. The last thing he remembered, he was on the ledge overlooking the prison camp, cradling Spear's dead body in his arms. Then Red appeared and...

Anger fought the fogginess in Caesar's mind. Forcing himself to concentrate on his new surroundings, he found himself sprawled on the frigid floor of what appeared to be an old railway depot. Iron train tracks cut through the base of a large cavernous structure. The rusted-out carcass of a dead locomotive gathered dust nearby. Looking up, Caesar saw a huge curved ceiling overhead. The yellow glare of sodium-vapor security lamps invaded the depot through a rip in the ceiling, melting the snow dripping through the gap onto the floor.

At first Caesar thought he was alone. Then he noticed a figure standing guard a few feet away. As his vision cleared, Caesar saw that it was Preacher, one of the human soldiers whose lives he had spared before. The youth looked tense and uncomfortable as he watched over Caesar while carrying a military-grade crossbow. Caesar wondered if Preacher was prepared to offer the same mercy he had been granted before.

Probably not, the ape guessed.

Before Caesar could say anything to Preacher, a familiar voice emerged from the shadows. Footsteps marched through the slush toward Caesar.

"Grant and Lee," he said. "Wellington and Napoleon..."

Caesar had only heard the voice once before, in his violated dwelling back at the fortress, but he recognized it instantly. His eyes widened as the Colonel stepped out of the shadows into the light.

"Custer and Sitting Bull... You're probably not much of a reader," he said, "but *this*, this is a big moment." He paused for emphasis. "This is... *beyond* historic."

Caesar glared fiercely at the murderer of his wife and firstborn. All awareness of his physical pains was incinerated by the white-hot rage ignited at the very sight of this particular human.

No camo paint obscured the Colonel's hated features as he coolly examined the prone ape. He had white skin, weathered by sun and wind, and a sidearm holstered at his hip. His voice was calm, bland even. Only a gleam in his cold azure eyes hinted at how dangerous he was.

"Where were you?" he asked Caesar. "We came upon your herd. We got lucky, to be honest, but I was surprised you weren't with them."

Caesar just stared at the bald, bearded human, who

was also responsible for the crucified apes on the ledge, the death of Spear, and the imprisonment of Caesar's people. He wasn't interested in answering this man's questions or waging a war of words. He just wanted the Colonel's blood.

He started to crawl toward his enemy, intent on ripping out his throat, but was yanked back hard by something around his own throat. Gasping, he realized too late that there was a collar around his neck and cold metal shackles upon his wrists. Glancing back over his shoulder, he saw Red at the other end of the chain connected to the collar. The turncoat gorilla tugged cruelly on the chain, obviously enjoying Caesar's humiliation and discomfort.

Revenge for Koba—and for Red's own outcast status?

Preacher stepped forward, leveling his crossbow at Caesar, who glared at him scornfully. Their situations had once been reversed, not so long ago.

"I hope you don't come to regret sparing his life," the Colonel said. "He's quite a good shot."

His tone was casual, but Caesar once again caught a gleam of genuine madness in the man's eyes that reminded him disturbingly of Koba. There was something wrong, *damaged*, about this human.

Which made him all the more dangerous.

"Have you finally come to save your apes?" the Colonel asked.

"I... did not know they were here," Caesar said, seething with fury and frustration. His green eyes blazed murderously. "I came for *you*."

His meaning was not lost on the Colonel, who paused to consider the ape's blunt statement. Understanding dawned on his face.

"I see," he said. "I kill somebody close to you that night?"

Caesar looked the human squarely in the eyes.

"My... family."

The accusation jolted the Colonel, who appeared taken aback by the revelation. He stepped closer to Caesar, maddeningly so, and stared silently at the ape with an inscrutable expression on his face. Caesar could tell that he had struck a nerve somehow, but had no way of knowing what unhinged thoughts and emotions were churning behind the human's icy blue eyes. Red cautiously tightened his grip on the chain.

"I'm sorry," the Colonel said, in seeming sincerity. "I was there to kill you."

Caesar ignored the worthless apology. He glowered at the Colonel, who was almost but not quite within reach. Simian muscles tensed as the human inched ever nearer, seemingly fascinated by the legendary ape he had been hunting for years.

"My God, look at your eyes... they're *almost* human." He considered the prisoner before him. "How did you know I was here?"

Caesar saw no reason to dissemble. "I was told you were coming. That others would be joining you here."

"Joining me...?"

"To finish us off," Caesar said, "for good."

The Colonel smirked, as though at a private joke. "Who told you that?"

Caesar held his tongue, not about to betray Bad Ape's confidence, let alone alert the Colonel to the presence of Maurice and Rocket and the others. Caesar wondered how long he'd been unconscious. If the sun hadn't risen yet, then his friends would still be waiting in the woods just beyond the canyon. He had told them to leave and join the others, but that was before he'd discovered that the exodus was already doomed. He wasn't sure what he wanted them to do now.

They were on their own now: just three apes and a

human girl. *Up against the Colonel and his army?*

The Colonel sighed in resignation, acting none too surprised by Caesar's refusal to answer his question. He nodded at Red.

"Okay, let's go."

Red yanked Caesar roughly to his feet, causing his head to spin momentarily. The collar dug into Caesar's throat, choking him.

"Okay!" Red rasped. "Okay, *Kerna*!"

Preacher also moved in toward Caesar, keeping a close watch on the captive ape, as he and Red marched Caesar out of the depot into the frozen prison yard beyond, which Caesar had previously only viewed from above. Peering about, despite the chain attached to his neck, he tried to take in as many details as he could manage.

It was still dark out, but electric lights lit the area harshly. The old railway tracks led away from the depot; glancing back at the moldering, hangar-like structure, Caesar spied a corroded metal sign identifying the building:

CA STATE BORDER QUARANTINE

DETENTION & RELOCATION CENTER,

PROCESSING DEPOT

In other words, Caesar translated, the human zoo where infected men, women, and children were brought to die. And where, according to Bad Ape, the guards had eventually died as well.

Leaving the depot behind, they followed the tracks past a string of dilapidated multi-level structures that had apparently been put to use as barracks for the Colonel's troops. Tiers of abandoned cell blocks, which had probably once been used to house infected humans under quarantine, were stacked on top of each other along both sides of a wide open yard that was littered with frosted rubble and debris. Many of the containment cells were missing doors, windows, and even walls. Human soldiers, huddled around campfires in front of the crumbling barracks, gave Caesar dirty looks as he passed them.

Beyond the barracks, a pair of two-story guard towers watched over the camp. Electrical wires and cables were strung across the yard. Searchlights swept the canyon, revealing more hateful, hand-painted slogans like the ones back at the Colonel's base camp.

MONKEY HUNTING SEASON!

EXTINCTION, NOT EVOLUTION!

KONGS BURN IN HELL!

MAKE THE WORLD HUMAN AGAIN!

Armed guards manned the watchtowers. They snapped to attention at the sight of them.

"Evening, Colonel!" one of the guards shouted down.

The Colonel did not bother looking up at the guard. "Any more trouble tonight?"

"No, sir!" the guard responded forcefully, eager to please. "Not anymore."

He pointed at the crucified apes on the granite shelf above. There were only eleven figures bound to the wooden X's now that Spear was gone. None of them appeared to be moving.

The Colonel finally peered up at the guard. He scowled slightly.

"You could use a haircut there, son." He scrutinized the other guard. "You too, soldier."

"Sir, yessir!" they answered in unison, demonstrating that what Red had said earlier, about the human soldiers' devotion to the Colonel, had not been an exaggeration. As a primate, Caesar recognized a display of dominance when he saw one. The Colonel's command over his troops appeared unchallenged.

There would be no human Koba usurping his authority.

Caesar slowed to consider this, earning him a sharp tug on the collar from Red. Caesar stumbled forward, toward where his people were being held against their will.

Countless chimpanzees, gorillas, orangutans, and bonobos were crowded into several large holding pens. Masses of apes, representing practically the entire population of their one-time fortress, were shackled to each other like an old-fashioned human chain gang, making it impossible for them to climb out of the fenced enclosures. They stared aghast at Caesar through the metal bars of the fences, stunned to see him. His heart aching for his people, he tried to meet their eyes, to let them know that he shared their distress, but, to his surprise and dismay, the majority of the apes averted their gaze. Sullen expressions and resentful scowls greeted Caesar.

They've lost faith in me, he realized. *Because I was not there for them when they needed me most.*

The realization that his own people felt that he had abandoned them jolted Caesar to his core. He staggered numbly, on the verge of losing all hope, when a frenzy of plaintive shrieks from another pen seized his attention. Turning rapidly, he saw that one of the pens was filled exclusively with ape children, heartlessly separated from their parents. Helpless and frightened, the children gazed pitiably at Caesar, looking to him for deliverance. One small chimpanzee pushed his way through the others to press himself against the fence, trying desperately to keep pace with Caesar, who was devastated to behold the terrified face of his only surviving son.

Cornelius!

Cornelius's tearful eyes pleaded for his father. His tiny fingers stretched through the bars of the fence, pathetically trying to reach Caesar, who wanted nothing more than to comfort his motherless child. His son needed him.

Caesar wanted to lunge toward his child, chain or no chain, but forced himself to hold back. He glanced anxiously at the Colonel, terrified that he would take note of the little chimp's frantic reaction to Caesar and figure out that he hadn't killed all of Caesar's family just yet. Better that the Colonel thought that he was just another ape child of no special importance.

He shook his head urgently at Cornelius, trying to quiet him, just as the Colonel started to turn toward the commotion. Caesar longed to comfort his child instead; it was torture to keep silent.

I have no choice, Caesar thought.

He turned his back on Cornelius, walking on as though his son's panicky cries meant nothing to him. The heartbreaking shrieks, as well as those of the other children, tortured Caesar, who could still feel his little son's eyes upon him as he left him alone in that dismal cage.

Just like Will left me alone in the primate shelter so many years ago.

Caesar remembered just how confused and betrayed he had felt on that nightmarish day. And he knew exactly what Cornelius had to be feeling right now, watching his father abandon him without a word.

Forgive me, my son. This is the only way to keep you safe.

If any of us is truly safe now...

The door to the adult ape pen slid open, the ice on its hinges cracking as it did. The Colonel sneered at the chained and dispirited apes confined to the pen, who shuffled anxiously at its opposite end, getting as far away from the soldiers as possible.

"Your apes didn't put up much of a fight," he informed Caesar. "You should have been with them." He snickered at his new prisoner. "Well, you're with them now."

He nodded at Preacher, who handed Red a key from his belt. The turncoat hurled Caesar to the ground with more force than was strictly necessary. Grabbing Caesar's leg, he yanked on it roughly as he began shackling Caesar to the other apes. Caesar winced in pain.

"Hey," Preacher muttered under his breath. "Take it easy, donkey."

Red looked irritably at the young soldier, but clearly knew better than to directly challenge a human. Preacher glanced nervously at the Colonel, as though he feared that his half-hearted show of compassion might incur a rebuke, but the Colonel merely observed the exchange in silence.

His work done, Red returned the key to Preacher. Caesar discreetly kept a close eye on the key as Preacher clipped it back onto the crowded ring on his belt, while trying hard not to make his interest too obvious. He shot a glance at the Colonel, who lingered for a moment before exiting the pen without another word. Preacher and Red followed as the door to the pen slammed shut behind them. A heavy padlock clicked in place.

Caesar found himself reunited with his people, but there was no heartfelt homecoming, joyous or otherwise. The captive apes all but ignored his presence, at most casting furtive glances at him while murmuring and signing amongst themselves. Caesar wished he could blame them for holding his departure against him, but given that he had finally returned not as a liberator, as they might have hoped, but as simply another helpless prisoner, was it truly any wonder that he had lost the confidence of those who had once revered him?

But, just as he was convinced that he was now a king without a country, a kind hand reached down to help him to his feet. Caesar looked up into the wizened face of Percy, the orangutan elder from his council. Percy offered

Caesar a sad, world-weary smile, while gesturing vaguely at the other apes.

Forgive them, he signed. *We've been through a great deal.*

That much was obvious. Heartsick, Caesar surveyed what was left of his people—and saw Lake among them. The female chimp was shackled further down the chain, but was close enough to grant Caesar a look of sympathy, even as Cornelius's anguished squawks and shrieks drew her gaze toward the penned children across the yard from the adults. Her lovely face filled with regret.

I'm sorry, she signed to Caesar. *I tried to keep him safe. They separated us from the children as soon as we got here.*

Caesar did not judge her. She had kept Cornelius alive at least, for which he would always be grateful, no matter how short always might turn out to be. He was confident that Lake had done her very best to protect Blue Eyes' little brother. It was a miracle that any of them were still alive at all, let alone little Cornelius.

Caesar stared bleakly across the agonizing gap between him and his son, who was still pressed up against the fence several yards away. Chains, fences, armed guards, and the Colonel's genocidal campaign divided them, just as so many other apes' families were divided.

But to what end?

17

"Hu-uh-left! Left-right-left...!"

A chanting voice greeted the dawn, rousing Caesar from uneasy dreams. He woke to find himself lying on the icy ground of the pen, still chained to the other apes, who were stirring as well. The sound of marching boots accompanied the stern voice ringing out with a distinctly military cadence.

Still slightly disoriented, Caesar looked around at his fellow prisoners, who all looked anxious, as though they knew—and dreaded—what was coming next. His eyes found Percy, who shook his aged head somberly. The old ape could offer only sympathy, not hope.

The noise from the pounding boots built in volume, drawing Caesar's attention to the grounds outside the ape pens, where at least three hundred human soldiers were marching in tight formation. Rising to his feet, Caesar observed the intimidating faces of the soldiers. Stony expressions allowed no weakness. Intense, blazing eyes exposed a common sense of purpose. Caesar could tell that any one of them would gladly die for the cause—and their Colonel.

Caesar knew that look. He had once seen it on the faces of his own people.

The chanting ceased and troops halted in unison. Executing a sharp about-face, they stared reverently up at the warden's station atop the central watchtower. The vandalized state flag hung below the empty balcony surrounding the station. The soldiers fervently saluted the banner and what it now stood for.

$A\Omega$.

Chilled, and not just by the brisk mountain morning, Caesar watched as an executive officer, whom the ape did not recognize, led the massed troops in some sort of ritual or ceremony.

"Blood...!" the lieutenant called out.

"MAKES THE GRASS GROW!" the soldiers responded.

"We...!"

"MAKE THE BLOOD FLOW!"

"We are the beginning...!"

"AND THE END!"

The ominous rite unnerved Caesar; even the most brutal humans he'd encountered in the past had never displayed this kind of fanaticism. The soldiers and survivors back in San Francisco, after the plague, had just been scared and desperate and angry. Caesar had understood what had driven them to violence, even if he'd had to fight back against them.

But this was something... different. Something wrong.

And even more terrifying.

"Oo-rah!" chanted the soldiers as the Colonel finally stepped out onto the balcony high above his troops. He was bare-chested, despite the cold, as though he hadn't finished dressing yet. Casually shaving his skull with a straight razor, he gazed down at his cheering soldiers, who chanted and whooped at the mere sight of him. "OO-RAH!"

Shrill army whistles cut through the roar, calling the troops to action. Breaking formation, the soldiers stomped toward the pens and unlocked them. Armed guards, accompanied by Red and a few other turncoat apes, stormed into the enclosures and forced the lines of chained apes to their feet and out into the yard. Barked commands were backed up by vicious leather whips, which were employed freely and indiscriminately, regardless of whether they were needed or not. The whips cracked against the backs and shoulders of the prisoners, brutally reminding Caesar of the ugly welts across Spear's back before he died. The sight of apes whipping apes turned Caesar's stomach.

Apes do not hurt apes!

The Colonel coolly watched the savagery unfolding below him. Putting down his razor, he retrieved a small stainless-steel flask from his hip and sipped from it slowly before retreating back into his tower.

The soldiers marched the apes across the snow toward the far end of the camp, away from the mountain looming above the railway depot. Armed guards paced menacingly on large railcar tankers lined up along one side of the camp; Caesar guessed that the tanks provided fuel for the camp's generators, keeping the lights on at night.

Humans and their fossil fuels, he thought. *Apes don't need electricity.*

Not that this does us any good now.

His jaw dropped as they passed beyond the tankers and a tremendously high wall came into view. Sealing the front end of the canyon, the colossal structure was like nothing Caesar had ever seen, before or after the humans' civilization crashed. Part of it, consisting of large cracked slabs of weathered concrete erected many years ago, appeared to be man-made, but the bulk of the wall was obviously *ape-made*. Building on the original construction, massive tree trunks had been fastened together to form an enormous framework into which huge chunks of stone were being set, one by one. The sheer amount of manual labor required was astounding—and explained why exactly the Colonel hadn't killed all the apes yet.

He's using us as slave labor, Caesar realized. *To rebuild the wall.*

The soldiers herded the apes toward the wall. Caesar noted that one old concrete slab, still standing amidst the newer timber and stone construction, was marked by graffiti. $A\Omega$ had been painted in red upon the slab, while large blood-hued letters spelled out a chilling message:

HUMANITY'S LAST STAND. Built on the backs of captive apes.

Caesar soon experienced firsthand what his unfortunate people had been enduring for days. The sun beat down on him, despite the wintry climate, as he toiled ceaselessly upon the wall, now just another slave in a suffering mass of apes forced into hard labor by the Colonel's soldiers. Huge rocks, too heavy for the average human to lift, were passed from ape to ape, while other apes strained on ropes to lift the boulders into place high upon the ever-growing wall. Armed soldiers supervised the construction, their weapons discouraging any opposition from the overworked apes, while Red and his fellow turncoats stood ready with their whips in case any of the ape workers slackened. Squinting into the sunlight, Caesar saw even more apes perched precariously on a rocky shelf overlooking the tanker cars, where they were being compelled to quarry more stones from the ledge using picks and hammers. Armed guards ensured that the tools were not converted into weapons.

At least our children are not being worked to death,
Caesar thought grimly. *Yet.*

The back-breaking labor went on for hours without
respite. Not far from Caesar, Lake panted in exhaustion
as she passed yet another boulder along the line; she was a
young ape, in her prime, but Caesar could see that all of the
apes had been pushed to the limits of their endurance. They
were weary, gaunt, on the verge of collapse. He had only
been at it for less than a day and he was already bone-tired
and ready to drop; he could only imagine how fatigued the
other apes were, especially the weak and the elderly.

He lifted his eyes to the upper reaches of the wall, where
Percy could be seen among the apes pulling the boulders
up on ropes. The geriatric orangutan was gasping for
breath, barely pulling his weight; Caesar was astounded
that the old ape was managing to work at all, given his
advanced age and how arduous the task was. His heart
ached to see his people abused this way. His jaw tightened.

Lake noticed his dismay.

We haven't had food or water since we got here, she
signed.

No food? Caesar thought. *That can't be...*

He had not thought that he could be any more shocked or
angry. Even the worst labs and zoos back in the old days had
at least fed and watered their animals; how did the Colonel
expect the apes to keep working without food and water?
He glared furiously at the mammoth structure that was
practically consuming his people's lives before his very eyes.

And for what reason?

Caesar didn't understand. *Why do they need a wall?*

Lake shook her head, not having any answers for him,
even as she strained to pass another hefty stone along the
chain gang. The stone passed through Caesar's hands as

well as he pondered the need for the wall. Was it to keep the apes in—or someone else out?

His musings were interrupted by the arrival of the Colonel, who strode onto the scene to inspect the progress of the work. His eyes quickly located Caesar, fixing on the captured ape leader, only to be drawn away by a harsh shout from the upper heights of the wall.

"Hey!" an angry soldier yelled. "Hey!"

High above, Percy was at the end of his rope… literally. Swaying unsteadily upon shaky legs, the old orangutan lost his grip on a thick rope hauling up yet another painfully heavy boulder. As the Colonel and the others looked up in alarm, Percy collapsed and the boulder swung into the wall, smashing into the framework and knocking loose the other stones stacked there. An entire section of rock wall came crashing down in an unplanned avalanche that was many times louder than the screams and shouts it provoked. Panicked apes and humans alike dived out of the way of tumbling boulders, which landed in a heap at the base of the wall, raising a choking cloud of dust and grit. Caesar backed away from the collapse, instinctively shielding Lake and the other members of the chain gang with his body. As the dust cloud cleared, he looked anxiously for Percy and saw the ape lying in the rubble where the avalanche had come to rest.

"Stupid monkey!" a red-faced soldier shouted at Percy before turning his rage on Red as well. "Don't just stand there, you useless donkey! Teach him a lesson he'll never forget!"

"Okay, Boyle," Red grunted. "Okay."

Caesar couldn't believe his eyes. Instead of tending to the injured old ape, Red and the other turncoats roughly dragged Percy from the rubble and brought him out into the yard where the Colonel could see. Down on his knees, clutching his wounds, Percy looked as though he

THE OFFICIAL MOVIE NOVELIZATION

couldn't even stand on his own, but that didn't stop Red from dutifully lashing the feeble orangutan with his whip. Percy spasmed and shrieked as the whip cracked against his weak and battered body.

Caesar glanced desperately at the Colonel, hoping against hope that the human commander would call a halt to this pointless brutality, but the Colonel simply looked on, seemingly unmoved by the sadistic spectacle, even as the whip came down on Percy again, wrenching an agonized howl from him.

The horrific scene drew Caesar forward, dragging the rest of the chained apes behind him. His own rage boiling over, he pulled himself up onto one of the prodigious tree trunks comprising the immense framework and finally gave voice to the volcanic fury that had been building up in him for hours.

"LEAVE HIM!"

18

A stunned hush fell over the worksite at Caesar's outburst, broken only by the sound of loose gravel and scree tumbling down the wall in the wake of the avalanche. All heads turned toward the furious chimpanzee as he glared down at the Colonel from the wooden timbers, unconcerned for his own safety. Apes and humans alike stopped dead in their tracks, stunned by Caesar's booming command. Even Red lowered his whip, forgetting about Percy's punishment for the moment.

Caesar locked eyes with the Colonel for long seconds, neither leader budging, when, one by one, the other apes began to rally behind Caesar. It started quietly, with just a few low grunts and growls, but then more apes joined in, hooting and shrieking defiantly, until the sound rose into a deafening chorus that echoed off the granite walls of the canyon. Scowling apes dropped the stones they'd been burdened with or angrily tossed aside their ropes and tools.

The spontaneous demonstration shocked Caesar. He turned in surprise to see his people, who had previously rejected him, rising in open rebellion behind him, standing in solidarity with their fellow apes. His heart swelled with pride and gratitude. His people had not given up on hope… or him.

Apes together strong.

Down on the icy floor of the prison yard, Percy gazed up in awe and admiration, despite his many grievous injuries, as the human soldiers appeared at a loss as to how to deal with this unexpected turn of events. The fierce cries of the apes rising to a fever pitch, the troops looked to the Colonel for guidance, but he just stared balefully at Caesar.

In desperation, a soldier shouted at Red and the other turncoats, pointing urgently at Caesar.

"Get him!"

The ape enforcers, accompanied by Preacher and a few other humans, scaled the heaps of rubble to approach Caesar, who stepped down to meet them, unafraid of whatever consequences lay ahead. That he had roused his people from despair, and inspired them to stand up to their oppressors, outweighed whatever punishment the Colonel might have in store, up to and including a summary execution. His only regret was that he would not be able to say goodbye to Cornelius—or guarantee his son's safety.

The other apes in the chain gang, including Lake, chanted and hooted in unison as the turncoats seized Caesar, taking hold of his arms. They started to lunge forward, but were held at bay by the raised weapons of Preacher and his fellow soldiers. To Caesar's relief, the shackled apes did not invite the soldiers' fire by trying to protect him; they could only roar in protest, along with the rest of the enslaved apes. A few of the gorillas beat their chests. Chimpanzees angrily slapped the ground. Orangutans shook their fists.

Visibly nervous, Preacher sweated and swallowed hard, keeping a close watch on the angry apes as he unclipped a key from his belt and tossed it over to Red, who dutifully unlocked Caesar from the chain gang. Casting a grateful look at Lake and the others, Caesar stepped away from them, glad that they would not be sharing his punishment, or at least not right away.

He couldn't imagine that the Colonel would take this uprising lightly.

The enemy apes and humans dragged Caesar down to the yard, where Red shoved Caesar onto his knees beside Percy. The Colonel took a moment to contemplate the kneeling chimp before calmly gesturing at Red and the other turncoats. Traitor apes tightened their grip on Caesar's arms as Red stepped behind him, bearing his whip.

Caesar braced himself for what he knew was coming.

The whip cracked savagely against Caesar's back, the force and pain of it even worse than he had anticipated. He clenched his jaw to keep from crying out; the Colonel was trying to make an example of him, as he had the crucified apes, so Caesar was determined to put up a brave front for as long as he could. He could not—would not—surrender before the eyes of his people.

Even so, the defiant hooting of the apes faltered as they witnessed their king being whipped. Other apes gasped and moaned in sympathy, even though Caesar made no sound.

Equally mute, the Colonel nodded at Red, who whipped Caesar again, just as hard as before, with all the strength of a gorilla. More of the protesting apes fell silent, shocked into speechlessness by the brutal spectacle. Beside Caesar, Percy dropped his eyes and stared bleakly at the dirty slush, his spirit seemingly as broken as his body.

But Caesar refused to give in. Gritting his teeth against the searing agony ripping across his back, he stared stubbornly into the Colonel's eyes as the two leaders confronted each other, neither willing to back down.

The Colonel nodded a third time, and even Red

hesitated for a moment, as though surprised by the command, before lashing Caesar once more. The sharp crack of the whip rang out in the appalled hush that had fallen over the camp. Wincing in pain, Caesar stubbornly endured the blows without a sound, even as he felt his own blood streaming down his back, wetting his fur. His tortured back felt like it was on fire. His whole body trembled, succumbing to shock. He couldn't remember ever experiencing pain like this, not even when Koba shot a bullet into him. He didn't even have the strength to brace himself against the blows anymore. He tottered unsteadily upon his knees, but kept his head high.

But how much longer could he stand up to this beating? He was only flesh and blood...

Coldly, impassively, the Colonel nodded again, eliciting gasps even from his own soldiers. Preacher looked away, unable to watch. Red gulped, shaken by how far he was being asked to go, but slowly raised his whip again and did as instructed. The lash came down on Caesar's shredded back with the vengeance of the entire human race.

Caesar's strength faltered; even he couldn't stand up to this much physical punishment. Mournful gasps and murmurs rippled through the other apes as his head sagged at last.

Satisfied, the Colonel nodded at the turncoats, who finally released Caesar. The tortured ape crumpled to the ground, his face landing in the cold, muddy slush.

"Okay," the Colonel said. "Back to work."

The soldier yelled at the apes to resume their labors, but the apes ignored them. They stared anxiously at their fallen leader instead, as though afraid that he might never rise again.

Caesar lifted his head. Mud smeared his features, clinging to his flesh and fur, but he was not finished yet.

He looked back at his people, who were counting on him, then glowered furiously at the Colonel.

"Apes need *food*," he growled. "*Water*."

The Colonel contemplated the recalcitrant apes, as well as his own hesitant troops, then looked down at Caesar.

"Please," he said. "Tell them to work."

Caesar's body had surrendered, but not his will. Defiance seethed in his voice as he repeated his demands.

"Give them food and wat—"

Before he could finish, the Colonel drew his sidearm and shot Percy in the head, killing him instantly. The orangutan's body dropped onto the snow beside Caesar, who barely had a heartbeat to react to the gunshot— and Percy's sudden demise—before, with chilling speed and efficiency, the Colonel placed the barrel of his pistol against Caesar's temple. The cold metal felt hard against his skin and skull.

"Tell them," the Colonel said calmly. His voice was eerily contained and level, unlike those of the agitated apes, who vocalized in fear, even as the sharp report of the gunshot still rang in Caesar's ears.

He glared at the Colonel fearlessly, hating him as he had never hated any human or ape before. Percy's pointless death was one more atrocity to add to the Colonel's list of crimes against the apes. No human words or speech could convey the depths of Caesar's fury. His abused body trembled with rage.

"Five," the Colonel began. "Four…"

The gun pressed against Caesar's temple, but he didn't flinch. If he had to die to prove to the Colonel—and his people—that apes could not be treated like animals, then so be it. He had given his life to the defense of his people. He would gladly do so one last time.

"Three… two…"

Loose stones clattered by the wall as a lone ape picked up one of the fallen boulders, straining under its weight. Turning his head, Caesar saw that it was Lake, frantically returning to work in a desperate attempt to save his life.

No, he thought, distraught. *Don't do this for me.*

But it was too late. Another ape bent to lift a rock from the pile, then another and another. As Caesar watched in dismay, his people resumed their labors on the wall, reclaiming their burdens and tools, making all his suffering in vain.

I failed, and he's won.

The human lowered his gun, putting it back in its holster. He turned toward Red and barked out a command.

"String him up, donkey."

19

A platform had been erected in the center of the prison yard for all to see. Red bound Caesar to the tall wooden X on it, tying his wrists and ankles with thick lengths of rope, while armed humans stood guard. Caesar put up no resistance, but merely sagged weakly upon the cross. Dried mud caked his face.

That's not like him, Maurice thought. *What have they done to him?*

The orangutan lowered the binoculars, horrified by what he had just witnessed. He and the others peered down at the sprawling camp from a ledge overlooking the bottom of the canyon. Rocket and Bad Ape lay beside him, keeping low and out of sight from the humans below, while the girl clung to his back as usual. Maurice had spotted among the guard one of the human soldiers Caesar had spared before.

So much for gratitude, he thought.

Rocket watched his expression, anxious to know what Maurice had seen. The orangutan handed him the binoculars so he could see for himself, too shaken by what he had just witnessed to speak or sign.

"*Bad* place," Bad Ape insisted, not for the first time. When the other apes did not respond right away, he addressed his warning to the girl instead, fearfully seeking anyone who might listen. "Bad, bad place."

The girl stared at him blankly.

Peering through the binoculars, Rocket grunted unhappily.

"What?" Bad Ape asked anxiously, looking as though he was on the verge of fleeing at any moment. He fidgeted restlessly, too frightened to keep still. "What you see…?"

Rocket turned the lenses away from Caesar toward the front of the canyon. Maurice knew what he saw there: masses of chained apes laboring on an immense wall. And not just any apes, but the apes from the fortress, the ones who were supposed to be on their way to a new home. The ones Caesar had ordered them to seek out if he did not return.

Our people, Maurice thought. *Enslaved.*

The situation in the canyon had proved many times worse than they had feared. They had descended the cliffs searching for Caesar, defying his orders to abandon him if he didn't return before dawn, only to discover that there was no exodus to rejoin. All of their people were here in this forsaken place, held captive by the Colonel and his troops.

Rocket set the binoculars down.

Must do something, he signed. *We are the only ones who can save them now.*

Maurice nodded gravely, although it was unclear what they could do under the circumstances. They had already lost Luca, and perhaps Caesar as well. How could only three apes free their people from an army of humans?

"Oh no!" Bad Ape exclaimed.

Maurice turned to see the addled chimp squinting into the wrong end of the binoculars with a look of horror on his face.

"Why they so small?"

Shuddering, he lowered the binoculars. Maurice and Rocket looked at each other; it would have been comical had Bad Ape not been their only remaining ally at this point. Sighing, Rocket reached out and flipped the binoculars around before handing them back to Bad Ape, who still looked puzzled as he lifted them to his eyes once more.

"Ohhh," he said.

Red finished binding Caesar to the X, tugging on the knots to make sure they were tight. Caesar winced, but said nothing, too exhausted and discouraged to object. Preacher frowned at the rough treatment.

"All right," the human said. "That's good."

Red looked at Preacher, who cocked his head toward the steps leading down from the platform. Red glanced back at Caesar, his lips curling as he gave the other ape a contemptuous sneer before heading down the steps. Lingering, Preacher watched Red depart, then approached Caesar hesitantly. He glanced about to make sure no one was watching and lowered his voice.

"Look, I owe you one," the soldier said, "so let me set you straight here, okay? I think he respects you, he does… that's why you're still alive. But believe me, he can do a lot worse than this. I've seen it."

A haunted look in his eyes hinted at past horrors. His voice descended to a whisper.

"You do *not* want to agitate the man. Understand? So just…"

Back off, he gestured.

Still glancing about nervously, Preacher retreated down the steps, leaving Caesar alone upon the platform. The young soldier's disturbing warning made Caesar all the more fearful for his people's safety. If even the other humans were afraid of what the Colonel was ultimately capable of, what did that mean for the apes?

Hours passed as Caesar hung upon the cross, with nothing but pain, hunger, thirst, and despair to keep him company. His lips were cracked and dry, while the welts on his back rubbed painfully against the wooden beams, making any true rest or sleep impossible. His wrists and ankles chafed against the ropes. A cold winter wind chilled him to the bone. Darkness fell, dragging the temperature down with it. A diesel generator coughed noisily to life. Harsh security lights assaulted Caesar's eyes.

Averting his eyes from the glare, he was startled by a loud commotion heading toward him from the rear of the camp, where the mountain resided. Puzzled by the clamor, he saw a large contingent of soldiers rolling various pieces of heavy artillery toward the wall—and the apes working there. Missiles, rocket launchers, and other lethal hardware provided more than enough firepower to destroy every ape in captivity. The sight jolted Caesar, despite his exhausted state. He strained helplessly at his bonds.

Was this it? Had the Colonel decided to end his war against the apes once and for all?

The other apes were alarmed by the approaching weaponry as well. Chained and unarmed, they didn't stand a chance against the soldiers and their artillery. More soldiers, toting heavy M2 machine guns, appeared and hoisted the formidable weapons up to the tops of the sentry towers, where they were positioned atop sturdy steel tripods. These chores the humans wisely handled themselves, not wanting to place the high-powered guns in the hands of the apes. Caesar feared he was about to witness a bloodbath.

It would be just like the Colonel, he thought, *to make*

me watch my people being slaughtered.

But then he noticed something odd.

All the artillery was pointed outward, away from the camp.

Not at the apes then, but at whom? Relieved to realize that the weapons were being placed to defend the canyon, not massacre his people, Caesar grew perplexed. There was more here than met the eye. What was the true purpose of the artillery—and the wall for that matter? Could it be that—?

Footsteps intruded on his ruminations. Caesar looked away from the soldiers' preparations to see Red climbing the steps of the platform toward him, gripping a machete in one hand. The smug, vindictive expression on the gorilla's face promised nothing in the way of mercy.

But was Red seeking his own revenge or acting on the Colonel's orders?

Fearing the worst, Caesar lifted his eyes toward the Colonel's watchtower and saw the human commander framed in the window, gazing down at the platform. Caesar remembered how casually the man had shot Percy only hours ago—and Caesar's family before that.

My turn, Caesar guessed. *What's another dead ape to him?*

He looked back at Red, determined to face his executioner. Red paused before him, savoring the moment. The machete in his hands looked sharp enough to avenge Koba, but Caesar would not surrender to fear. He looked Red squarely in the eye and spoke hoarsely.

"What did the Colonel promise you? You really think he will let you live... after we are gone?"

Red's hair bristled aggressively. He glared murderously at his former leader.

"No matter what you do," Caesar taunted, "you'll never be one of them." He snorted derisively. "You let them call you 'donkey.' You are *ape*."

Sneering, Red raised the machete and ran a finger along the blade, testing its edge. Disgust contorted his face.

"Koba right," he snarled. "You think you *better*... than rest of apes. But look you now." He bared his teeth. "You *nothing*."

He angrily raised the machete above his head. Caesar braced himself for the fatal blow as the weapon came swinging down—and sank into a wooden beam only inches from Caesar's wrist. The blade hacked through rope instead, freeing Caesar's arm. He gaped at Red in surprise.

"Kerna... want see you," the gorilla said.

Caesar looked back up at the watchtower, where the Colonel was still watching from above, his hands clasped behind his back. Had he expected Caesar to beg for his life? Was he pleased or disappointed that Caesar had not?

He respects you, Preacher had said.

Whatever that meant.

The Colonel lingered behind the window for a moment, then turned and vanished into his lair. Caesar's eyes narrowed suspiciously.

What did the Colonel want with him now?

20

A door at the top of the watchtower swung open, admitting Caesar to the Colonel's command center. Red and Preacher escorted him into the premises, alert to the first signs of rebellion. The young human kept his crossbow at the ready to guarantee Caesar's cooperation. Red had Caesar on the chain again.

The Colonel did not acknowledge their arrival. His back to Caesar, he leaned over a long table on top of which a large map had been spread out. Fragrant smoke rose from a smudge of sage and grass burning in a tin bowl. The incense struck Caesar as an incongruous touch, out of character with the man's brutality.

Searchlights situated around the camp swept over the cliffs outside, periodically lighting up the windows of the watchtower. One such sweep briefly illuminated a small chamber just off the command center; Caesar caught a fleeting glimpse of some sort of private sanctuary. A grisly collection of ape skulls, with every breed of great ape represented, were piled upon an altar. The word HISTORY was scrawled across the wall in bold, jagged letters— possibly by the Colonel himself?

The search beam moved on, throwing the grotesque sanctum back into shadow, but Caesar's momentary look at the morbid collection had been enough to send a chill down the chimpanzee's spine. Examining the Colonel by the interior lights of the command center, Caesar noted for the first time that the human had old marks on the backs of both hands that looked as though they had been branded there by a red-hot iron.

A scarred his right hand; Ω scarred his left.

"Interfere with the work again," the Colonel said finally, not looking up from his map, "and I'll begin slaughtering the apes, one by one. Understand? I need that wall."

He turned to look at Caesar, perhaps to make sure the ape was listening, then nodded at Preacher to indicate they were done here. Red and Preacher started to lead Caesar away, but the ape was not ready to leave yet.

"Apes... need food... water."

The Colonel kept his eyes fixed on the map. "They'll get food and water when they finish the work."

"Give them food or water," Caesar argued, "or they will not be *able* to finish."

The Colonel turned away from the table, facing Caesar at last. He chuckled and shook his head, seemingly amused by the prisoner's audacity.

"You know you're very emotional." He looked over the shackled, unarmed, and outnumbered chimpanzee. "What makes you think you're in a position to make demands?"

Caesar had no ready answer, so the Colonel went back to his map. Preacher prodded Caesar with his crossbow.

"C'mon..."

Preacher had warned Caesar not to provoke the Colonel, hinting at dire possibilities if he exhausted the human commander's patience, but Caesar didn't care. Despite the chain tugging on his collar, he refused to budge.

"The soldiers who are coming here... are not coming to *join* you, are they?"

That got the Colonel's attention. He turned back toward Caesar, looking more intrigued than before. He smiled at Caesar in what might have been grudging admiration, while Red warily tightened his grip on Caesar's chain.

"I saw men outside by the wall... preparing for battle..."

It was the only explanation that made sense. Winter had been mistaken when he'd said that the Colonel's troops were planning to meet up with reinforcements from the north; the Colonel was building the wall to defend himself from the approaching forces.

"I was told you were smart," the human said appreciatively, "but... that's *impressive*." He paused briefly before confirming Caesar's suspicions. "No, they won't be joining me."

Caesar didn't care about impressing the Colonel. He just wanted to understand the situation, for his people's sake.

"They are *against* you?"

"They fear me," the Colonel said.

"Why...?"

The Colonel did not reply, but Caesar could guess the answer.

"Because you kill your own men?"

Preacher tensed nearby, clearly not liking where this conversation was going. The Colonel stared at Caesar in surprise, stunned by how much the ape had deduced already.

"We found bodies." Caesar recalled the snow-covered corpses by the trail and the makeshift cemetery along the shore, as well as that one panicked survivor who seemed to have lost the power of speech. "Something *wrong*... with these men."

The Colonel shook his head in amazement.

"Jesus Christ, you are impressive." He smirked at Caesar,

as though he was almost enjoying this encounter. "Well, you paint quite a picture. What must you think of me."

"I think… you have no mercy."

The smirk vanished from the Colonel's face. His expression darkened.

"You came here to kill me. Were you going to show me mercy?"

"I showed you mercy," Caesar said, "when I spared your men. I offered you peace… and you killed my family."

"*Mercy*." The Colonel grimaced as though the word tasted bad on his tongue. "Do you have any idea what your *mercy* would do to us?"

Caesar tensed warily. He wasn't sure what he had said to provoke the Colonel, but the human's wry amusement had been replaced by a simmering rage that had Caesar keeping one eye on the man's sidearm while remembering Preacher's warning earlier. There was no telling what this man might do.

"You're much stronger than we are," the Colonel said venomously. "And you're smart as hell. No matter what you say, you'd eventually replace us; that's the law of Nature. And the irony is, we *created* you. We tried to defy Nature, bend it to our will. And Nature's been punishing us for our arrogance ever since. *Testing* us. Even now."

Caesar could have defended Will's experiments, explained that Will had been a good man who had only been trying to cure a terrible disease, but that was ancient history now, gone with most of humanity. Instead he held his tongue and let the Colonel go on. The more the man talked, the more Caesar learned about what was driving his enemy.

"Ten months ago, we sent out recon units to look for your base. They found nothing. My own son was a soldier with one of the groups. One day he suddenly stopped speaking. He became... *primitive*, like an animal." A muscle twitched beneath his cheek. "They contacted me, said that they thought he'd lost his mind, that the war was too much for him. But the man taking care of him stopped speaking too. Their medic had a theory, before *he* stopped speaking: that the virus that almost wiped us out—the virus that every human survivor still carries—had suddenly changed. Mutated."

He peered at Caesar, scanning the ape's mud-splattered face to see if he was following this. Caesar understood, but the Colonel spelled it out anyway.

"And if it spread, it would destroy humanity for good this time. Not by killing us, but by robbing us of the things that make us human. Our speech, our higher thinking. It would turn us all into beasts, not unlike what you all used to be. You talk about *mercy*?" he accused Caesar. "What would *you* have done?"

Caesar thought of the mute girl Maurice had adopted, and the wild-eyed soldier grunting like an animal before escaping into the woods with a bullet in his back. He recalled the caked blood beneath the noses of the dead soldiers and recognized belatedly the telltale symptoms of the virus. The idea that the mutated virus could now reduce humans to animals was a sobering one. Caesar had gone to great lengths to raise his own people's intellect, elevating them from their primitive origins. How far would he go to keep them from slipping back into savagery?

"Well, it was a moment of clarity for me," the Colonel said. "I realized I would have to sacrifice my own son, so that humanity could be saved. I held that gun in my hand and I pointed it at my only child." His eyes moistened at the memory; raw emotion cracked his voice. "He looked at me with trust in his eyes, which was all he had left in his primitive gaze. And I pulled the trigger."

He took a deep breath, regaining his composure. He blinked to dry his eyes.

"It purified me. It made my purpose clear."

Caesar had no response. Knowing that the Colonel had killed his own son as well as Caesar's was almost enough to make Caesar pity the man, but only almost. And he understood now, more than ever, just how ruthless this human was. If the Colonel could execute his own son, he was capable of anything. The glint of madness lurking in his eyes made perfect sense now. Killing his son had twisted the Colonel's mind somehow. He didn't realize it, but it seemed to Caesar that the Colonel had *already* lost his humanity...

"I gave orders to kill the others infected, all of them, and anyone who might have been in direct contact with them, even if they showed no symptoms. We burned their belongings, anything that might spread contamination."

The torched personal effects at the cemetery, Caesar remembered. *The charred dog tags and belt buckles.*

"Some of the men questioned my judgment," the Colonel continued. "I was asking them to do what I had done: to sacrifice their families, their friends. They refused... so I had them killed too."

No wonder Preacher is so afraid of his own leader, Caesar thought. *The Colonel will kill anyone, human or ape.*

Even his own soldiers and their families.

"Others with children deserted into the woods," the Colonel said darkly, still quivering with resentment. "One of those cowards fled to my superiors up north. They sent officers down to restrain me. They tried to convince me that this plague could be dealt with medically, that they were already looking for a cure." He let out a bitter laugh. "That's when I realized that they had learned *nothing* from our past."

Caesar could predict what happened next.

"You killed them too…?"

The Colonel looked at the young soldier standing guard with his crossbow. "What did I do, Preacher?"

Preacher gulped before answering.

"You severed their heads, sir."

"Except for the one I spared," the Colonel clarified, "so he could return to deliver my message: if they wanted to relieve me of my command, they'd have to meet me here, and do it themselves."

Why here? Caesar wondered. *Why this place?*

The Colonel responded to the ape's baffled expression. "This place used to be a weapons depot. They turned it into a relocation camp when the crisis was just beginning. But the weapons are all still here, inside that mountain."

The artillery, Caesar realized. *That's where it came from.*

"This is a holy war," the Colonel declared. "All of human history has led to this moment. And if we lose, we'll be the last of our kind. It will be a planet of apes… and we'll become your cattle."

Caesar tried to imagine it: a world ruled entirely by apes, with the last remnants of humanity no more than animals, treated perhaps as humans had once treated apes, as zoo exhibits or lab specimens or circus performers, confined to cages or hunted to near-extinction. An endangered species.

It was an… unsettling vision of the future.

"Look at you," the Colonel said, noting the ape's troubled visage. "You think I'm sick, don't you?"

Caesar forced himself to focus on the crisis at hand. "How many… will be coming?"

"Probably all of them. But don't get any ideas; the only thing they fear more than me is you apes." He chuckled bitterly. "They never questioned my methods when it came to *you*."

He stepped closer to Caesar, his tone softening to a degree.

"I didn't mean to kill your son…"

Caesar stayed totally still, waiting for his enemy to get just a little bit closer. His near proximity to the Colonel was agonizing. Caesar was acutely aware of the chain holding him back and of Preacher's crossbow, both keeping him from his revenge.

"But if his destiny was to inherit your unholy kingdom," the Colonel said of Blue Eyes, "then I'm glad I did."

The Colonel's callous words unleashed the fury Caesar had been carrying since he'd lost his wife and son. All thought of caution and patience and self-preservation fled from his mind as he lunged for the Colonel, reaching for his throat. The startled human threw himself backward barely in time, so that Caesar's nails only grazed the Colonel's neck before his target tumbled out of reach, crashing onto the floor as Red hauled on Caesar's chain with both hands, yanking Caesar backwards with all his strength, so that the collar dug into Caesar's neck, choking him. The Colonel's flask fell from inside his jacket. Preacher leveled his crossbow at Caesar while crying out frantically.

"Hey! Hey-hey-hey!"

Caesar strained against the chain, but Red was too strong and he was too weak after his ordeals. Consumed by rage, he growled and bared his teeth, maddened by the need to lash out at the insane human who had murdered his family without regret.

How dare he brag about killing my son!

Shaken by his close call, the Colonel recovered his flask and tucked it back into his jacket. He backed further away from Caesar and staggered to his feet. Grimacing, he reached up and touched his neck where Caesar had scratched him, probing the shallow nicks with his fingers, which came away stained with blood. He smiled, no doubt realizing just how much worse things could have turned out for him. He regarded his assailant, who was still struggling against the chain holding him back. Caesar would have given everything for just a few more feet— and time enough to do far more to the Colonel than just scratch him.

He needs to die, Caesar thought, *at my hands.*

"So emotional!" the Colonel said, mocking him.

Caesar's furious battle against the chain slowly ebbed. After being whipped and strung up on the cross, he lacked the endurance to keep up his attack. Not with a gorilla at the other end of the chain.

"I can see how conflicted you are," the Colonel said, his smile fading. "You're confused in your purpose. You're angry at me because of something I did that was an act of war. But you're taking this all much too personally."

He walked toward Caesar, seemingly unconcerned for his safety. He got too close to the vengeful ape for Preacher's comfort.

"Sir…"

The Colonel held up his hand to silence the nervous soldier. He stepped closer to Caesar until he was just out of reach. Caesar seethed, tortured by the agonizing gap between him and his revenge. The Colonel scowled at Caesar, a trickle of blood dribbling down his neck.

"What do you think my men would have done to your apes… if you had killed me?"

Despite his fury, Caesar grasped what the Colonel was saying. Killing the Colonel would surely cause all of the other apes to be slaughtered in retaliation. Was his own revenge worth the lives of his people?

What about Cornelius? And Lake? And the rest?

Confident that Caesar had gotten the message, the

Colonel tempted fate by stepping right up to the ape, within striking range. His gun remained holstered at his hip... Caesar guessed because he knew he wouldn't need it.

"Or is killing me more important?"

Caesar knew this was probably his best and last chance of avenging his family. Every muscle in his body ached to attack the Colonel, to tear him apart before Red or Preacher could stop him.

I could do it. I could kill him now.

But at what cost? He would gladly sacrifice his own life to destroy the Colonel, but was he willing to sacrifice his people as well?

No, Caesar thought. *And the Colonel knows that.*

With titanic effort, the ape restrained himself while the Colonel lingered tauntingly before him, until it was obvious that he had made his point. He brusquely dismissed Preacher and Red, who led Caesar back down to the yard. The chill of the night came as a shock after the shelter of the Colonel's lair. An unhappy Preacher shook his head as soon as they were out of earshot, and muttered, "Didn't I tell you not to agitate him? That was not smart, man..."

Caesar was not a man, but he accepted the remark in the spirit in which it was intended. Alone among the Colonel's followers, Preacher still seemed to have a spark of goodness and compassion in him. Caesar felt a twinge of sympathy for the young soldier, who reminded him, to some degree, of the best humans he had encountered in his life: good, caring individuals like Will and Caroline and Malcolm and Ellie. Glancing back at Red, Caesar lowered his voice.

"If this battle is coming," he told Preacher, "you should leave while you still can."

"Leave?" Preacher stopped and stared at Caesar. "What are you talking about?"

Caesar addressed him gently. "You are not like him."

Preacher reacted as though he had been slapped. His voice took on a harsher edge.

"He was right, you do think he's sick, don't you?" he accused Caesar. "You're just like them. He's not crazy. The *world's* gone crazy. And he's the only one with the vision to get us through this. He sacrificed everything for us. You can't judge him. Who are you to judge him?"

The soldier's face flushed with anger.

"I was trying to give you a heads-up, keep you out of his way. I don't even know why. But if you think you and I have some sort of relationship… that you're gonna give me, what, advice? You can disavow yourself of that notion right fucking now."

Preacher's virulent response stunned Caesar—and disappointed him.

Not like Will, he realized. *Or Malcolm.*

Preacher gestured with his crossbow, sneering at the disillusioned ape. Whatever compassion he'd displayed had evaporated completely. Or maybe it had never really run as deep as Caesar had let himself hope.

"C'mon, kong," Preacher snarled.

21

Rocket growled under his breath as, through the binoculars, he watched Red and an armed human march Caesar past the soldiers' barracks, where the lights were going out one by one as the humans apparently retired for the evening after a long day of supervising the apes' slave labor. Rocket wished them bad dreams and guilty consciences.

Concealed behind snow-topped boulders, the hairless chimp crouched on a ledge overlooking the camp. Maurice, bearing the human girl on his back, and Bad Ape climbed down the rocky cliff-side to join Rocket as he spied on the scene below. Worry showed on the orangutan's face.

How is he? Maurice signed.

Rocket shook his head dolefully. Caesar didn't look good, but at least he was still alive.

And badly in need of our help, Rocket thought.

He was not sure how they could rescue Caesar, let alone the rest of the apes, but he knew they could not do it by lurking on this ledge. They would have to go lower, to where Caesar needed them.

Rising and gesturing to the others, he started down the

slope again. They set off to follow him.

Even Bad Ape.

Confined to the pen, chained to the other apes, Lake watched as Red and a human soldier brought Caesar back to the base of the platform where he had been strung up before. She was relieved to see that he was still alive, but her beaten-down spirits sank even further at the sight of Caesar, their great leader, being dragged about on a chain. He stood stoically at the bottom of the steps as the gorilla unshackled his wrists under the watchful gaze of the soldier, who was armed with a vicious-looking crossbow. She winced at the ugly welts crisscrossing Caesar's back.

He suffers for our sake, she thought. *For what little good it does.*

Her fellow prisoners also pressed against the fence, watching Caesar's ordeal. Like her, they were tired and hungry and thirsty and without hope. Caesar had tried to protest their treatment, and had briefly inspired them to stand up to the humans, but look what had become of him. Lifting his eyes, he returned their regard, taking in the sight of his people penned up like the animals they once were. The sorrowful expression on his face broke Lake's heart.

You look weary, she signed to him.

He swept his gaze over his downtrodden people. A look of renewed determination came over his majestic features. Glancing furtively at his captors, he discreetly signed to the apes behind his back:

Do not lose hope. Some way, somehow, we will finish the journey to our new home. I will find a way to get us out of here.

Lake experienced a surge of hope, and knew that her

fellow apes had to be stirred by their leader's bold promise as well. She was too young to remember when humans had once ruled the world, back in the days when Caesar first led their people to freedom, but she remembered him saving the apes from Koba's madness and shielding them from the humans who had been hunting them for years. Caesar had always found a way to protect them. She refused to lose faith in him now.

I believe in Caesar, she thought, *just like Blue Eyes would want me to.*

Over by the platform, Red finished removing Caesar's shackles and returned the key to the human, who ordered Caesar to begin climbing the steps back up to where the cruel wooden X awaited him. Despite her confidence in Caesar, Lake wondered how he could possibly save them while roped to the cross. And how long could he truly survive the ordeal?

Weak and in pain, his shoulders slumping, Caesar started up the steps, only to lose his balance and stumble backward into the human soldier, who shoved him away forcefully, as though repulsed by the very feel of an ape body against his.

"Get off!"

The sheer disgust and anger in the human's voice made Lake fear for Caesar's life. She watched in terror as Red yanked violently on Caesar's chain, dragging him away from the human and down onto the icy steps. Caesar lay there for a moment, at the mercy of his irate captors, before he slowly lifted his head and shot a furtive look at Lake and the others. Then, apparently recovering from his moment of weakness, he rose to his feet once more and continued slowly up the steps to the platform.

Lake was puzzled, not entirely sure what she had just witnessed. She couldn't blame Caesar for stumbling; after everything the humans had done to him, she was amazed he was still standing. But what had been the meaning of that sly look he had given her? Was she missing something?

Then Caesar slipped his hand behind his back and subtly opened his hand to reveal a small metallic object hidden in his palm. Her eyes widened as she realized that it was the key to his shackles, which he must have stolen from the soldier during his "fall." The key was on a ring, which was now looped around Caesar's middle finger.

Lake couldn't believe her eyes. It was hard to conceal her jubilation as she quietly pointed out the key to the other apes. A ripple of excitement spread through the prisoners, who gazed intently at Caesar as he reached the top of the platform, where his captors remained oblivious to what he had just done.

Lake kept silent, but she was hooting and doing somersaults inside. The humans thought they had beaten Caesar. They thought the apes had given up, that making an example of Caesar had broken their spirits. That killing Percy and Spear and Blue Eyes and the others had won this war.

But they were wrong.

A vast frozen expanse stretched before the unfinished wall guarding the entrance to the canyon. Large rocky outcroppings jutted up from the plain, which was bisected by obsolete railway tracks leading to a depot beyond the wall. Past rock falls had deposited a fringe of boulders at the foot of the slopes, along the edges of the expanse. The heaps of rubble helped to hide Rocket and the others as they crept down from the hills to scout the sleeping prison camp. Darkness was their ally, despite the searchlights and guard towers.

Better now than by day, Rocket thought.

Moving furtively, they snuck along the base of the huge wall until they found a gap where the construction had recently collapsed. Keeping low, they peered around the fallen rocks and timbers to spy on the camp's interior. Anger burned inside Rocket's chest as he saw Caesar strung up on the platform like a trophy on display and the rest of their people chained and locked up. Rocket was reminded of the cage he had once been kept in, back at the primate shelter in the city, before Caesar had freed him and the other apes. Seeing apes in cages again, after all their years of struggle and accomplishment, sickened Rocket to the core.

Never again, he vowed.

He was scoping out the sentries on the guard towers, trying to figure out the best way to slip past them and get to Caesar and the others, when the sudden clatter of pounding hoof beats, approaching from inside the camp, caused the apes to scramble away from the wall and dash across the expanse toward a mammoth outcropping about a hundred feet away. Hearts pounding, they hastily climbed the rocks, ducking for cover, as a mounted human soldier galloped out of the camp to patrol the surrounding terrain.

Rocket exhaled a sigh of relief. That had been a close call; if they had been just a little slower, they would have been spotted for sure. Along with Maurice, he peered out from behind the rocks at the heavily guarded prison camp.

How will we get in? the orangutan signed. *Humans everywhere.*

Rocket refused to be deterred. *Must get in somehow...*

He noted Bad Ape watching them anxiously, studying their finger movements in hopes of interpreting the signs. Rocket felt sorry for the illiterate ape and wondered just how much he understood. Did he have any idea what had to be done? A worried expression suggested that Bad Ape got the gist of the discussion. He tapped Maurice on the shoulder and tentatively mimicked the sign for "get in" by pointing with two fingers at the camp.

"'In'…?" he whispered. "'In'?"

Maurice nodded in confirmation.

"No!" Bad Ape's eyes went wide with panic. "No go *in*—!"

Rocket disregarded the other chimpanzee's warning; as far as he was concerned, they had no choice but to try to liberate Caesar and the other captive apes. But Bad Ape backed away fearfully.

"Friends!" he pleaded. "Friends! No go in! No go iiii—"

Without warning, he abruptly dropped out of sight, his hysterical voice trailing off as the ground opened up beneath him. Shocked, Rocket and Maurice rushed to where he had been standing only moments before—and found him hanging by his fingertips on the lip of a deep, dark pit that Rocket could have sworn hadn't been there before.

What is this?

Rocket reached down and grasped Bad Ape's forearm. Grunting, he pulled the chimp out of the pit, while hoping that more of the ground would not give way beneath them. To his relief, the snow-covered earth stayed where it was.

"Thank you, friend!" Bad Ape said when he was back on solid ground. "Thank you!"

Rocket ignored him. He was less interested in the silly chimp's gratitude than in exploring the newly revealed pit. Squinting in the dark, he made out something in the hole and gestured for Maurice to come see.

An old rope ladder hung down the side of the pit, staked to one of the frozen dirt sides of the hole. The ladder descended into the utter blackness at the bottom of the pit. Rocket assumed that frozen leaves and branches had covered the hole until Bad Ape had inadvertently stepped on it.

Good for him, Rocket thought grudgingly.

A flicker of hope sparked inside him as he and Maurice exchanged knowing looks. The orangutan looked just as intrigued by the pit as Rocket was.

Perhaps they had found a way past the guards.

22

Whistles greeted the sunrise, jolting Caesar from what meager sleep he'd managed to obtain while hanging on the cross. To his relief, he discovered that the pilfered key was still hidden in his hand, which remained bound to one of the wooden beams making up the X. The shrill shriek of the whistles pierced his ears, adding to his woes.

Caesar felt more dead than alive. He couldn't remember the last time he'd had anything to eat or drink. Sometime before venturing down the cliff to find Spear and the other crucified apes? His mouth was so dry that even the dirty slush and mud puddles around the base of the platform tormented him. His empty stomach growled fiercely; he was more than just hungry, he was starving. His back still stung where Red had whipped him, over and over again; his muscles ached from hanging on the cross, his whipped back and tied wrists and ankles worst of all.

Human soldiers, responding to the whistles, banged on the bars of the pens, rousing the apes, who rose wearily to their feet to face another day of back-breaking labor upon the wall. Chained together, they were herded out of the pens into the yard. Watching helplessly from the cross, it pained Caesar to realize that they had been starved for even longer than he had. He yearned to lead them in battle against the humans, but knew he needed to bide his time. The stolen key was their only hope; he couldn't afford to waste it on a doomed show of resistance.

Wait, he thought. *Our moment will come.*

The Colonel appeared on the walkway outside his watchtower. He looked down at the soldiers awaiting his commands and nodded to one of his lieutenants who signaled the other soldiers. Puzzled, Caesar watched as men approached the apes pushing wheelbarrows and toting pails. Water sloshed over the rims of the buckets as the soldiers spread out among the chain gangs, scooping out portions of what looked like horse feed and setting down the pails of water.

Caesar couldn't believe his eyes. *Could it be...?*

Confused apes glanced at each other uncertainly, understandably suspicious of the humans' intentions, until one hungry chimpanzee worked up the nerve to hold out his hands. A scowling soldier dumped a small mound of dry oats and barley into the open palms of the ape, who greedily bolted it down before anyone could take the precious food away from him.

His success set off a stampede as famished and thirsty apes shoved forward, cupping their hands to receive the unexpected bounty and gulping down water from the buckets. Their desperation tore at Caesar's heart, even as he took pride in the fact that his people were not fighting amongst themselves for the food, as humans might have. It took more than starvation to turn apes into animals.

Lake held back, however. When a turncoat ape brought a wheelbarrow toward her and the rest of her chain gang, she signed urgently instead of helping herself:

No, no. The children first, please!

The ape shrugged and turned the wheelbarrow toward the pen holding the children, holding Cornelius. Caesar doubted that a human soldier would have heeded Lake's plea and was grateful to her for thinking of the children first.

Blue Eyes chose well, he thought sadly. *Lake would have been a fine mother to my grandchildren.*

She looked across the yard to Caesar. Gratitude radiated from her eyes.

You *did this*, she signed.

Had he? Caesar had certainly confronted the Colonel in his tower last night, demanding that he provide the enslaved apes with food and water. The Colonel had seemed indifferent to Caesar's arguments, but had he indeed managed to get the uncaring human to see reason?

It seemed so.

Not that Caesar was foolish enough to think that the Colonel's change of heart had anything to do with mercy or compassion; he was under no illusions as to the man's motives. At best, Caesar had merely reminded the Colonel that even apes could not work indefinitely without food or water.

He just wants his wall finished, Caesar realized, *before his enemies arrive.*

Red ascended the steps of the platform, bearing a pail of water. He paused before Caesar and looked up at the Colonel, who gazed down on them from his tower. Red slowly lifted the pail toward Caesar's cracked, dry lips. Caesar scowled at Red, skeptical of the offering and reluctant to accept succor from the same renegade ape who had whipped him so savagely less than a day ago. But Caesar's parched throat and ravaged body craved relief, so he swallowed his pride and parted his lips.

Perhaps, he thought, *the Colonel intends to put me back to work as well?*

Then Red tipped the bucket, spilling the precious water onto the platform before Caesar's eyes. Anger warred with anguish as Caesar saw it splatter uselessly and drain away through the floorboards. He could practically taste it as the last few drips fell from the pail.

Red snorted at Caesar's distress.

Caesar's face hardened and he glared balefully at Red with bloodshot eyes. He knew, however, that this sadistic joke was not the gorilla's idea. Lifting his eyes, he stared angrily at the Colonel, who watched in silence from his balcony before retreating back into his lair.

No work for me, Caesar guessed. *Just punishment.*

He held onto the hidden key, concealing it from Red.

Patience, he reminded himself.

A flashlight beam pierced the inky blackness of the forgotten underground tunnel. Maurice held the light as, grunting, Rocket cleared away more of the rubble blocking the way ahead. It was hard, laborious work, but the two apes had been at it for some time now; several yards of tunnel stretched behind them, all the way back to the bottom of the pit. Rocket shoved aside another rock, then paused to inspect their surroundings.

Looks like it caved in, he signed.

Maurice nodded in agreement. Using the flashlight, he peered past the obstruction they had just cleared. Frozen wooden planks reinforced the tunnel, which led away into darkness. A shattered kerosene lamp, which looked like military issue, rested on the floor of the tunnel, the cracked glass reflecting their beam of light. Maurice guessed that the broken lamp had been lying there a long time. No whiff of kerosene remained in the air.

It keeps going, he signed to Rocket. *Wonder how far?*

There was only one way to find out. Avoiding the broken shards of glass, the apes went deeper into the tunnel.

Bad Ape watched the beam of the flashlight recede down the tunnel as he fidgeted anxiously at the bottom of the pit. He was not at all convinced that exploring the tunnel was a good idea; he only descended into the pit after the other apes because he didn't want to be left alone on the surface so close to the humans' bad place. Glancing around nervously, he pined for the comfort and safety of his former home in the mountains. It was good to have friends again, after being alone so long, and he had wanted to help Caesar find the bad human, "the Colonel," who had killed his child, but now Caesar was a prisoner and they were all in danger.

And taking even more chances.

The other apes' peculiar way of talking with their fingers baffled Bad Ape, but he understood that Rocket and Maurice intended to free Caesar and their other friends, despite his warnings to stay away from the camp. Bad Ape wished the prisoners could be saved, too, but trying to find a way into the camp was not smart. It was a bad idea. Bad, bad, bad.

Why won't they listen to me?

A scrabbling noise, along with the sound of falling dirt, made him spin around to check on the human girl, whom Maurice had asked Bad Ape to look after. His eyes bulged in alarm as he saw the child climbing the rope ladder back toward the surface. Snowflakes fell from above, drifting past her. She craned her neck to look up at the cloudy morning sky beyond the pit.

"No, no, no!" He rushed to the ladder, crying out to her. "No climb!"

But, like the other apes, the girl didn't listen to him. She clambered up the ladder, almost as agilely as any ape child, and climbed out of the pit, leaving Bad Ape flustered and distraught at the bottom of the ladder. He clutched his head and paced around the hole, torn as to what to do.

Do I stay down here? Do I go get her? What if the bad humans see her? What if they see me?

He still wasn't entirely sure why the other apes had a human child, but he knew she wasn't safe up there by herself, which meant he had no choice.

Maurice told me to watch her…

Muttering unhappily, he reluctantly climbed the ladder after her. He emerged from the pit to find the girl standing nearby, staring up at the falling snow with a look of wonder on her face. Transfixed by the snow, she seemed oblivious to all else, lost in her own world. She opened her mouth to let the flakes land on her tongue. Belatedly noticing Bad Ape's arrival on the surface, she turned and offered him a slight smile.

Bad Ape was charmed despite his fears. Relaxing slightly, now that he saw that the girl had not gone far, he mimicked her by sticking out his own tongue as well. Leaning back against a boulder, he enjoyed the amusing sensation of the wet snowflakes dissolving on his tongue. Grinning, he turned toward her, his tongue protruding comically from his muzzle.

See, he thought. *I can play this game too.*

But she was not looking at him or the sky anymore. Instead she was squinting at something beyond the fallen boulders that shielded them from view. Worried, he crept forward to see what she was looking at, while hoping against hope that none of the bad humans would spot them.

"What?" he whispered. "What you see…?"

She didn't answer, of course. Bad Ape had already

figured out that the girl couldn't talk for some reason. Following her stare, he saw that she was squinting at one of the gaps in the giant wall guarding the prison camp. She squeezed forward through the rocks, trying to get a better look at whatever had caught her interest. A gray, overcast sky hung over the frozen expanse between them and the camp. The falling snow also made it hard to see very far.

An idea struck Bad Ape.

"Stay!" he told her. "Stay here!"

Hoping she would be a good human child and not go anywhere, he scrambled back to the pit and hurried down the ladder to retrieve the binoculars. Carrying them back up to the surface, he was relieved to see that the girl was still staring through the gap in the wall, a worried expression on her dirty, hairless face. He held out the binoculars to her, nodding in encouragement.

She didn't understand at first, regarding the glasses with bewilderment, but then she reached out tentatively and took them from his hand. He smiled in approval as she lifted the binoculars to her eyes, as she had seen the apes do, and looked back at the distant camp.

Where Caesar hung limply upon the cross.

23

This is as far as we go, Rocket thought. *Or is it?*

Their exploration of the underground tunnel had reached a dead end. Tons of poured concrete blocked the way ahead and, unlike the rubble he and Maurice had dug through to get this far, the solid concrete was obviously impassable. It would take picks and drills or explosives to tunnel any further. The weary apes paused to assess the setback.

Probably caught the humans trying to escape, Maurice signed. *Filled it in.*

Rocket nodded. He wondered how many sick humans had managed to escape the detention center before the guards sealed off the tunnel—and how long they had managed to survive outside the prison walls.

Not long, he guessed. Pushing such somber ruminations aside, he glanced around the blocked tunnel, trying to estimate how far they had traveled beneath the earth. It was difficult to judge the distance without any landmarks to position themselves, not even the sun. He could only chart their course by instinct and memory.

Must be under the camp by now, he signed.

But where? Maurice asked.

The orangutan turned the flashlight beam on the ceiling. He looked speculatively at Rocket, who climbed up Maurice's shaggy back and set to work clawing at the tunnel roof. His fingers were already raw and tired from clearing their way through the tunnel, but Rocket did not let that stop him. Caesar needed him. Their people needed him.

And the only way in was up.

Unfortunately, they were too deep below the earth to make this an easy task. Hours passed as Rocket dug upward through the hard, frozen soil, inch by inch, foot by foot, until at last he was practically standing on top of Maurice's shoulders to reach the top of the shaft he had excavated. The hefty orangutan bore Rocket's weight stoically, without complaint, even though Rocket knew that the burden had to be wearing on his friend. Dire possibilities weighed on Rocket's own mind as he worked. What if they were digging in the wrong place, directly under the depot's foundation? Or in plain view of a guard tower? There was no way to tell what exactly was above them at this particular spot. It was very possible that all his efforts would result in failure—or worse.

No. Don't think like that.

Still, he was beginning to wonder if he was ever going to reach the surface when a slurry of ice and gravel spilled from above, showering down upon the apes' heads and shoulders. Faint sunlight penetrated the tunnel through a small hole at the top of the shaft; muffled noises filtered down from the camp.

Yes! Rocket thought. *We did it!*

He stopped digging immediately for fear of attracting attention from any nearby soldiers. They needed to know where precisely they had broken through and how far they were from Caesar and the others. Rocket glanced down briefly at Maurice before peering cautiously up through the hole.

The first thing he saw was a rusted metal pole looming against a gray winter sky. Blinking, it took Rocket a moment to identify the pole as a train signal switch leftover from the days when the railway tracks had still been in use. Rocket remembered trains; he had been transported to the primate shelter in one, many years ago, caged and boxed up like freight. He didn't miss them.

Rocket shifted his position on Maurice to find different angles of view. From what he could tell, they were in an exposed area of the prison yard, looking out through a hole in the gravel between two rusty iron train tracks. Armed soldiers loitered nearby, oblivious to the apes lurking practically beneath their feet.

That's it, Rocket silently urged the humans. *Don't look down.*

The sun was sinking behind the mountains, but the girl kept looking at the camp through the binoculars. Bad Ape wondered what she was seeing at the bad place.

Nothing good, he was sure.

He was tempted to take the binoculars away from her, so that she wouldn't have to see the terrible things happening in the camp, but then she finally put them down.

Good, Bad Ape thought. Children, even human children, should not see bad things. Noting the concerned, preoccupied look on the girl's face, he could tell that what she had seen had already affected her. All the more reason, he decided, to steer her back down into the pit where the other apes were. They would be safer there, hidden from sight, and the girl wouldn't be able to spy on the prison camp anymore.

He was about to beckon to her when, without warning, the girl squeezed out from behind the rocks and started walking toward the wall. Bad Ape watched in horror, taken completely by surprise by the child's unexpected actions.

"No, no, no…" Bad Ape whispered. "No, no, no!"

She paused briefly, gazing up at the looming wall, then looked back over her shoulder at Bad Ape, who gestured frantically for her to turn around and come back. He wanted to chase after her, but he was afraid that would just make things worse. Plus, he was just afraid, period.

Come back, girl! Come back!

Caesar sagged upon the X. He tried to keep his head up, to remain aware and conscious, but he was fighting a losing battle against hunger and fatigue. His head lolled on his shoulders, while his heavy eyelids drooped. It was a struggle to keep them open.

Just close them for a moment, he thought. *Just a moment.*

A shadow passed over him, registering vaguely on his senses, and he awoke abruptly, startled to discover that night had fallen at some point. The camp was eerily still and silent, lit only by the harsh glow of the security lights. He blinked in confusion, trying to figure out how long he had been unconscious.

What have I missed?

But before he could fully take stock of the situation, the vague figure of an ape stepped into view before him, haloed by the camp's lights. A pair of hairy simian hands reached out to gently cradle Caesar's face as he squinted into the light, trying to bring his blurry vision into focus.

Was this Red again? Come to taunt him some more?

The ape came closer, his head blocking the glare from

the lights. An ugly scar ran down one side of his face, across his mutilated right eye. Caesar gaped in surprise and confusion as he recognized the other ape at last.

"Koba," he whispered hoarsely.

The ape's one good eye gazed tenderly at Caesar. He leaned in toward his former friend and enemy and pressed his lips to Caesar's ears.

"Sleep," the dead ape said softly.

Caesar shook his head. He had to stay awake. His people were counting on him to free them. He couldn't surrender to exhaustion, no matter how little strength he had left, or how easy it would be to drift away and never wake up.

"Let go," Koba tempted him. "There is no hope." He glanced over at the apes in their pens. "Even *they* will know that soon enough."

Caesar considered his people. He had given them hope by stealing the key. Was Koba suggesting that he was doomed to fail them once more?

"No..." he said weakly.

"Yes!" Koba insisted. "*Join me...*"

In death?

Caesar squeezed his eyes shut, trying to block out the disturbing apparition, who could not possibly be real. Koba was dead. He couldn't be here.

This can't be happening.

A blinding light shone in his eyes, startling him. His eyes snapped open in time to see a gleaming machete swinging toward him. The blade chopped into the rope binding his right wrist with a loud thwack. His freed arm dropped numbly to his side, leaving him hanging from only one wrist. Pins and needles stabbed the liberated limb.

Disoriented, Caesar looked for Koba—and saw Red instead. The Colonel and Preacher had appeared as well, the latter shining a flashlight at Caesar as Koba sliced through the ape's remaining bonds. Caesar collapsed onto the platform, too weak to do anything else.

A dream, he thought. *Koba was just a dream.*

But the Colonel and his henchmen were very real.

"If he's still alive in the morning," the Colonel said, "he goes back to work or you shoot him." He gazed down at the debilitated ape. "Keep him separate from the others."

Preacher nodded obediently as Red came forward to carry out the Colonel's orders. Caesar did not fight back, but, with what little strength he had left, he closed his fist around the key.

Koba was wrong, Caesar thought. *There is still hope. For me* and *my people.*

24

Maurice and Rocket emerged to find Bad Ape crouched behind the craggy outcropping hiding the pit from the humans on the wall. The orangutan was surprised to find Bad Ape up on the surface, instead of waiting for them at the bottom of the pit, and looked with growing concern for the girl, whom he had left in the strange chimpanzee's care. His eyes searched the surrounding rocks for any sign of the child, but she was nowhere to be found.

Where is she? What's become of her?

Bad Ape heard them exit the pit. Turning toward them, he pointed hysterically at a gap in the huge uncompleted wall guarding the camp. His motions were so frenzied that it took Maurice a moment to realize that the chimp was crudely making the two-fingered sign for "go in." The distraught ape jabbered at them as well.

"*In!* She go *in!*"

To the camp? Maurice froze in shock as he grasped what Bad Ape was saying, even as he struggled to understand why the girl would do such a thing. He looked at Rocket, who appeared equally stunned by the news. Maurice knew that his friend had not grown as attached to the child as he had, but even so Rocket understood the severity of the situation.

Now the girl was in danger, too.

Maurice snatched the binoculars from Bad Ape and turned them toward the wall, where human soldiers were working through the night to secure heavy artillery in place, sweating and straining as they hoisted rocket launchers and machine guns up the wall. Searchlights were concentrated on the wall to assist the soldiers in their labors. Intent on the arduous operation, none of the humans appeared to notice as the girl entered the camp undetected. Maurice could not believe her luck.

But how much longer before they noticed?

Confined to a small cage directly beneath a guard tower, isolated from the other apes, Caesar found his new accommodations only slightly more comfortable than the cross on the platform. He sprawled face-down upon the cold, frigid earth, too weak to move, let alone try to make use of the key. Both sleep and wakefulness eluded him as he hovered in a semiconscious daze, dreading whatever dreams might be creeping up on him, knowing that Koba might be waiting for him there.

No sleep was almost better than that.

Something flew through the bars of his cage and thudded softly onto the ground beside him. Puzzled, Caesar lifted his head and was surprised to see the human girl's pitiful rag doll lying in the frozen slush.

What?

He looked up to see the human girl standing right outside the cage, gazing at him with a worried expression on her dirty face. She'd carried the doll in her parka pocket all the way there, until she had apparently lobbed it into his cage.

To comfort him?

Baffled by the girl's presence, Caesar wondered if he was dreaming again. He looked around anxiously for Koba, but saw only the girl, who appeared as real and tangible as the metal bars between them. She was no figment of his imagination, rising up from his guilty conscience like Koba, he realized. She was really here, looking at him with sad blue eyes.

How is this possible? Where did she come from?

He wanted to ask her how and why she was here, but he knew that she couldn't answer him. The Colonel had revealed the secret to the girl's perpetual silence; Caesar understood now that the mutated virus had indeed taken away the child's capacity for speech. Despite his own dire circumstances, he pitied her for her loss, and was glad that Will was not here to see what his best intentions had led to. Will had wanted to save human minds from a terrible disease, not turn humans into mutes.

But where is Maurice, he wondered, *and Rocket and Bad Ape?*

He had ordered his friends to flee these mountains if he did not return to them, so what was the girl doing here? He glanced around again, but there was no sign of his allies. He looked quizzically at the girl, who astonished him by sliding a tiny finger along her neck, tentatively mimicking the sign Maurice had tried to teach her before.

Thirsty? she signed.

Caesar was both floored and touched by the child's query. He had not thought her capable of communicating in such a manner. He lifted a shaky hand to respond, but before he could sign back to her, the girl abruptly turned and wandered out of sight. Caesar craned his neck, looking anxiously for her, but was unable to see where she had gone. The depth of his concern took him by surprise; he had never wanted her along on his quest in the first place, but he waited tensely until she finally returned, lugging a heavy pail of water in both hands. The water sloshed over the sides of the bucket as she raised it and held it up to the bars.

The sight of the water gave Caesar the strength to lift himself from the ground and crawl over to where the girl was standing. He pressed his mud-caked face against the bars and she tilted the pail, spilling the water into his gaping mouth. He guzzled it thirstily, rejoicing as it soothed his parched throat and tongue, which had been without a drop of water for days. He couldn't remember ever drinking anything sweeter.

Thank you, he thought. *Good girl.*

As he drained the bucket, reducing its weight, she was able to hold onto it with just one hand. Her other hand reached through the bars to touch Caesar's face… just like Cornelius once had. Caesar felt his heart melting.

Low grunts came from the ape enclosure across the yard. As Caesar gulped down the last of the water, he saw the other apes pressing against the bars of their pen, staring in wonder and curiosity at the girl and Caesar. A few of the apes, desperate for relief, beckoned silently to the girl, who turned toward them.

Careful, Maurice thought. *Don't let the soldiers see you.*

The fearful orangutan spied on the scene from around the edge of the camp's towering front gate. He and Rocket and Bad Ape clung to the shadows at the base of the wall after creeping out from behind the nearby outcropping protruding from the plain. Maurice was torn by mixed emotions as he watched the girl come to Caesar's aid; he was proud of her bravery and compassion, and found himself deeply moved by the sight, while also terrified for her safety. As she crossed the open yard toward the other apes, she seemed oblivious to the danger she was in, leaving Maurice to worry for her.

If the guards spot her...

25

Caesar watched with mounting anxiety as the girl communed with the apes trapped in the pen. Her back was turned to him, so he couldn't quite see if or how the girl was communicating with the prisoners, but the longer she lingered by the pen, the greater the risk that she would be caught infiltrating the camp. His worried gaze swept over the guards posted by the wall; the soldiers remained unaware of the girl's presence, but Caesar knew that she was tempting fate by remaining in view. She could be spotted at any moment.

And then...?

The girl could expect no mercy from the Colonel once he realized she was infected. The man had killed his own son and ordered his soldiers to kill their own families. He wouldn't hesitate for a moment before having the girl put down like a sick animal, which, now that Caesar thought of it, might explain why that ragged deserter had been hiding out in the ramshackle oyster farm with the girl. Had he been a former soldier concealing the mute child from the Colonel and his troops? *Probably*, Caesar guessed. He felt a twinge of regret for shooting the man.

Not that he gave me much choice.

After what felt like an eternity, the girl finally turned away from the pen and wandered back toward Caesar, cradling something in her small arms. Caesar squinted at the approaching child, unable to make out what she was carrying. Puzzled, he looked past her to the other apes, who were watching expectantly for reasons Caesar couldn't quite grasp.

He was about to sign to them when the girl stepped up to his cage. She leaned forward carefully, as though trying to spill the contents of her arms through the bars of the cage. Curious, Caesar reached out to catch whatever it was—and a long stream of grain poured into his palms.

Food!

Surprised and grateful, Caesar looked up at the girl, then back at the apes, who were nodding in encouragement. He realized that the apes must have been hoarding the oats, perhaps to stretch them out in case they were not fed again, and had seen an opportunity to share their meager stores with him, using the girl as a conduit. A gorilla in the pen raised his hands and pressed his fists together.

Apes together strong, he signed.

A wave of emotion, even more powerful than his hunger for the grain, washed over Caesar as he hastily wolfed down the food. Pride filled his heart as, one after another, the other apes raised their fists as well, joining in solidarity despite their captivity. A smile lifted Caesar's lips for the first time in too long; this was food for the spirit, not just for the body. He could practically feel his strength returning already.

He had never been so proud to be an ape.

The girl watched the exchange with interest. Her flat, hairless brow furrowed in concentration as her gaze swung back and forth between Caesar and the defiant apes. Uncertainly, she lifted her own tiny fists and pressed them together too. A smile broke out across her face as she successfully signed along with the others.

Apes together strong.

Caesar did not correct her. She had risked death to ease his suffering, and was in just as much danger from the Colonel as any of his people. She had earned the right to consider herself an ape.

Even if she could never speak the word.

Apes together strong, the girl signed, amazing Maurice as he and Rocket and Bad Ape watched from their hiding place. Deeply moved by the poignant scene playing out in the prison yard, he wasn't sure what he was more proud of: his fellow apes' perseverance in the face of adversity or the human girl's loyalty to her newfound tribe. Male orangutans, by instinct, did not play much of a role in raising their offspring, but Maurice couldn't have been more touched by the girl's spirit and signing if she had been his own child. He resolved to keep teaching her to the best of his abilities.

Assuming any of them survived until dawn.

The warm glow in his chest turned to ice, however, as he spotted the Colonel and his lieutenants heading toward Caesar and the other penned apes, who did not yet appear to be aware of the soldiers' approach. The humans conferred with each other as they walked across the camp, apparently engrossed in conversation. Rocket stiffened beside him, having clearly noticed the Colonel and his men as well. Maurice gestured at the girl, who was still standing right outside Caesar's cage. He could not imagine that the ruthless Colonel would tolerate any unwanted intruders aiding the apes.

If the humans see her, Maurice signed, *they will kill her...*

Footsteps crunching across the frozen yard alerted Caesar barely in time. Spinning around inside his cage, he saw the Colonel and his officers coming towards them, accompanied by Red and a few of his fellow renegades. Only ten feet away and closing, the humans appeared to be deep in discussion of some vital issue or another, keeping their attention elsewhere, but it was only a matter of moments before they or the turncoats spied the girl.

Unless...

Caesar grunted urgently at the girl and gestured for her to hide herself behind the guard tower's nearest leg. Responding quickly, she darted behind the long steel leg and pressed her small body against it just as the Colonel and his men paused along the route passing Caesar's cage. None of the humans were looking their way yet, but Caesar averted his eyes from the girl to avoid betraying her presence by mistake. He was suddenly grateful that the girl was mute; her silence was the only thing that might save her.

He kept quiet too, hoping to avoid attracting the Colonel's attention, but fearing that the girl was bound to be discovered before long. Quiet as she was, she was deep behind enemy lines. The odds were not on her side.

Angry shouts from the direction of the wall came to the girl's rescue, distracting the Colonel and his lieutenants. The Colonel lifted his head, scowling at the commotion, and Caesar looked to see what was causing the disturbance. Was this good news or bad for the apes?

A squad of five soldiers, toting pistols and rifles, marched toward the Colonel. The guards were in an agitated state, shouting at an unseen prisoner in their midst, who was hidden by the humans' bodies. They roughly prodded the captive with their weapons. Although grateful for the distraction, Caesar couldn't help wondering what the uproar was all about. Had one of the enslaved apes attempted to escape, or was another human showing signs of the virus?

Caesar hoped for the latter.

As the soldiers neared, he eventually managed to peer through their ranks. His heart sank as he saw who the prisoner was.

Rocket.

Outnumbered and held at gunpoint, the chimpanzee held his head high as he was brought before the Colonel, who cast a suspicious look at Caesar, no doubt suspecting that the other chimp had braved the camp on Caesar's behalf. For himself, Caesar was dismayed to find his friend in the hands of the enemy. As the girl's arrival had already suggested, it was obvious that Rocket and the others had not fled the region as he had ordered, but what about Maurice and Bad Ape? What had become of them?

He longed to question Rocket, but that was impossible with the Colonel looking on and the girl hiding only a few yards away. Caesar endured the Colonel's scrutiny while praying that the madman's gaze did not drift toward the tower leg concealing the child. Bad enough that Rocket had somehow been captured; Caesar did not want the girl's summary execution on his conscience.

Getting no reaction from Caesar, the Colonel examined Rocket from a safe distance. Scratches on the human's neck reminded Caesar of how close he had come to killing the man before. The Colonel nodded at Red, indicating that he should take custody of the captive chimp, and Red knuckle-walked toward Rocket, who bared his teeth and gums at the renegade ape.

Red glowered back at Rocket. There had been a time, Caesar reflected, when the two apes had been allies, united in a single tribe under Caesar's benevolent rule. But Koba's revolution had torn apart that unity, pitting ape against ape. The bad blood left over from that bitter conflict was still very much in evidence in the almost palpable hostility between the apes as Red attempted to restrain Rocket's arms, provoking a sudden violent response from Rocket, who thrashed wildly, throwing off Red's grip and butting his head into the startled gorilla's face. Red stumbled backwards, clutching his head, before launching himself back at Rocket in a rage.

Snarling, the apes battled viciously, pummeling each other with their fists and rolling across the ground, while the soldiers stood by, keeping their guns trained at the grappling apes. A few of the humans laughed callously, enjoying the brutal spectacle, while others looked on apprehensively. Bets were made on which ape would come out on top. The other turncoat apes circled warily, uncertain whether to come to Red's aid. Caesar suspected that they didn't want to get shot by mistake if the humans lost patience and opened fire on both apes. He was actually surprised that the soldiers hadn't done so already.

All eyes were on the savage brawl, even the Colonel's. Seeing an opportunity, Caesar furtively signaled the girl to make a run for it. It pained him to make use of Rocket's solitary struggle, but perhaps some good could come from the violence. There was nothing he could do for Rocket right now, but the girl at least had a chance to get away.

Responding quickly, she darted away from the tower and crossed the yard to the crumbling multi-story barracks along one side of the canyon. She kept low, ducking behind heaps of accumulated rubble and debris, as she sprinted for the wall and safety. Caesar forced himself not to track her progress with his eyes.

Keep going, he thought. *Don't stop.*

The two apes still fought, with neither gaining an advantage. The gorilla was bigger and heavier than the chimpanzee, but Rocket made up for the difference with his guts and ferocity, despite knowing that he would still find himself surrounded by enemies even if he prevailed. Caesar had battled Rocket himself, years and years ago, and knew just how fast and hard the wiry chimpanzee could hit; he hoped that his friend could keep on fighting long enough for the girl to make it past the wall, even as he yearned to go to Rocket's aid. The vicious battle reminded him of his own frenzied one-on-one clashes with Koba, before the rebel ape finally fell to his doom. Caesar felt as though that ugly history was replaying before his eyes, but even more pointlessly.

Apes should not fight each other.

The human commander frowned, clearly growing impatient with the ape-on-ape violence. Drawing his sidearm, he took aim at the warring simians. Fear gripped Caesar, remembering how the Colonel had gunned down Percy without remorse yesterday.

No! he thought. *Not Rocket, too!*

The Colonel pulled the trigger. A shot rang out, the sharp report cutting through the guttural snarls and barks of the apes. Both Red and Rocket froze at the sound—as a cloud of dirt and ice erupted where the bullet slammed into the frozen ground. Caesar gasped in relief.

A warning shot, not a kill shot.

But the interruption gave Red a chance to get the upper hand. Taking advantage of his greater strength and bulk, the gorilla forced Rocket's face into the ground, pinning him. Rocket struggled to break the hold, and might even have succeeded, but the Colonel walked over, gun in hand, and stared down at Rocket, who was smart enough to know that the Colonel and his soldiers were the real menace, not the malevolent ape on his back. The foul odor of gunpowder hung in the air like an unspoken threat.

"How many of you are out there?" the Colonel demanded. "Are there others?"

Despite the guns surrounding him, Rocket kept silent. His face betrayed no hint of fear, only stubborn resolve. Caesar knew that no power on earth could get Rocket to betray Maurice or even Bad Ape. This was hardly the first time Rocket had risked death for his fellow apes. He could not be threatened into talking.

The Colonel must have sensed this, too. Scowling, he stepped away from the pinned chimpanzee and addressed his soldiers.

"Sweep the area," he ordered, then nodded at Red. "Put him in the pen."

The Colonel walked off, turning his back on the apes. Red abruptly sprang to his feet and grabbed Rocket roughly by the ankle, starting to drag him across the icy ground toward the pen. Rocket flailed wildly, but Red had him where he wanted him, on the ground and off his feet.

And then the other turncoats joined in.

Caesar watched in horror as the renegade apes piled on Rocket, beating him into submission. Hooting and jabbering like the savage beasts they once were, they showed the downed chimpanzee no mercy. Simian fists rained down on Rocket, hammering him relentlessly, until the outnumbered ape stopped resisting. Caesar winced at every blow. The apes in the pen stared aghast, or else looked away from the barbaric onslaught.

Red unlocked the gate of the pen. The enclosed apes backed away from the entrance as the turncoats seized Rocket's battered body and hurled him roughly into the enclosure, where he smacked to the ground at the feet of the other apes. Barking out at them, warning them not to interfere, a traitor chimp shackled Rocket to the chained apes. Red waited until Rocket was securely fettered, then savagely kicked him one last time. Rocket grunted in pain as the kick collided with his ribs. He lay crumpled on the ground inside the pen.

Red snorted in disdain.

Locked away in his own cage, Caesar felt a growl forming at the back of his throat. He had never thought he could hate another ape as much as he'd hated Koba at the end, but Red had proven him wrong about that. Even Koba, at his worst, had always been on the side of the apes—at least from his own twisted, hate-crazed perspective—but Red? He brutalized other apes in the service of a human who wanted to exterminate Red's own kind.

He made Koba seem like a hero.

After locking Rocket up with the other captives, the turncoats departed, leaving their fellow apes behind. Caesar stared ruefully at his injured friend, tormented by the bars and distance separating him from Rocket, who slowly stirred himself and staggered to his feet, bloody but unbowed. The chimp's face was bruised and swollen and torn and bleeding; Caesar had never seen him in worse shape, not even when he had been mistreated by humans back at the primate shelter. That he was still standing after taking such a beating, and from other apes no less, was a testament to the chimp's indomitable nature. He leaned against the bars of the pen, looking back at Caesar, and *smiled*.

Feeling better? Rocket signed.

Caesar's jaw dropped as it suddenly occurred to him that Rocket might have let himself be captured on purpose—to give the girl a chance to escape undetected?

Certainly, the commotion Rocket had set off had kept the Colonel and any other human from discovering the girl, saving her life.

Clever, Caesar thought, *and crazy too.*

Caesar managed a slight smile. He nodded at Rocket. The food and water the girl had brought him had indeed restored him to a degree.

Good, Rocket signed. *Then we can talk about escape.*

He brought his fists together.

Apes together strong.

26

The morning came too early as far as Caesar was concerned. As before, the soldiers paraded in formation as they mustered themselves before the Colonel's tower, even as the caged apes dreaded the day to come. The assembled soldiers looked reverently up at the tower, waiting for their leader to step out onto the balcony above them. Caesar expected another disturbing ritual such as he had witnessed yesterday, with the soldiers once more declaring themselves the Beginning and the End. He frowned in anticipation.

I do not need to witness that again.

The sound of a metal door swinging open broke the expectant hush. Surprised soldiers shifted their gaze to the base of the tower, where the Colonel emerged unexpectedly. Instead of surveying his troops from on high, he stood directly before them atop a low flight of steps leading down to the ground.

His attire was different as well. Instead of his usual rumpled fatigues, the Colonel was decked out in his full dress uniform, complete with a single-breasted coat, gleaming brass buttons, and matching trousers.

Freshly polished medals glittered upon his chest. Crisply pressed green fabric looked practically brand new, as though the formal uniform had barely been worn before. Caesar wondered—and worried—about what might have prompted the Colonel to dress up for the occasion. He exchanged wary looks with Rocket. Was something momentous on the horizon?

Whatever this means, it cannot be good for apes.

The Colonel gazed out at his soldiers, studying their puzzled faces. He took a deep breath before addressing them in an oddly reflective tone.

"For two years we've fought relentlessly against these beasts, and when we are done with them, we will bring an end to their kind. But now we find ourselves on the eve of battle… against our *own* kind. So you may ask: who is the *real* enemy, who are we fighting here? And I'll tell you. It's not the apes. It's not the men who are on their way here right now to altercate with us. The battle we've been waging all this time is against ourselves."

He paused to let his words sink in, descending the steps to walk among his troops, just as Caesar had often walked among his own people in challenging times, such as after the human raid on the apes' trench. The Colonel glanced briefly at Caesar in his cage, making eye contact with the captive ape leader, before continuing to speak to the devoted men and women under his command.

"They say we are inhumane," he told them. "Indecent. They call us a death squad. But they'll never understand our sacrifice. How agonizing it has been to do what must be done, even as it tears away at our very souls. Because there are times when you must abandon your humanity in the fight to save humanity. All of you have shown the courage to do that… and now we must take the fight to them, or this hellish trial will all have been in vain."

He moved steadily, assuredly, through the ranks, speaking loud enough to be heard by humans and apes alike. That the apes could also hear him speak plainly of his plans for their total extermination did not seem to concern him. Their demise was a foregone conclusion, apparently.

"We cannot fail. We're the last defense. Somewhere in this world there are more survivors. And whether they know it or not, they are counting on us. To show the will to protect them against this new plague." He shook his head pensively. "We've seen it here. And it's already spreading up north. If we lose this battle, there will be nothing to stop it from spreading everywhere. If we lose, in a matter of months, the human race will gasp its last words and go silent. Just another dumb animal, left to roam a godforsaken world."

He came to a stop in the midst of his troops. Preacher stood close by, listening intently to his leader with a rapt expression on his youthful face that dashed whatever illusions Caesar might have had about the soldier's innate decency. Like the rest of the humans, he was committed to the Colonel's genocidal crusade.

"Most of you are still young men and women," the Colonel said, adopting a more intimate, almost affectionate tone. "And if we win, years from now, you may be sitting somewhere with your children, your grandchildren, and they'll ask you: what did you do in the greatest war? And you can tell them, you fought—viciously—for a gentler world."

Preacher swallowed hard and lifted his chin in pride. Like the other soldiers, he appeared genuinely inspired by the Colonel's speech. Despite the army bearing down on them, their eyes shone with a fervency that scared Caesar to the marrow of his being. It was clear that they would gladly commit any atrocity to maintain humanity's dominance over the planet and bring about the idyllic future the Colonel foretold. A peaceful world where humanity could thrive and grow as it had before the virus.

A world without apes.

Whistles shrieked as the Colonel's executive officer dismissed the troops from the rally and set them to work forcing the chained apes out of the pens and into the yard, where the apes dragged their feet and knuckles, in no hurry to resume their labors. The Colonel waded through the chaotic operation, accompanied by Preacher and Red, until he reached Caesar's cage.

Drawing his sidearm, he signaled Red. The gorilla dutifully unlocked the cage for Caesar, who remained on the floor.

He gave the Colonel a hard, weary look, making no move toward the open gate. He was in no hurry to help the humans build their wall, for when the wall was finished, so were his people. If the Colonel wanted him to budge, he would have to do more than send Red to fetch him.

I'm a prisoner, he thought. *Not a slave.*

The Colonel proved up to the challenge. Scowling, he cocked his gun.

Caesar considered his options. Working on the wall was giving the Colonel what he wanted, and hastening the end of the apes' usefulness, but then again, Caesar could do nothing to save his people with a bullet in his brain.

I must lose this battle if I hope to win the war.

Sighing, he reluctantly rose to his feet and stepped out of the cage, tottering slightly upon shaky legs. Despite the food and water the girl had brought him last night, he was still recovering from his recent ordeals. Just walking upright required more effort than it should have.

The Colonel regarded him coldly.

"Send him up to the quarry," he ordered. "Alone."

Caesar remembered the apes he'd seen prying rocks out of the cliffs for use on the wall; apparently, the Colonel didn't think that working on the wall was hard enough labor for Caesar. Or perhaps he simply wanted to keep Caesar isolated from the other apes to forestall any further insurrections.

Probably a smart move, Caesar conceded. *I would do the same if I were him.*

Red fastened shackles back onto Caesar's ankles and wrists, which were already rubbed raw by the ropes that had bound him to the cross. He tried his best not to flinch as the tight metal restraints clamped shut, but was not sure he succeeded.

Wanting to lock the shackles into place, Red looked to Preacher for the key. Caesar maintained a poker face as the young soldier searched through the key rings on his belt, looking more and more concerned as he failed to find the key to the shackles. Sweat beaded on his forehead and he licked his lips nervously as he checked over and over again, as though hoping that the missing key would somehow miraculously reappear. He glanced anxiously at the Colonel, no doubt terrified of screwing up in front of his unforgiving leader.

Caesar *almost* felt sorry for him.

"Is there a problem, soldier?" the Colonel asked impatiently.

"I'm sorry, sir," Preacher said. "Just give me a minute."

Frowning, the Colonel called out to another soldier, who was herding a gang of chained apes past them, jabbing them with the barrel of his rifle to keep them moving. He seemed, at a glance, to be even more impatient than the other guards.

"Boyle!" he barked and nodded at Caesar. "His cuffs."

The other soldier, a blond, white-skinned human with a surly expression, hurried over to lock the shackles, leaving a couple of fellow soldiers to watch over the other apes. Preacher flushed in embarrassment as Boyle carried out the Colonel's orders with a key from his own belt. The Colonel looked on, apparently wanting to make sure the job was done to his satisfaction, as the locks clicked shut. He started to turn away when his gaze fell on the cage behind Caesar—and something lying inside it. His head jerked up in surprise.

The doll, Caesar suddenly realized. *I forgot about the rag doll.*

Striding forward, the Colonel reached into the cage and plucked the discarded toy from the ground. He stared at the dirty, beaten-up doll, visibly perplexed. Caesar would have enjoyed the man's obvious confusion if not for the danger the doll's discovery posed to the girl, Maurice, and Bad Ape, not to mention Caesar's plans to free the other apes. The colonel's soldiers were already on the lookout; what if the Colonel took this as confirmation that Caesar still had more allies on the loose?

The Colonel thrust the doll in Caesar's face.

"What is this?" he demanded.

Caesar did not answer. He racked his brain for a plausible explanation, but there was nothing he could say that would not put his friends at risk. He mentally kicked himself for not trying to hide the doll somehow, although he had been distracted by everything that had transpired last night. The doll, lying in the dark, had completely slipped his mind.

Frustrated by Caesar's silence, the Colonel turned on Preacher, presumably because he was the human who had helped cage Caesar in the first place.

"How did this get in there?"

The blood drained from Preacher's face. Already in hot water over his inability to produce the key, the soldier gulped and fidgeted nervously, looking utterly miserable. His voice quavered as he responded.

"I really don't know, sir."

The Colonel examined the doll, unable to make sense of its inexplicable appearance in the cage. Caesar could see how this odd, aberrant detail might leave the human commander at a loss. Hostile forces, rebellious apes, even a mutating virus... those were things that his military training and experience had equipped him to handle. A crude, handmade shank hidden in the cage would have been cause for concern, but perfectly within the realm of expected possibilities. But a floppy rag doll, appearing as though by magic...

Caesar didn't blame the Colonel for looking confused.

Could be worse, he consoled himself. *Better the doll than the key*. The cold steel of it pressed against his palm, hidden from view.

The Colonel eyed Caesar suspiciously, staring at the chimpanzee's inscrutable face as though the answers were somehow hidden in his enemy's simian features. Caesar maintained a stony expression, his face an impenetrable mask revealing nothing. He stared back at the Colonel, not giving an inch.

The human blinked first. "Get him to work," he said irritably.

Red shoved Caesar forward, toward the waiting quarry where hours of back-breaking toil surely awaited him. Glancing back over his shoulder, he saw the Colonel staring in silence at the doll in his hands, whose button eyes looked back up at him.

Good, Caesar thought. *Keep thinking about the doll. So you won't see what's truly under your nose.*

27

High above the prison yard, on a dangerously narrow perch, Caesar strained to quarry heavy rocks from the icy cliffs. The granite ledge had been roughly hacked out of the side of the cliff, above the camp, but below the slopes where the apes had been crucified before. Chimpanzees did not perspire as profusely as humans did, but now sweat dripped into his eyes, stinging them. Slippery palms made it hard to keep a tight grip on the handle of his pick as he chipped away at the frozen stone face of the canyon, wresting more building materials from the stubborn granite. A savage part of his soul wished that he were swinging the pick at the Colonel's skull instead. Only the armed guards keeping watch on him from below prevented him carrying out his bloodthirsty fantasies.

His precarious position upon the ledge required him to watch his footing, a task made all the more difficult by the heavy iron shackles around his ankles. Caesar was not afraid of heights, having scaled towering redwoods and skyscrapers in the past, but he respected gravity. One wrong step and he could plunge to his death more than a hundred feet below.

Careful, he told himself. *No accidents.*

He toiled beneath a bleak winter sky. The day had barely begun and he was already tired and thirsty. If the girl hadn't smuggled him a modicum of food and water last night, there was no way that he could have managed this arduous chore on top of everything he had already endured. Was the Colonel hoping that he would drop dead of exhaustion? Caesar still wasn't quite sure why the Colonel hadn't simply executed him the way he'd casually killed Percy. Was he afraid of turning Caesar into a martyr... or did he simply think that it sent a better message to the other apes to show that even Caesar had been reduced to toiling for the humans?

The pick tore loose a hefty chunk of rock from the cliff. Caesar scooted backward to avoid getting a foot crushed beneath the falling stone, but the bulk of his concentration was directed elsewhere. He peered furtively at the yard below, where impatient human overseers were still trying to get the weary, slow-moving apes over to the wall. Scanning the crowded, hectic scene, Caesar spotted Rocket among a chain gang that was just now being dragged out of a pen. That the hairless chimp had been beaten badly only hours ago did not exempt him from being put to work along with the other apes, it seemed.

Just as well, Caesar thought. *That fits our plans.*

Rocket surreptitiously made eye contact with Caesar, confirming that he was ready to play his part. Confident that Rocket would get the job done, Caesar next sought out Lake. As planned, her group had paused not far from the children's pens to pick up their tools and ropes for the day. Lake lingered at the task, stalling until she was sure Caesar was watching, before letting her gang be poked and prodded toward the wall by the unsuspecting humans.

Good, Caesar thought. *Everyone is in place.*

Turning his gaze back toward Rocket, he observed carefully and covertly as the other chimp trudged ploddingly toward the wall, his downcast eyes fixed on his furry feet, counting every step as his group approached an obsolete train signal switch posted by the old railway tracks running through the center of the yard. The same switch, Caesar knew, that marked the location of the underground tunnel Rocket had told him about last night. He couldn't help looking for the peephole Rocket had dug near the switch, but it was far too small and inconspicuous to be glimpsed from this distance.

Probably just as well, he thought.

Rocket passed the switch and signed to Caesar.

Thirty-seven.

Caesar nodded back at him and committed the number to memory before shifting his gaze to Lake. As she and her group were led past the switch, she looked up from her feet and signed to Caesar.

Fifty-five.

He acknowledged the message with a nod, adding it to the information he had just received from Rocket.

That's all I need to know, he thought. *The rest is up to me.*

He began to scale the icy cliff face, pulling himself up onto a higher ledge above. Before he could climb any further, however, gunfire from below slammed into the stones around him, pelting him with bits of shattered rock and ice.

Caesar froze and looked down at the guards below, who were posted on the large, stationary fuel tanker railcars. One of them lowered his rifle and shouted angrily at Caesar:

"That's high enough, kong!"

Relieved that the guards had not simply killed him, Caesar raised his hand submissively to show that he had gotten the message: this far but not farther. The soldiers watched him carefully as, making no sudden movements that might provoke them, he returned to his work, just a little higher up the cliff than he had been before.

But maybe just high enough.

He waited until the guards had lowered their rifles and relaxed their vigilance to a degree, letting them think that he was doing nothing more than continuing to pry rocks from the cliff, before finally peering out over the wall at a distant outcropping beyond the camp, where Rocket had told him the others would be hiding and waiting. The monumental rock formation squatted like an island on the vast frozen waste past the canyon. If Caesar squinted, he could just make out a large shaggy form lurking behind the boulders...

Maurice spotted Caesar upon the ledge. He had been monitoring the camp for hours, ever since Rocket had bravely walked right into the humans' base to distract the soldiers and, hopefully, make contact with Caesar. The plan all along had been for Rocket to find some way to signal Maurice from inside the camp, perhaps even from the wall or quarries. Seeing Caesar, the orangutan prayed that Rocket had been able to share their plan with Caesar at some point, so that their captured leader knew what to do.

His prayers were answered when Caesar put down his pick and paused long enough to sign to Maurice across the distance between them:

Thirty-seven steps to adult cage... fifty-five to the children.

Maurice nodded, even though he knew that Caesar could not see him doing so without binoculars. That was the information that Rocket had promised to transmit to him in some way: the precise distances between the pens and the signal switch near the tunnel opening.

Now we can get to work.

Lowering the binoculars, he crept further back among the rocks, where the girl and Bad Ape waited for him. Maurice was relieved to see that Bad Ape had not managed to misplace the girl again. Perhaps he had learned his lesson after letting her get away from him before.

Maurice pointed to the child, then up at his eyes. He pantomimed looking around to indicate that he wanted her to keep a lookout and gave her the binoculars. He hoped that by giving her a job he would encourage her to stay put. Plus, they really did need someone to watch out for any approaching soldiers who might come this way. Security in and around the camp had increased noticeably since Rocket's incursion last night. Maurice and the others had been dodging the humans' patrols ever since Rocket had been captured.

Nodding gravely, the girl accepted the binoculars. Maurice was amused by the seriousness of her expression.

My little soldier, he thought.

Leaving the girl safely concealed among the boulders, or so he hoped, he led Bad Ape down into the tunnel he and Rocket had excavated until they were directly below the train switch they were using as a landmark. Bad Ape employed the flashlight while Maurice consulted the compass Luca had salvaged from the oyster farm, taking a moment to thank his lost comrade for his foresight. The device proved useful when it came to orienting their position with respect to the camp above. Maurice double-checked the readings before finally pointing out two different locations along the wall of the tunnel.

There, he indicated, *and there.*

Bad Ape nodded eagerly. Moving to one of the spots

Maurice had indicated, he began to tentatively dig at the wall. He looked over at the orangutan, who nodded back in approval, appreciating Bad Ape's enthusiasm and cooperation; despite his intense fear of "the bad place," the hermit chimp seemed willing to do whatever was necessary to help Caesar, Rocket, and the other apes.

Good, Maurice thought, *I need his help.*

Lumbering over to the other location, he began digging too.

28

The wall was finished, but the work continued into the night as the exhausted apes were forced at gunpoint to roll massive pieces of artillery across the camp from the depot under the mountain to the wall at the entrance to the canyon. Enslaved gorillas were made to hoist cumbersome steel rocket launchers to the top of the wall, where both soldiers and apes wrestled the powerful weapons into position, in anticipation of the encroaching forces from the north. The feverish activity told Caesar that the enemy army was very near; the Colonel was obviously running out of time to complete his fortifications and prepare for the assault.

War is on the way, Caesar thought, *and apes are caught in the middle.*

He did not delude himself into thinking that the approaching humans were coming to liberate his people. The Colonel had made that clear enough; he had crossed a line only by executing infected humans, not because of his brutal campaign against the apes. Caesar could expect no mercy from the other humans, even if they managed to defeat the Colonel and his troops.

Our only hope is escape.

He contemplated the formidable weaponry being deployed on the wall as Red and Preacher marched him back toward his solitary confinement in the cage. Most of the other apes, the ones not currently employed in hoisting the weapons, were finally being returned to their pens as well, after being worked practically into the ground. They were being used up without concern for the future. Caesar doubted that they would be fed again, now that the wall was complete.

Arriving at the cage, Preacher unlocked it with one of his other keys, while Red kept Caesar on a tight leash. An angry red welt over Red's right eye marked where Rocket had head-butted him the night before; the mark was disturbingly reminiscent of the scar over Koba's dead eye. Caesar made a point to look directly at the welt, earning him a dirty look from the gorilla. Irking Red was feeble revenge for the traitor's crimes, but Caesar took some small pleasure in it nonetheless.

You deserve worse, he thought. *And have it coming, perhaps sooner than you think.*

Preacher opened the cage and Red shoved Caesar inside. Stepping closer to Caesar to unhook the chain from his collar, Red snarled in his face.

"You know Kerna shoot apes tomorrow... before battle begins."

Caesar looked past Red at Preacher, who averted his eyes. Caesar took this as clear confirmation that Red was telling the truth.

Tomorrow, he thought. *The slaughter is planned for tomorrow.*

The revelation was alarming but not surprising. The Colonel had made no secret of his intention to exterminate the apes once he no longer needed them, but now Caesar

234

knew for certain that there could be no hesitation or delay when it came to freeing his people. The time for action was rapidly slipping away.

Tonight, he thought. *It has to be tonight.*

Red seemed to think that he had shocked Caesar into silence.

"What?" he scoffed. "Caesar nothing say?"

The ape's gloating was pathetic, actually. Did he truly not see the bigger picture here—or understand the full consequences of what was coming? Caesar shook his head sadly. A note of genuine pity entered his voice as he finally spoke.

"I wonder... how long they will wait... before they shoot you?"

Red's spiteful expression gave way to a look of uncertainty as Caesar's words struck home. It looked to Caesar as though Red was struggling to come up with a dismissive reply, but couldn't find a convincing one. All he could manage was another hostile glare before wheeling about and exiting the cage. The malignant gorilla lumbered past Preacher in a foul mood. Caesar doubted that Red would sleep well tonight.

Nor should he.

Preacher kept avoiding Caesar's accusing stare as he locked the door of the cage. He turned to leave, then turned back to look at Caesar one last time. Despite everything, a trace of regret could be seen on his face.

"You must've known this fighting would never stop," he said quietly. "It was always going to come down to this. It was going to be you... or us."

Caesar had never believed that. He still didn't want to believe it.

But could he say for certain that Preacher wasn't right?

He looked back at the young soldier, wishing that

matters had not come to this. In a better world, Preacher might have been a good man, maybe even an ally.

But this was not a better world.

Whistles blew, calling the work crews away from the wall. Caesar felt time bearing down on them. Had Maurice received the vital information he had signed to him from high upon the cliff? Without binoculars, Caesar had no sure way of knowing whether his signs had been seen by his allies outside the camp. He could only hope that the plan was proceeding on schedule.

Otherwise, there was no hope.

The girl watched the apes come down from the wall. Bad men with guns made them go back toward their cages. Bigger guns now sat on top of the wall, which no longer had any holes in it. She realized that she could not sneak into the bad place anymore, even if she wanted to.

She lowered the far-seeing glasses and stared silently at the distant camps, worried about the apes. The bad men had too many guns.

And they hurt her friends.

Her other friends had been under the ground for a long time now. Had something happened to them? Concerned, she climbed down into the pit and went searching. The tunnel was scary and dark, but she kept on going until she came to a wall of cement blocking the way. Two new tunnels headed off in different directions.

Which way to go?

She paused for a moment, then chose one at random. She followed it, worried that she might have chosen the wrong way, but was soon reassured by the comforting glow of a flashlight up ahead. Drawn to the light, she found Maurice digging away at the wall with his bare hands. Dirt covered his shaggy hide. More dirt was piled to the side of the tunnel.

He was working very hard.

Soft footsteps alerted him to the girl's arrival. Maurice paused to look back at her and acknowledge her presence. It dawned on him that they had perhaps left the child alone on the surface for longer than they should have.

But there is so much digging to do, he thought, *and so little time.*

Concerned over what might have prompted the girl to seek him out, he searched her face and pointed toward the ceiling, wanting to know if everything was still quiet and secure up on the surface. She still knew very little sign language, but he liked to think that they were getting better at communicating with each other.

She nodded solemnly, which Maurice took to mean that no humans had discovered them yet. He smiled at her, pleased that she had apparently understood him.

You are very brave, he signed.

She stared at his large, expressive fingers in confusion, and he patiently repeated the sign:

Brave.

Her brow furrowed as she concentrated on the gesture, then hesitantly mimicked it.

Brave? she signed back.

Maurice nodded, proud of her progress. She had come far in the days since they had first found her hiding in that rundown shack. He still didn't understand what had made her mute, but there were other ways to speak, and she was proving to be a fast learner.

The girl beamed at him, happy to have gotten the sign right. Then her smile dimmed as a new thought seemed to occur to her, dampening her spirits. She raised her small hands in inquiry.

Ape?

Maurice wasn't sure what she was asking. He gave her a puzzled look.

Me? she signed again. *Ape?*

He understood now. The child was mute, not blind. She had obviously noted that she looked more like a human than an ape, despite her present company. He couldn't blame her for being confused, although he was uncertain how to respond. There was no easy answer here, or at least not one that wouldn't leave her more conflicted about her own identity than before. Humans were the enemy. Apes were her protectors. So what was he to tell her?

You are…

At a loss for words, he noticed a shiny silver solution poking out from the pocket of her jacket. Leaning forward, he gently plucked the chrome car emblem from the pocket and showed her the trinket. The gleaming steel letters spelled out a name from a vanished world of cars and consumerism:

"Nova," he said aloud, pointing at her.

The girl took the emblem back. She turned it over in her hands, watching it catch the glow of the flashlight, and a smile broke out across her face. She knew who and what she was now.

She was Nova.

An urgent grunt intruded on the moment. Bad Ape appeared at the mouth of the tunnel, looking worked up for some reason. For a moment, Maurice was afraid that something had gone wrong, but then he realized that the chimpanzee appeared more excitable than alarmed.

"Come!" Bad Ape said eagerly. "Come see!"

Maurice and Nova hurried to find out what had the

chimp so worked up. In their haste, they failed to notice a trickle of water seeping through the dirt where Maurice had been digging.

The water kept coming, even with no one to see it.

29

"...thirty-five... thirty-six... thirty-seven!"

Bad Ape counted out his steps, intent on his feet, as he led Maurice and Nova down a freshly dug tunnel. Reaching the end of the passageway, he turned around and threw out his hands to show off his handiwork. He looked very pleased with himself.

As he should be, Maurice thought, admiring the chimpanzee's progress. He had quietly counted the number of steps himself, just to double-check Bad Ape's calculations. It was not that he'd distrusted the chimp's ability to do the job correctly, at least not too much, but better safe than sorry. While Nova beamed at Bad Ape, mutely sharing his jubilation, Maurice consulted the compass to verify that Bad Ape had indeed tunneled in the right direction. To his relief, the compass needle confirmed that they were in the correct place.

He nodded approvingly at Bad Ape.

Good job, Maurice thought. *Perhaps he's not as much of a clown as he seems.*

Bad Ape basked in his success.

"What now?" he whispered.

Maurice surveyed the new tunnel, gazing up at the ceiling. In theory, they should be directly underneath the pen holding the adult apes. Getting down on his hands and knees, he gestured for Bad Ape to climb onto his back, as Rocket had done before. With any luck, the scrawny chimp weighed less than Rocket. Maurice's back was already sore from all the digging.

But Bad Ape didn't seem to understand. He stared at Maurice with a baffled expression, scratching his head in confusion.

"What?"

Maurice sighed, wishing the other ape was more fluent in sign language. He pointed at the ceiling, then patted his back impatiently. There was no time to waste. Caesar and Rocket and the other apes were counting on them.

Understanding dawned on Bad Ape's face, along with a look of utter horror. Terrified eyes practically bulged from their sockets as he backed away from Maurice in fear, almost stepping on Nova, who had to dart out of the way.

"Ohhh, no," he whimpered. "No, no, no…"

He looked to Nova to back him up, but she just looked on wordlessly.

"Nooooo…"

Maurice revised his earlier estimates of Bad Ape's intelligence and courage. Had the chimp truly not grasped the purpose of this undertaking until now, that the plan was to burrow up into the camp from below? What had he thought this entire operation had been all about?

Who knows, he thought irritably. *Anything could be going through that childish brain of his.*

Or nothing at all.

Shaking his head, Bad Ape kept backing away, but Maurice had neither the time nor the patience to put up with his foolishness. Spinning around in the tunnel, he grabbed Bad Ape by the ankle, startling the frightened chimp, who had never seen Maurice behave aggressively before. Bad Ape stared at the orangutan in shock.

Don't look surprised, Maurice thought. He considered himself a gentle soul, but he was still an ape, and a battle-tested ape at that. A low, menacing growl issued from his throat. His meaning was clear.

Don't test me.

Bad Ape got the message. He took a deep breath to steady his frazzled nerves.

"Okay."

Bad Ape was scared and tired.

But mostly scared.

Standing on Maurice's wide shoulders, his long arms stretched above his head as he reluctantly dug a shaft up toward the surface, he couldn't believe that he was actually working to claw his way into the bad, bad place. He understood now that they were trying to free Caesar and the others, but didn't Maurice realize how hopeless that was? The camp was full of angry humans with guns, who beat apes and tortured them and sometimes even shot them in the head. It was no place for an ape... or even the little human child they were calling Nova now.

You don't go into the bad place! he thought. *You run away from it! Caesar went into the camp, to get even with the Colonel, and look what happened to him! Rocket went into the camp and the bad apes beat him!*

Not for the first time, Bad Ape wished that he had stayed on his mountain where it was safe. He had been alone, without any friends, but at least he hadn't been afraid all the time.

Loose dirt rained down on his face. His fingers ached

from tearing at the hard, frozen earth. His nails were cracked and bleeding. Worse yet, he knew that every inch he gained brought him closer to the bad place and the bad humans waiting there. He almost thought that he would rather keep digging forever than actually reach the surface, so his heart sank when his fingers finally pushed through one last layer of dirt and ice to touch cold, empty air instead. Harsh electric light shone down through the tiny hole he had just created above his head.

Oh, no! I did it.

He yanked his fingers back before anybody saw them. Straining his neck, he peered up through the hole—at a human soldier's boot right before his eye!

No, no, no!

He clenched his jaw to keep from yelping in fright. He started to shrink away from the hole, then realized that one of the gorillas being herded into the pen had spotted him. The imprisoned ape blinked in surprise.

Ssssh! Bad Ape pressed a finger to his lips, terrified that the gorilla would accidentally alert the guards to his presence. *You don't see me!*

The gorilla understood. He glanced covertly at the oblivious soldiers and held up his palm to indicate that Bad Ape should stay put and keep still. He moved closer to the hole, positioning himself as a lookout, even as the other apes gradually spotted Bad Ape and realized what was happening. They too moved to discreetly block the humans' view of the hole, while pretending not to have seen anything unusual.

Smart apes! he thought with gratitude. *Very smart apes!*

He felt Maurice shifting his weight impatiently beneath him. Bad Ape knew that the orangutan had to be wondering what was taking so long, and why Bad Ape wasn't digging anymore, but there was no way he could say anything to Maurice without risking being overheard by the soldiers.

Have to be quiet now, he thought. *Maurice will have to wait.*

Bad Ape held his breath until the soldier's scary black boot stepped out of the chimpanzee's line of vision. Bad Ape kept his gaze glued to the gorilla serving as his lookout, who was still stealthily signaling him to hold tight. The gorilla's own eyes were busy watching something Bad Ape could not see, but he was pretty sure it had to do with the soldiers locking the apes into the pen. He listened anxiously to the sound of boots crunching through the snow, but it was impossible to tell what was actually happening.

What were the humans doing? How far away were they? Did he need to jump down into the tunnel and run away as fast as he could?

His heart was pounding so loudly that he couldn't believe the soldiers couldn't hear it. He felt like he had been hiding forever by the time the gorilla finally glanced back down at Bad Ape and indicated that it was safe for him to show himself.

Okay, he thought. *If you say so…*

Standing on his tiptoes, he nervously poked his head up through the hole in time to see the departing soldiers marching away from the pen. The sight relaxed him slightly, allowing him to focus instead on the gang of apes crowding around the hole, gaping down at him. Suddenly feeling self-conscious about being covered in dirt, Bad Ape took off his colorful wool cap and brushed it off before putting it back on his head.

That's better, he thought. *Need to make good impression.*

He smiled sheepishly at the other apes, not sure what

to say, as one of them shoved his way through the crowd to get to Bad Ape, who was briefly spooked before realizing that the ape coming at him was Rocket.

Rocket's face was a mess, all swollen and bruised from what the humans and turncoat apes had done to him. Bad Ape cringed in sympathy as the other chimpanzee stared at him, as mutely as Nova might. Bad Ape feared that he was in trouble, until an enormous grin lit up Rocket's battered features.

I did good? Bad Ape thought. *Yes, I did good!*

Rocket had never been so glad to see that silly ape in his ridiculous hat. He had been starting to worry that Maurice had not received Caesar's message after all, but apparently the digging had just taken longer than Rocket had hoped. He excitedly signed to the other apes.

This is the ape I told you about!

The other apes stared at Bad Ape in fascination; Rocket had to admit that Bad Ape wasn't the most impressive of liberators, but beggars, as the humans used to say, couldn't be choosers. He assumed that Maurice and the girl were waiting down in the tunnels, out of sight.

The gorilla who had first spotted Bad Ape came forward to greet him.

Thank you, he signed.

But Bad Ape didn't know that sign, Rocket realized. He stared blankly at the gorilla, looking slightly uncomfortable, until the gorilla shrugged and reached down to offer Bad Ape his hand.

Bad Ape regarded the hand uncertainly. Rocket recalled that the timid chimp had fled from Caesar and the rest of them when they had first met. He'd lived as a hermit for years, cut off from other apes. This was probably the biggest crowd of apes Bad Ape had encountered since he'd escaped the zoo too many years ago. No wonder he appeared a bit insecure.

For a second, Rocket thought it might all be too much for Bad Ape, but then the other chimp seemed to overcome his trepidation. He eagerly clasped the gorilla's hand while beaming from ear to ear. He thumped his chest with his palm and shook the gorilla's hand energetically.

"Bad Ape," he introduced himself. "Bad Ape."

More apes jostled forward to get a look at him, greeting him warmly, and Bad Ape shook each of their hands in turn. His earlier bashfulness evaporated and it seemed as though he couldn't meet his new family fast enough. His eyes grew moist, betraying the powerful emotions behind the never-ending stream of introductions.

"Bad Ape… Bad Ape… Bad Ape…"

Rocket, who even caged had enjoyed the company of other apes back in the bad old days, could only imagine what Bad Ape must be feeling now.

He's one of us now, Rocket thought. *He just needs a better name.*

If any of us live to see another day.

Maurice peered up the shaft, trying to figure out what was happening high above his head. Bad Ape was practically dancing on the orangutan's overworked shoulders, while beams of artificial light invaded the tunnel. Maurice assumed that meant that Bad Ape had reached the surface and gained access to the interior of the ape pen, but Maurice would have been much happier if the chimp would just inform him what was going on.

And perhaps get off of me, he thought.

Nova tugged at his fur to get his attention. Turning

his head, he saw her pointing down the tunnel at a small stream of water flowing toward them. Maurice reeled back from the sight, hooting in alarm, as the muddy brown water started to pool around his feet. Anxious to find out where the water was coming from before it flooded the entire tunnel, he rushed forward to investigate, momentarily forgetting the chimpanzee on his shoulders. Bad Ape tumbled down into the mud.

Sorry, Maurice thought. *My mistake.*

He turned around to make sure Bad Ape was unharmed, but the chimp seemed more confused by the water spreading everywhere than shaken by his fall. He stared at the muddy stream, looking utterly baffled by the pooling water. Maurice sympathized as he bent to help Bad Ape to his feet, but the chimp was too busy staring up at the shaft to notice Maurice's outstretched hand. The orangutan looked up as well and saw Rocket peering over the rim of the hole, no doubt worried by Bad Ape's sudden tumble. Making eye contact with Maurice, the perceptive chimp quickly picked up that something was amiss.

What's wrong? he signed.

30

Trapped in his cage, cut off from his people, Caesar could only look on in frustration as the apes in the pen huddled around the hole Maurice and Bad Ape had dug. He waited impatiently for news until Rocket finally broke away from the crowd to report to Caesar. He signed to Caesar from across the yard.

There's a problem, he said.

Caesar frowned. This was not what he wanted to hear. *Tell me*, he signed back.

Muddy water gushed from a widening fissure in the tunnel wall where Maurice had been digging before. The flood had grown from a trickle faster than the orangutan wanted to think about; he could only assume that he had accidentally hit some underground pool or stream, which was now pouring into their diggings.

Working together, Maurice and Bad Ape struggled to plug the leak with whatever dirt and rocks were on hand, as the icy water stung their hands and feet, turning them numb. Nova clung to the orangutan's back, trying to keep above the freezing muck. It was hard to tell if they were making any progress in damming the flow, but even if they could stop the water from flooding in, Maurice wondered, what then?

They were supposed to be digging up to the children's pen by now, not fighting a flood. The entire plan was in jeopardy, thanks to this unplanned disaster.

What were they supposed to do?

Caesar pressed against the bars of his cage, the better to take part in an urgent discussion with the apes in the pen. Grunting softly, Rocket and the others stared back at him through the bars of their own prison. The need for stealth made Caesar grateful that apes preferred sign language to speech; if they were discreet, the guards might not notice that the apes were communicating at all.

We can't dig any further, Rocket insisted. *It will flood the whole tunnel!*

But Lake and many others refused to accept that.

If we don't dig further, she signed, *we'll never get to the children! How are we going to get them out?*

Anxious parents grunted in agreement, sharing her concern. The plan had been to dig a separate shaft up to the children's pen, allowing them to escape via the underground tunnels as well, but the unexpected flooding had made that impossible. The agitated grunting grew louder as distraught apes demanded that their offspring be rescued no matter what, despite the seemingly insurmountable obstacle posed by the leak. Caesar grew concerned that the increasingly noisy debate would attract the attention of the guards.

He held up his hand to quiet the other apes, while glancing around at the various guards posted within earshot. His people's survival depended on silence and secrecy; the last thing they wanted to do was alert their foes on the very brink of their escape. But was it already too late? Rocket and the others looked up at the guard tower directly above Caesar's cage as a soldier stomped over to the edge of the catwalk to investigate the noise. Caesar heard the human named Boyle mutter irritably under his breath; he could well imagine the human's suspicious expression as he spied on the apes below, who suddenly did their best to appear docile and defeated. They milled about aimlessly, not speaking or signing, until Boyle backed away from the ledge and sought shelter inside the guard tower to escape the biting winter wind.

Careful, Caesar warned his people. *Wait*.

Minutes passed before Lake dared to resume the discussion. She kept her hands low as she subtly signed to the others:

We have to keep looking down there, see if there's another way to reach our children...

Caesar appreciated her concern for Cornelius and the other children, but decided that the discussion had gone on long enough. Morning would come too soon and, with it, death at the hands of the Colonel and his killers.

We have no time, he signed, shaking his head. *We must leave tonight. This is our last chance. We'll have to get the children out above ground.*

The other apes watched his hands intently, hanging on his every word. Rocket eyed him curiously. He signed back to Caesar:

How?

Lights went out in the soldiers' barracks, one by one. Scowling, Boyle envied the men and women who were getting a good night's sleep while he was stuck in a goddamn guard tower keeping watch over the monkey cage.

Just my luck, he groused silently. *Wanna bet plenty of the other guys are getting lucky tonight, what with the big battle practically knocking on our front door? Might as well get some before the shooting starts.*

At least the kongs had quieted down after making a racket earlier; he wondered if they'd guessed that they were all going to be slaughtered tomorrow and that was what had gotten them worked up. He could see how knowing that this was their last night on earth might be a tad upsetting.

Tough, he thought.

After tomorrow, what the apes knew or didn't know wouldn't matter anymore because they'd just be dead meat. He was looking forward to seeing every filthy kong put down—with extreme prejudice.

But in the meantime, he still had to keep an eye on them for one more night. He didn't figure that the stupid kongs would be any more trouble than they'd been before, but the Colonel expected every soldier to do his duty and Boyle wasn't about to disappoint him. The Colonel was a great man, as far as Boyle was concerned, and the only hope humanity had of stopping the damn apes from taking over the planet.

Too bad those spineless losers up north don't realize that.

He glanced at an old-fashioned windup clock somebody had installed in the tower and saw that he was probably overdue to eyeball the apes again. Groaning, he stirred himself from his seat, where he had been leafing through a stack of old skin magazines salvaged from the ruins of an abandoned convenience store, and steeled himself to face the wintry air outside the enclosed shelter atop the tower.

Time to check the monkey house, he thought sourly.

Taking a thermos of hot coffee with him, he exited the shelter and stepped out onto the catwalk outside where he discovered, much to his annoyance, that it had started to snow again. His breath frosted before his lips as the cold instantly leached away whatever body warmth he'd managed to hang onto in this frozen hellhole. He sipped from the steaming thermos as he stared out over the apes penned up below him. Searchlights swept past the pen periodically, revealing nothing amiss.

Looks quiet enough to me, he decided. Before heading back inside, he took a moment to admire the massive wall defending the camp from the hostile forces coming for the Colonel. The fortifications looked impressive, and had enough artillery mounted on them to repel a small army, but would it be enough to turn back whatever the Colonel's enemies might throw at them?

Guess we'll damn well find out soon.

He was turning away from the railing to head back indoors when, without warning, something cold and wet smacked into the back of his head, hitting hard enough to hurt. He lost his grip on the thermos, spilling coffee onto the catwalk.

What the—?

He reached back to see what had hit him and came away with a handful of thick, gooey mud. Disgusted, he wiped the muck off on his trousers and spun back toward the railing. Surprise ignited into fury as he stormed over to the rail and glared down at the ape pen below. His face flushed with anger. An engorged vein throbbed furiously at his temple as he shouted in rage:

"Hey! You animals!"

Thirsting for payback, he charged down the ladder and across the yard to the pen, where he unlocked the gate and slid it to one side. Storming into the pen, he maintained the presence of mind to shut the gate behind him before raising his rifle and waving it at the kongs, who shuffled away from him fearfully, as they damn well should.

"WHO DID THAT?" he bellowed.

The apes cowered, shaking their heads to proclaim their innocence and jabbering like monkeys. Frustration ate at Boyle as he tried to figure out how to force the truth out of them. He was tempted to shoot just any ape at random, but he really, really wanted to get the stinking kong who had nailed him with the mud.

Wait a minute... mud?

It briefly occurred to him to wonder where the hell the kong had gotten the soggy mud anyway, especially on a freezing night like this. But before he could put his brain to work figuring out that mystery, another wad of muck smacked into the side of his head, knocking out of it the train of thought. The mud splattered against his profile and got in his ear, oozing down onto his neck and under his collar.

"SUNUVA—!"

He swung his rifle wildly at the chained apes, who scampered out of the way, exposing the culprit who had been hiding among them: the bald chimpanzee who had been caught sneaking into the camp the night before, the same one Red and the other donkeys had delivered a major ass-whupping to. The ugly chimp, still sporting bruises and scabs from his well-deserved beatdown, sneered at Boyle as he clutched another goopy fistful of muck. He bared his teeth and gums defiantly.

"You..." Boyle snarled.

Livid, he took aim at the rebellious ape, who obviously hadn't learned his lesson yet. His finger tightened on the trigger.

Say goodbye, asshole.

But before he could fire, a large shaggy hand reached up from beneath the ground and seized Boyle's ankle, yanking the startled soldier out of sight. The other apes, no longer cringing in fear, gathered around the hole expectantly. A heavy thump, coming from below, suggested that Boyle would not be threatening any more apes, tonight or ever. A moment later, a set of keys were tossed back up through the hole.

Rocket dropped the mud, half-disappointed that he hadn't had the opportunity to use it, and snatched up the keys. Knuckle-walking over to the hole, he peered down at Maurice, who handed him the soldier's rifle.

Boyle wouldn't be needing it anymore.

31

While Rocket distracted the guard, Caesar retrieved the stolen key from the metal strip above the cage door, where he had hidden it. Bending over, he hastily began unshackling his feet. He had just managed to free his right leg when the sound of approaching footsteps sent his heart racing. He quickly turned toward the noise and was dismayed to see the Colonel heading toward him, despite the late hour.

What does he want? Caesar wondered. *And why now?*

He straightened, palming the key, and shot a warning look at Rocket, who immediately hid the captured rifle behind his back. Caesar hoped the Colonel had not already spotted the weapon. If so, the apes' escape attempt would be over almost before it had begun. Armed with the rifle, Rocket might be able to hold off the soldiers long enough for some of the apes to escape via the tunnel, but the humans' superior firepower would gun Rocket down almost as soon as the alarm was sounded—and there would be no chance of rescuing the children.

But the Colonel didn't even glance at the ape enclosure. Instead he simply gazed pensively at the completed wall looming at the far end of the canyon, taking the sight in. Caesar assumed that he was too worried about the upcoming battle to give much thought to the apes in their pens.

Good, Caesar thought. *Maybe he will move on soon.*

The Colonel's late-night stroll was unexpected, but perhaps it would only cause a temporary delay in the apes' plans—unless he noticed that Boyle was not at his post in the guard tower.

Caesar watched tensely, silently urging the Colonel to return to his lair atop the watchtower, but the murderous human commander seemed to be in no hurry to escape the cold night air. He simply stood there, as still and silent as a statue, as though rooted to the spot. Caesar began to fear that the Colonel was never going to move.

He can't stand there all night. Can he?

At last the Colonel turned away from the wall, but instead of heading back to his tower, he detoured toward Caesar's cage. As the Colonel drew nearer, Caesar could see that the man was still lost in thought, appearing barely aware of his surroundings, let alone the frigid temperature. His lips moved silently as though he was conversing with himself. One hand grasped his stainless-steel hip flask.

Is he drinking? The night before a battle?

The Colonel walked up to the bars of the cage and began speaking in an oddly vacant tone, without any preamble. There was a far-off look in his bloodshot eyes, which gazed past the ape on the other side of the prison bars. His uniform was rumpled and disheveled, in marked contrast to his crisp appearance when addressing his troops several hours ago. Caesar smelled whiskey on his breath.

"Least you can take comfort," he mused. "Your struggle ends. Ours goes on. Nature still has the power to wipe us off this planet at any moment. Killed the dinosaurs off with a single meteor…"

His unfocused eyes swept over Caesar's wiry frame.

"You apes are so strong. I wonder... what kind of world you would have built... on our graves..."

His voice trailed off for a moment, leaving Caesar to ponder the man's odd demeanor. Was he drunk or feeling guilty or just contemplating his mortality in anticipation of the battle? He seemed to be talking more to himself than to Caesar, who remained still in order to avoid revealing that his right leg was free.

"You know," the Colonel said, gazing off into space, "when I first got to the city, a man said he had to see me. He said he knew you. That you had worked together."

Caesar's eyes widened. There was only one person the Colonel could be referring to.

"Malcolm...?"

Caesar had last seen his human friend in the grim aftermath of Koba's attack on the human colony in San Francisco. Caesar had urged Malcolm to take his family and flee the war that both he and Malcolm had tragically failed to avert, the war that had inevitably led to this very moment.

The ape's voice jarred the Colonel from his reverie. He looked directly at Caesar for the first time. His brow furrowed as he searched his memory.

"I think that was his name, yes."

It would be just like Malcolm, Caesar reflected, to reach out to the Colonel in hopes of preventing further bloodshed, no matter the risk to his own safety. Malcolm had done the same when he'd bravely ventured into the forest to try to negotiate with Caesar and search for a way humans and apes could coexist peacefully. And when he'd risked his life to help Caesar defeat Koba.

"He... was a friend," Caesar said.

"He said you were remarkable," the Colonel replied. "More than just an animal... that you were a great leader."

He shook his head at the memory. "I thought he was crazy... but I almost see what he meant..."

His eyes began to lose focus again, his gaze turning inward as it looked back through the years.

"He pleaded with me to find you. To make peace with you."

Caesar was stunned by this revelation. This was the first he'd heard of Malcolm attempting to make peace between the apes and humans after the war began, but, in retrospect, it made perfect sense. The Malcolm he'd known would have never stopped trying to keep humans or apes from being harmed. He'd cared too deeply about taking care of people, human or simian. Caesar was almost afraid to ask where Malcolm was now.

"What... happened to this man?"

The Colonel didn't answer at first; he just stared mutely at nothing in particular, lost in his own thoughts and memories. Caesar wasn't sure the Colonel had even heard his query until the man finally answered casually, shrugging as though he barely recalled the incident.

"I shot him."

Sorrow, laced with anger, descended on Caesar. He had often wondered what had become of Malcolm and his family, but had always preferred to think that they were alive together somewhere, safely distant from the war. Caesar had never expected to see Malcolm again, but finding out for certain that his friend was dead—killed by his own kind—still came as a painful blow. Caesar could only pray that Malcolm's lover, Ellie, and his son, Alexander, had not accompanied Malcolm when he went to see the Colonel. He wanted to think that they were still alive at least.

But the Colonel had killed Malcolm, too? As well as Cornelia and Blue Eyes and Percy and so many others? The enormity of this knowledge sank in, refueling Caesar's determination to destroy the Colonel before he could kill anyone else Caesar cared about. Intent on saving his people, Caesar had almost forgotten his quest for revenge, but knowing that the Colonel had also murdered Malcolm, on top of so many others, was a bitter reminder of just how much this man deserved to perish at Caesar's hands.

Not that the Colonel seemed to care, let alone show any trace of remorse. He fell silent for a moment, then abruptly snapped out of his daze. His head jerked up and he glanced around wildly, as though trying to orient himself. A suspicious, almost paranoid gleam entered his eyes.

"Wha—what's going on here?"

Caesar held his tongue, unsure how to respond to the Colonel's erratic behavior. Was the alcohol to blame or was this evidence of some deeper fracture in his damaged psyche? The man almost seemed to be melting down like one of the many untended nuclear reactors that had reportedly burned out of control after the plague, contaminating other parts of the country. Caesar knew he needed to tread warily here; there was no telling what might provoke the seemingly unhinged Colonel to violence.

And at the worst possible time, Caesar thought. *Just when we need to make our escape!*

The Colonel's wary gaze darted about the slumbering camp. Caesar struggled to maintain a neutral expression and not betray his growing anxiety as the Colonel craned his neck to squint up through the falling snow at the guard tower where Boyle had been posted. The angle was steep enough that Caesar didn't think that the Colonel could see that the guard station was unoccupied, but he wasn't entirely certain. And what if the Colonel chose to check on the guard, or call out to him?

If he sounds an alarm, our plans are doomed.

A metallic clank interrupted the tense moment,

distracting the Colonel, who looked down at his feet to discover that he had dropped his flask. The odor of spilled whiskey wafted up from the adulterated snow. Frowning, the Colonel picked up the flask and peered at it in confusion, as though he'd already forgotten that he'd brought it with him. He shook it to see if it was empty or not. A few last gulps sloshed inside it.

He glanced around uncomfortably, perhaps worried that his embarrassing lapse had been observed. He noticed the apes in the pen watching him, then looked back at Caesar and winced at the chimpanzee's piercing gaze. His usual self-assurance was nowhere in evidence as he slowly backed away from the cage and retreated, with unseemly haste, back to his tower. Falling snow began to cover up his tracks.

Watching him go, Caesar was both relieved and puzzled by the Colonel's sudden departure. He turned toward Rocket, who appeared equally perplexed.

What was that? Rocket signed.

Caesar shook his head, having no idea, but, ultimately, it didn't matter. The important thing was that he was gone now and they could get back to their plan. Caesar bent down to liberate his other foot from the heavy shackles, then tossed the key to Rocket, who deftly reached through the bars of the pen to catch it. Wasting no time, Rocket set to work freeing himself from the chain binding him to the other apes. He grunted with satisfaction as he stepped free and lobbed the key to Lake, who followed his example before passing the key along to the rest of the chain gang. One after another, the other apes eagerly unchained themselves.

Thank you, Preacher, Caesar thought wryly.

Moving freely, Rocket made use of Boyle's keys to unlock the gate of the pen. Caesar was briefly reminded of their "jail break" from the primate shelter more than a decade ago. He hoped this escape would prove just as successful.

Apes together strong.

Rocket tossed the keys over to Caesar, who received them gratefully. He had been caged enough in his life, as had his people. He was ready to leave these bars behind.

No more cages, he thought. *Never again.*

He was unlocking the gate when the lights of the Colonel's watchtower came on and Caesar saw something that caused him to instantly signal the other apes to stay where they were, at least for the moment. He nodded at the tower where the Colonel could be seen standing before the window, lit by a lamp behind him. Only his shadowy outline was visible, making it impossible to tell if he was gazing down at the prison yard or staring out into the distance.

Rocket looked across the yard at Caesar. *Do you think he knows we're up to something?*

Caesar wished he knew. If the Colonel had observed something suspicious a few minutes ago, wouldn't he have dispatched soldiers to investigate by now? But the apes could hardly carry out their escape plan, and rescue the trapped children, with the Colonel standing watch from his tower. They'd be spotted for sure.

Long minutes passed before the Colonel turned away from the window and vanished into the private eyrie, but the lights in the tower remained on, suggesting that the Colonel had not yet retired for the evening but was instead sleeplessly moving about his lair—and might return to the window at any moment.

Rocket hoisted his rifle, anxious to get going.

Now? he signed.

Caesar shook his head. He shared Rocket's frustration; the night was not getting any younger and their time was running out, but they couldn't risk attempting the rescue while the Colonel was still up and about.

Wait, Caesar signed back, *till he turns off his lights.*

The snow began coming down harder. A rising wind howled in the night as the apes gazed up at the tower, waiting... and waiting... and waiting...

32

Hours passed and the snowstorm became a blizzard. A fresh layer of white blanketed the camp and fell upon the shivering apes, who huddled and paced within the pen, trying to keep warm while staring anxiously up at the Colonel's watchtower. The snow frosted the apes' furry hides, making them look nearly as white as the late, unlamented Winter.

And still the Colonel's lights remained on.

The endless waiting tortured Caesar, who knew their time was running out. The escape tunnel under the pen was ready, providing a route to safety, but only for the adults, who were not about to flee the camp without the children. But how could they get to the children's pen with the Colonel potentially watching from above? It was possible that the man was indeed sleeping, despite the lights on in the tower, but they couldn't count on it, especially given how oddly the Colonel had been acting earlier. Caesar could readily imagine the man spending a sleepless night on this, the eve of battle. Perhaps he was poring over his maps and strategies one last time, or meditating before that grotesque shrine of his? Or maybe he was simply passed out drunk on his cot?

There was no way of telling.

Tearing his burning gaze away from the tower's lights, Caesar looked over at Rocket, who was coiled tensely at the gate of the pen, clutching his rifle. The hairless chimp shook off the snow clinging to his head and shoulders as he gazed back at Caesar.

The sun will be up soon, Rocket signed.

Caesar was all too aware of this. The storm made it difficult to tell if the sky was lightening yet, but the dawn could not be too far away. Caesar looked at the watchtower one last time, hoping that it would finally go dark, but realized that they could not delay any longer.

We go now, he signed to Rocket. *Or die trying.*

Rocket nodded grimly. He waited until a searchlight swept past the pen, then darted out, rifle in hand. Crossing the yard quickly, he came to Caesar's cage, and the ape leader exited it at last, glad to be finally free.

They wasted no time conversing. Keeping low, they dashed from the empty guard tower into a murky alley between the soldiers' darkened barracks and the pen containing the ape children, who were huddled together for warmth. Caesar hated leaving tracks behind in the fresh snow, but there was nothing to be done about it; as the Colonel himself had observed earlier, nature cared little for the plans of men or apes. Caesar could only hope that the tracks went unnoticed until it was too late for the humans to react.

Soldiers, patrolling the camp, marched past the children's pen, missing Caesar and Rocket by moments. The escaped apes ducked further into the alley, pressing their backs against the cold concrete wall, until the soldiers crossed out of sight. Caesar silently signaled Rocket and they darted over to the children's pen, where they were confronted by the heartbreaking sight of several small gorillas, orangutans, bonobos, and chimpanzees shivering beneath a heavy coating of snow.

Caesar's anger grew. The heartless humans had not even provided the young ones with blankets or a fire or any shelter from the storm. He assumed that the Colonel had only kept the little apes alive to help ensure the cooperation of their parents—and to avoid the riot that would have resulted had he simply butchered the children in front of the adult apes. The children were hostages, but they too had outlived their usefulness as far as the Colonel was concerned; Caesar knew that the genocidal commander would show the children no mercy when the time came. He wasn't going to leave a single ape alive.

He unlocked the gate and slid it open as quietly as he could. Even still, his actions stirred some of the children from their sleep. They sat up dozily, rubbing their eyes and shaking off the snow that had accumulated on their small bodies, then jumped to their feet at the sight of Caesar and Rocket. They scrambled wildly toward the adults, waking up their companions. Caesar worried that the children might get too excited, alerting the guards.

Quiet! he signed to them urgently. *Make no noise!*

To their credit, the children grasped the need for silence. Despite their age, they had learned too well that attracting the humans' attention was to be avoided at all costs. They kept quiet as the two adults furtively slipped into the pen, where Caesar and Rocket were immediately swarmed by the little apes. Their wide, hopeful eyes tore at Caesar's heart as he gently patted their heads and continued to shush them. His own eyes sought out Cornelius and were rewarded by the sight of his son at the back of the crowd. Cornelius broke into a run, clambering up and over the backs of the other children to practically leap into his father's arms. Overcome with emotion, Caesar embraced the son he had been forced to turn his back on only days ago. He hugged

Cornelius tightly, never wanting to let him go.

But reality dictated otherwise. Caesar shifted Cornelius onto his back in order to get all of the children to safety before it was too late. Rocket kept watch on the nearest guard tower, where a solitary sentry could be glimpsed through an open doorway. The guard appeared to be oblivious to what was going on beneath his nose as Caesar hustled the children out of the pen toward a tall iron lamp pole that was far too close to the guard tower for Caesar's peace of mind. He took a moment to mourn their original plans.

The tunnel would have been better, he thought ruefully, *but this will have to do.*

He hoisted the children, one by one, onto the pole. At his direction, they hastily scaled the pole and scrambled out onto an electrical line strung high above the guard towers and the camp. Strong winds and icy lines made this route more perilous than Caesar would have preferred, but once again Nature had other plans. As the heavy snow swirled all around the children, he watched in suspense as they made their way across the camp toward the adult pen, over the heads of the soldiers posted below, most of whom were probably more concerned with the snow falling down on them than with peering up into the storm.

Perhaps the blizzard was not entirely to the apes' disadvantage?

Arriving above the adult pen, the children began dropping silently down into the waiting arms of Lake and several other apes, who hastily handed them off to their respective parents. Each mother and father clutched their little ones joyously as they were reunited.

Caesar and Rocket waited until all the other children had made it safely over to the adult pen before following them. Cornelius clung tightly to his father, his small arms around Caesar's neck as they climbed the pole and crossed the swaying wire to join the others. A pair of burly gorillas caught the chimpanzees as they dropped from the wire. They lowered the chimps onto the snowy floor of the pen, where the escape tunnel awaited.

So far, so good, Caesar thought. *But we're not safe yet*. Not as long as the Colonel remained alive.

33

Cornelius did not want to let go of his father, not after Caesar had finally come for him. The young ape had been afraid that his father had abandoned him, leaving him alone in the cage with the other children, but he realized now that Caesar had just been waiting for a chance to sneak past the scary humans and rescue them all, like he was supposed to.

I should have known he would come, Cornelius thought. *My father is Caesar.*

But now Caesar was herding him and the other children toward a dark hole in the ground where Cornelius saw Maurice beckoning to him. Cornelius was glad to see the wise old orangutan again, but he still didn't want to leave his father's side to go down into the hole. The humans had already killed his mother and brother. His father was all he had left.

I can't lose him too! Not again!

But his father insisted that he go with the other children.

Be brave, Caesar signed as he pulled Cornelius off his back and handed him down to Maurice, who took him from his father. *Be safe.*

Cornelius didn't want to go without him, but he tried to be brave as his father had asked, as Blue Eyes had been. He was Caesar's son. He had to be as brave as Caesar.

Come soon, he thought. *Hurry!*

Maurice lowered Cornelius to the floor of the tunnel, where he joined several other children whom his father and Rocket had already handed down to Maurice. To his surprise, he found a human girl waiting for them underground, holding a flashlight. She took Cornelius's hand and began to lead the children down a long dark tunnel…

Away from his father.

Bad Ape shivered as he paced nervously around the top of the pit, clutching himself in a futile attempt to stay warm. The rocky outcropping shielded him from the humans' view, but provided scant protection against the freezing wind and snow. He missed the thick green parka he had given to Nova, even though he knew she needed it more than he did.

Maybe I can find a new coat someday, he thought, *if we get away from the bad place?*

A noise echoed up from the depths of the pit. Peering down into the hole, Bad Ape saw Nova guide a large group of little apes out of the tunnel to the base of the pit, where she steered them toward the ladder leading up to the surface. Snow fell past the children as they began to climb the ladder, one after another. They looked nervously up at Bad Ape, not recognizing him. He felt a pang in his heart as he recalled his own lost offspring.

"It's okay, little ones," he said softly, urging them on. "Come, come…"

Despite their apprehension, the children were anxious to leave the tunnels and get away from the humans. In no time at all, a whole troop of children were huddled together behind the outcropping. Maurice followed the last of them out of the pit, joining Bad Ape and Nova.

Is it clear? he signed to Bad Ape.

The chimp peered through the binoculars at a guard post along the giant wall. Human soldiers—with guns!—paced back and forth on the wall, maintaining a close watch on the horizon. According to Maurice, more human soldiers were coming to fight the ones in the camp; Bad Ape didn't entirely understand that, but he guessed that the humans on the wall were watching out for their enemies. And he did understand that none of the humans were friends to apes, so they needed to get away before the fighting started.

Which meant running for their lives.

"Go!" he whispered to Maurice and the children, waving them on with his hand while he lingered behind to keep watch on the camp. The soldiers were searching the horizon for enemy humans now; they weren't looking for any runaway apes yet. "Go, go, go...!"

Nova scrambled onto Maurice's back, settling into her usual spot, as the apes dashed out from behind the rocks and set out across an exposed stretch of flats toward the lower slopes of the mountain looming over the camp. They ran single file toward the snowy, wooded hillside as fast as their feet and knuckles could carry them, counting on the storm and the night to hide them.

But would that be enough?

Go, go. Away from the bad place!

After the children, it was the adults' turn. Rocket took charge of urging the other apes down into the tunnels. It was a tight squeeze for some of the larger gorillas and orangutans, but they managed. Many of the adults had wanted to stay with their children, but had been persuaded that it was better to get all the children clear of the camp first just in case the humans suddenly caught on to what was happening; nobody wanted any children left in the pen if the guards started firing on the escaping apes. The old and the injured were also given priority.

Almost there, Rocket thought.

It had taken longer than he liked to get everyone out, but finally the last of their people had exited the pen, leaving only him and Caesar behind. He turned toward his leader, more than ready to leave the hellish camp behind, and found Caesar over by the gate, staring up at the Colonel's watchtower, which was lit up from the inside. Rocket assumed that he was keeping an eye out in case the Colonel suddenly appeared in the window again. Rocket was glad to see that the window remained empty... at least for the time being.

Not wanting to push their luck, he went to fetch Caesar. He tapped the other chimp on the shoulder to get his attention.

Let's go, he signed.

But Caesar remained where he was, making no effort to move. His brilliant green eyes remained fixed on the lighted window high in the tower. Rocket was not sure why Caesar was delaying. The other apes were safely gone; there was no need to linger or keep watching out for the Colonel anymore.

Caesar? What's wrong?

Caesar kept one eye on the tower as he answered.

"By the time they wake, you'll all be up on the mountain." He turned to face Rocket, bearing a grim expression on his face. "Hurry, you must go."

Rocket suddenly realized that Caesar did not intend to join them.

Without you? No…!

A hint of regret showed upon Caesar's determined features, but he did not relent. His course was clearly set, as it had been since he had found his wife and firstborn murdered in their own home.

"Maurice was right," he said. "I *am* like Koba. He could not escape his hate." He turned his vengeful eyes toward the Colonel's tower once more. "And I still cannot escape mine."

Rocket wanted to change Caesar's mind, to convince him that their people needed Caesar more than Caesar needed revenge. But he remembered his own anger after Koba had killed Ash. If Koba was still alive and dwelling in that tower instead of the Colonel, Rocket knew he would feel just as Caesar did right now—and that he would make the same choice.

He nodded at Caesar, accepting the inevitable. He was tempted to join Caesar in his search for vengeance, as he had before, but their people were far from safe yet. Maurice and the others needed him.

I must go, he realized.

Even if it meant that he might never see Caesar again.

Caesar also seemed to realize that this might be their final farewell. He reached and gently grasped Rocket's head, pulling their foreheads together as they shared a moment of silent communion. Rocket's throat tightened with emotion as he recalled how he and Caesar had started out as rivals and enemies so many years ago, and what a long, winding journey they had taken together since.

Was this finally that journey's end?

Caesar pulled away from Rocket and looked his friend in the eyes.

"Go," he said.

Rocket reluctantly turned away from Caesar and returned to the tunnel entrance. Glancing back over his shoulder, he paused to look at Caesar one last time before descending into the tunnel after the others.

He wished his friend luck.

And he wished the Colonel death.

34

Hurry! Bad Ape thought. *Hurry, hurry!*

Remaining by the tunnel exit to assist the adults climbing from the pit, he watched Maurice lead the fleeing children onward across the icy waste to the base of the mountain. They had just reached the nearest foothills when the ground began to shake beneath Bad Ape's feet. An ominous rumbling grew louder and louder.

Confused and frightened, Bad Ape peered up at the immense wall guarding the entrance to the camp. The sentries on the wall appeared to be equally agitated by the approaching noise. They frantically scanned and pointed at the horizon, which was where the clamor was coming from. Following their example, Bad Ape paused and turned his binoculars toward the noise. A jolt of fear ran down his spine as the terrifying source of the rumbling came into focus.

The other humans! Bad Ape realized. *They're coming!*

Through the snowy haze, headlights appeared in the distance, cutting through the dark and the swirling white flakes. The lights preceded a huge convoy of large, imposing armored vehicles advancing toward the camp across the wide frozen tundra. Their heavy treads dug great trenches through the accumulated snow. Winter's fury failed to slow their approach.

Alarms sounded along the length of the wall. The battle between the warring humans was about to begin.

And the desperate apes were trapped in the middle.

Oh no, Bad Ape thought. *Not now!*

Sirens assailed Caesar's ears. Lights blinked on all over the camp, including the soldiers' barracks, which suddenly came alive with activity. Soldiers poured out of the barracks, clutching their weapons. Many of them were still tugging their ragged uniforms and winter gear into place as they charged toward the war, shouting wildly at each other.

"Holy shit!" someone yelled. "They're here!"

Crouching in the shadows by the barracks, Caesar cursed the bad timing of the attack—and his own protracted caution earlier. Getting to the Colonel, and remaining undetected, was going to be much harder now that the entire camp was wide awake and the Colonel was bound to be directing the battle. Caesar feared that he had waited too long to seek his revenge.

With no time to waste, he broke from cover and hastily scaled the side of the barracks to reach the roof. He raced along the edge of the snow-covered rooftop, tempting gravity as he headed toward the watchtower, even as the adrenalized soldiers rushed in the opposite direction to get to the wall. None of them looked up to see the agile chimpanzee making his way along the roof several stories above them. Their enemies were attacking by land, not air.

Because of the blizzard? Or have humanity simply lost command of the sky since the plague?

Caesar didn't know or care.

Just as long as they don't look up... until I've done what I have to do.

Reaching the far end of the roof, he paused on the brink of the precipice. The Colonel's watchtower lay before him, several feet away. Frantic shouts and banging drew his gaze down to the base of the tower, where a group of human officers were pounding on the metal door guarding its front entrance. They yelled up at the watch station high above them.

"COLONEL! COLONEL!" a lieutenant shouted, then turned and snapped at his fellow officers, "Why the hell is this door locked?"

Good question, Caesar thought.

Not that he'd been planning to walk in the front door anyway. He stared up at the open window four stories above, on the other side of the daunting gap dividing the barracks from the watchtower. Judging from the chaotic scene he had just witnessed, the Colonel was still holed up in his eyrie all by himself, for reasons known only to his own troubled brain. Caesar recalled the man's peculiar behavior earlier that night and was relieved to find out that the Colonel had not yet joined his forces on the wall. The ape knew he would never have a better opportunity to take his revenge—and protect his people.

No ape was safe while the Colonel lived.

The time had come. Caesar gauged the distance between the roof's edge and the window above, just as he had often calculated the gap between sky-high treetops and branches. Backing up to get a running start, he took a deep breath, mustered all his remaining strength and vigor, and launched himself off the rooftop toward the tower.

The sun was just beginning to rise as Preacher, along with his fellow soldiers, ran for the wall to defend the Colonel from his enemies. The young soldier was grateful for the few hours of sleep he'd managed to snag before the sirens had sounded, but he was not looking forward to the coming battle. Beyond the imminent danger to life and limb, he hated the very idea of having to fire on his brother and sister humans. He glanced over at the ape pen as he started to run past it. Fighting the kongs was one thing, but…

"Jesus Christ!"

Preacher froze in his tracks. His jaw dropped and it took his befuddled brain a moment to process what he was seeing: an empty pen where the apes had been locked up only hours before. Empty chains lay discarded in the snow. Swallowing hard, he remembered that lost key he had never actually managed to locate. His voice edged on hysteria as he shouted at the top of his lungs:

"THE APES! THEY'RE GONE!"

35

Racing the dawn, Caesar crept through the window into the Colonel's lofty abode. It occurred to him that his surreptitious home invasion echoed the way the Colonel had silently infiltrated Caesar's own dwelling back at the fortress, right before the merciless human had slaughtered Cornelia and Blue Eyes. Now Caesar was returning the favor with equally murderous intent. There was, perhaps, a certain poetic justice to be found there.

He glanced around, getting his bearings, and was immediately struck by a sight both incongruous and unnerving. The front door of the command center, which led to the stairs descending to the base of the tower, was barricaded by a heap of furniture—a desk, chairs, file cabinets—shoved up against the door from the inside. It appeared that the Colonel did not wish to be disturbed, but who was he trying to keep out: his enemies or his own officers?

The entire room was in disarray, as though the Colonel had lashed out in anger at his own lodgings. A stockpile of munitions, including belts of grenades, were strewn across the top of a messy table that had somehow avoided being added to the barricade. A tray of half-eaten army rations sat beside the disordered armaments, along with the Colonel's steel flask, which was lying on its side, spilling its pungent contents onto the table. Soaking in a pool of whiskey was a photo of a small human boy smiling at the camera. The Colonel's son, Caesar guessed.

Caesar felt an unwanted twinge of sympathy for the Colonel until he remembered that it was the Colonel himself who had murdered his own son, ruthlessly executing the infected soldier who had once been the smiling boy in the photo.

Just like he killed Blue Eyes and Cornelia and Percy and Malcolm...

The Colonel's medals were also scattered on the table, but the man himself was nowhere to be seen. Caesar's eyes scanned the eyrie, searching for the human he had come so far to kill. Caesar knew the Colonel had to be nearby.

But where?

Missiles blasted off from the top of the wall, targeting the approaching army, streamers of bright orange flame trailing behind them. Bad Ape watched the flames light up the wintry landscape before diving for the enemy convoy. Massive explosions rocked the ground and the armored vehicles erupted into smoke and flames. Mangled metal fragments flew like shrapnel through the falling snow. The humans in the camp had drawn first blood, but Bad Ape knew the battle was only beginning.

"Hurry!" he urged a few stray children, who had hung back waiting for the parents. "Go, go, go!"

A tremendous roar, accompanied by a blinding flash, announced that the invaders had returned fire. Artillery shells soared toward the wall as Bad Ape lunged to drape himself protectively over the children. The shells made impact thirty feet short of the wall. A deafening boom briefly drowned out the world, including the fearful gasps and pants of the frightened little ones. Pulverized rock and ice pelted the apes like hail. Bad Ape's ears rang from the echoes of the explosions.

This is no place for apes, he thought. *We need to be anywhere but here!*

Down in the tunnels, Rocket and the other adults reacted in dismay as a violent rumble shook the frozen earth surrounding them. Dirt rained down from the ceiling and the ancient timbers supporting the tunnel trembled and creaked, making Rocket fear for the structural integrity of the passage. It felt like an earthquake, but the battle-scarred chimpanzee guessed that they were feeling the shock waves from large explosions instead. He recalled the massive artillery the apes had been forced to haul up onto the wall, in anticipation of the coming battle between the Colonel and his human enemies.

We waited too long. The fight is underway. Now we must make our way through the humans' war.

More explosions shook the tunnels, which were crammed with apes, slowing their progress toward the waiting ladder. More of the ceiling began to give way, adding to Rocket's fear that the tunnels might soon collapse. Despite the conflict being waged on the surface, there was no safety to be found down here; they needed to keep moving and catch up with the children who had gone before them.

Just like Rocket needed to find out what was waiting for them above.

Gripping his rifle, he tried to push his way through the crush of bodies. It was a tight squeeze, but Rocket kept shoving, desperate to reach the surface. For all he knew, the children, along with Maurice and Bad Ape and the human girl, were trapped in the middle of the war—or had already been blown apart by the explosions. He needed to know what had become of them. He signed urgently to the apes in his way.

Let me through!

36

The thunder of war penetrated the walls of the watchtower.

Caesar wheeled about at the sound of the shelling. Racing to the window, he gazed in horror at the fierce battle being waged outside, practically at the Colonel's doorstep. Incoming missiles flew over the wall to explode inside the camp. Entire sections of the dilapidated barracks were blown apart, adding to the rubble piled along the edges of the yard. Fiery debris erupted where missiles struck, igniting numerous small fires despite the cold, wet snow everywhere. Pristine snow was blackened by smoke and ash. The lofty watchtower rattled and swayed beneath Caesar's feet, bleached simian skulls tumbling from the Colonel's morbid shrine. Caesar realized that the watchtower itself would be a tempting target for the enemy artillery.

Time is running out…

A muffled crash came from an adjoining room. Remembering that he was not alone in the tower, Caesar turned away from the destruction outside and advanced cautiously toward a partially open doorway. Although eager to finally rid the world of the Colonel, he knew better than to proceed rashly when his quarry might well be waiting with a loaded firearm on the other side of the door. Caesar had not come this far to have his quest for revenge ended by a bullet to his head or heart.

The end is near, he thought. *For one of us*. Steeling himself, ready to spring for cover at the slightest hint of a gun being cocked, he peered warily around the doorframe. The first thing he saw was a broken Coleman lantern lying at the foot of a small wooden table. Spilled fuel pooled around the fallen lamp with its cracked glass pane. The harsh odor of the kerosene invaded Caesar's nostrils, rendering his keen sense of smell useless. His eyes watered at the stink. Labored breathing came from beyond the door. Pushing it open as quietly as he could, Caesar peeked inside the room, which appeared to be the Colonel's private sleeping quarters. A hint of dawn came through a small window, lighting the room... and its occupant.

At last.

The Colonel was sprawled on his stomach on a simple military-issue cot. His head drooped forward, while a flailing hand groped blindly for something just out of reach. His outstretched arm and trembling fingers clutched at empty air, while his face sagged against the cot, making Caesar suspect that the man was indeed well and truly drunk. It was not hard to guess how the unlucky lantern had been knocked over. Caesar's alert eyes quickly spotted what the Colonel was actually reaching for: a loaded automatic pistol resting on the table by the cot. His heart racing, he crossed silently to claim the gun before the human could. His fingers closed on the grip as he snatched the weapon from the table.

That's better, Caesar thought. The pistol felt cold and heavy in his hand. Lifting it, he trained the weapon on the prone form of his mortal enemy, who was still groping uselessly. The Colonel seemed to not even be aware that Caesar was present, let alone aiming a gun at his head.

It was almost too easy.

Pitiless green eyes glared down at the Colonel as Caesar recalled all the innocent blood on this man's hands, all the friends and loved ones he had taken from Caesar: Cornelia, Blue Eyes, Malcolm, Percy, even Luca. Not to mention the countless other lives, ape and human, that had been needlessly destroyed by the Colonel's genocidal madness.

No more.

The ape's face was as hard as granite as he prepared to finish off the Colonel once and for all. It dawned on him belatedly that he had never actually learned the killer's name.

Not that it mattered anymore. In a moment, the Colonel would be history.

But before Caesar could pull the trigger, the human finally lifted his head from the cot. Caesar paused, wanting a chance to look his enemy in the eyes before killing him, so that the Colonel would go to his grave knowing that Caesar had made him pay for his crimes, but then Caesar noticed the fresh blood smeared beneath the man's nose.

Just like on the bodies of the infected.

And the mute soldier in the woods.

The Colonel's bloodshot blue eyes were wide with fright and desperation, like a wounded animal's. He opened his mouth as though to speak, but nothing emerged except meaningless gasps and grunts.

Caesar reeled back in shock. His foot found an object lying on the floor next to the cot. Glancing down, he recognized it immediately.

The girl's rag doll.

Flecks of fresh blood stained the doll, which the Colonel had carried away from Caesar's cage only hours ago. The doll the infected girl had been holding onto for who knew how long. Caesar recalled the pile of torched personal effects they had found by the impromptu graveyard near the coast. The Colonel had ordered the bonfire to try to contain the spread of the mutated virus.

But he hadn't known about the doll.

Caesar was thrown by this unexpected discovery. Of all the savage punishments he had meted out to the Colonel in his vengeful imaginings, the possibility that the Colonel himself might fall victim to the contagion had never crossed Caesar's mind.

This is worse than death for him, he realized.

Caesar started to lower the gun, then caught himself. The Colonel was still clumsily reaching for the weapon, but Caesar had no intention of letting the impaired human take it from him. Raising the gun once more, he aimed it directly at the Colonel's head. Diseased or not, the man still deserved to die.

The barrel of the pistol was only inches from the Colonel's face, but the man did not even flinch. Instead he lifted his head toward Caesar and pressed his sweaty brow against the muzzle of the gun. Garbled, inarticulate noises escaped his lips. Tortured eyes pleaded mutely for death.

Caesar stared back at the stricken human, his next action suddenly uncertain. He had visualized killing the Colonel so many times since his family had been murdered, but he had never expected that the Colonel would wish for death. Caesar looked long and hard at the Colonel's agonized features. His gaze drifted slowly to the gun in his hand. His finger rested tensely on the trigger.

Just one squeeze and it's over, he thought.

But he slowly lowered the gun and stepped away from the Colonel. His stony expression softened as he felt a terrible weight slide from his shoulders. For the first time since his family had been killed, his heart was no longer at war with his conscience. He felt like an ape again.

I don't need to do this. Not anymore.

The Colonel gaped at him helplessly. Caesar understood the man's confusion; he was just as stunned by what he had chosen not to do. He looked again at the pitiable creature the Colonel had become.

He wasn't a monster anymore. Just a sick animal.

In a moment of mercy, Caesar gently placed the gun down on the table. Within the Colonel's reach.

A look of primitive gratitude flickered across the man's agitated features. His hand fumbled for the weapon.

Caesar turned away and walked out of the room.

A shot rang out behind him.

37

Soldiers shouted impatiently at Red and the other apes, demanding more ammunition for their weapons as they hastily prepared for the firefight to come. Along with his fellow renegades, all of whom had once chosen Koba over Caesar, Red scrambled up to the top of the giant defensive wall. Multiple ammo belts were slung over his brawny shoulders, a rucksack packed with military gear and weaponry weighed heavily upon his back. He handed out a belt of .50 caliber cartridges to a gunner loading a big M2 machine gun mounted on a tripod.

Red envied the gunner. He wanted a gun like that.

The rising sun did little to alleviate the biting cold and wind. Swirling snow fell on humans and apes alike. Nearby, more soldiers launched another round of missiles at the attacking army from the north. The missiles struck a pair of large mobile rocket launchers at the head of the convoy, blowing the armored vehicles to pieces. Smoking debris scattered across the icy approach to the camp.

Raucous cheers greeted the direct hits. Soldiers high-fived each other, convinced that the tide of battle had turned in their favor. Red hoped they were right about that, despite what Caesar had said before.

The other humans are not my allies, Red thought. *And neither are the apes.*

Then the gunner beside Red spotted something below. His jaw dropped and his piggish human eyes bugged out beneath his ugly flat brow. Recovering from his shock, at least to a degree, he hollered at the other humans.

"LOOK! THE APES!"

Red looked too. To his amazement, a horde of apes could be seen scrambling out from behind a sizable outcropping of rock beyond the wall. Caught between the camp and the northern army, the apes were obviously making a dash for freedom after somehow escaping from the pen, trying to cross a flat stretch of frozen terrain toward the foothills to one side of the camp. Red blinked in confusion: how and when had the apes gotten free from their chains?

"Uh-uh," the gunner muttered. "No way."

He rotated his heavy machine gun toward the apes and opened fire.

High up in the watchtower, Caesar was about to climb out the window when he saw the apes taking heavy fire from the soldiers on the wall. From his elevated vantage point, he watched in horror, desperate for a way to keep his people from being slaughtered.

I have to do something, but what?

He scanned the camp below, searching for a strategy, and his eyes locked on the tanker cars lined up on the old railway tracks stretching all the way from the foot of the wall to the depot at the rear of the canyon. Tankers filled with hundreds of gallons of fuel...

An idea occurred to him and he rushed back into the Colonel's trashed command center. Fists pounded furiously on the other side of the barricaded door; the Colonel's officers had finally managed to break through the locked door below and make it up the stairs.

"Colonel!" a man shouted through the door. "Are you in there? Colonel!"

They were calling out to a dead man, but Caesar didn't care to inform them of that; they could find their leader's corpse on their own. Instead he snatched a bandolier of grenades off the cluttered table, even as the human soldiers smashed through the crudely constructed barricade. The piled furniture tumbled and skidded across the floor. Swearing profanely, the officers caught sight of Caesar and went for their weapons. Rifles and pistols swung toward the chimpanzee, and bullets slammed into the walls as Caesar leapt through the open window onto the ledge outside, where he barely noticed the brisk morning air in his haste to get away from the watchtower and save his people. He could hear the machine gun on the wall firing, cutting down the other apes.

No! he thought furiously. *No more dead apes!*

The desecrated state flag flapped in the wind below him; a stray spark or shot had set the banner afire, so that it was burning like a torch. Swinging down from the ledge, Caesar grabbed onto the flagpole, which only barely supported his weight, breaking his fall. The end of the pole tore loose from its moorings, but Caesar held onto it for dear life, riding it down toward the ground before letting go and tumbling onto the snowy floor of the canyon.

The rough landing knocked the breath from him, but he sprang to his feet immediately and took off across the yard, still clutching the grenade-laden bandolier, as the enraged officers fired on him from the tower window. Bullets slammed into the ground behind him, tearing up the ice and snow.

The Colonel was gone, but Caesar's people were still in danger.

Keep my son safe, he silently pleaded with Lake and the universe. *While I take the war to these humans.*

Hundreds of apes were pinned down behind the outcropping, driven back from the hills by the machine-gun fire from the wall. Not for the first time, Rocket wished that they could have made their escape under the cover of dark and before the other humans had arrived with their army. He fired back at the wall with Boyle's rifle, hoping to provide cover for the other apes, some of whom were still emerging from the tunnels to discover that there was nowhere to go.

Simian bodies, cut down by the humans' guns, littered the icy flats between the outcropping and the foothills. According to Bad Ape, Maurice and most of the children had managed to make it up into the mountains at least, but the rest of them were trapped here behind the rocks. The wooded hills called out to Rocket, but how could they cross the exposed flats without being gunned down?

If only Caesar were here, he thought. *Caesar would have a plan…*

A hail of bullets assaulted the machine-gun station on the wall, forcing the gunner to duck down behind his weapon as bullets tore into the wooden timbers and concrete around him. He swore obscenely before shouting at the other soldiers. His hairless pink face flushed with anger.

"Kill them, man! Kill them all!"

Keeping back, out of the line of fire, Red realized that the apes were fighting back. He wondered briefly how they had managed to get their hands on an automatic rifle before deciding it didn't matter. He flinched at the unbridled bloodlust in the gunner's voice. He was talking about killing those other apes, right?

The sight of the besieged apes coming under fire bothered Red more than he thought it should. He had no love for Caesar's people, who had chosen Caesar over Koba, making Red and his comrades into outcasts, but Red couldn't help recalling that Koba had always fought to protect apes from humans, not the other way around. Guilt pricked Red's conscience.

I have no choice, he thought. *None.*

But what would Koba do?

"Donkey! DONKEY!" the gunner bellowed at Red, jolting the gorilla from his bitter musings. Spittle flew from the soldier's ugly human lips. "Get the grenade launcher!"

Flustered, Red shrugged off his rucksack and turned to retrieve the launcher from the pack. As he fished out the weapon, he was startled by what he saw down in the camp far below.

Caesar was racing on all fours across the prison yard. A mortar shell, arcing over the wall, hit the ground and exploded in his path, but the chimpanzee kept on going. Darting hard around the empty ape pen, he charged fearlessly through the billowing smoke. Red watched spellbound despite himself as Caesar rushed toward a large tanker car sitting at the base of the wall. The gorilla's eyes widened as he spotted the bandolier of grenades Caesar had with him. The chimp was less than thirty feet from the tanker, and closing, when he plucked a grenade from the belt and reared back to throw it. Caesar reached for the pin on the grenade, but his face contorted in agony and he collapsed, clutching his side...

Blood leaked from a wound in his abdomen, staining

the snow red. He'd lost his grip on the grenade, which had landed harmlessly amidst the debris a few feet away. Reaching back behind him, Caesar discovered a crossbow bolt in his back.

Red could guess where the bolt had come from.

Preacher stalked through the smoke and snow, emerging from the empty ape pen. The soldier hesitated briefly, as though reluctant to finish off his foe, before loading another bolt into the crossbow. He advanced slowly toward Caesar, who gasped in pain as he snapped off the steel shaft piercing his body, leaving the point embedded in his flesh. Grimacing, the wounded ape turned to see Preacher approach him, ready to loose another bolt from his weapon.

Red couldn't look away. "Goddamn it!" the gunner screamed at him. "You stupid donkey! Where's my launcher?!"

Red stared down at the grenade launcher in his hands. Turning back, he saw that the irate human was still firing relentlessly at the apes pinned down outside the camp. The M2 machine gun chewed up ammo, spitting it out at the apes, who would stand no chance once the gunner got his hands on the launcher. Images of apes blown apart by the grenades filled Red's mind.

What would Koba do?

What would *Caesar* do?

38

Pain stabbed Caesar with every movement, every breath, but even worse was the knowledge that he had come so close to freeing his people, only to be brought down by a human whose life he had once spared.

Lying in the snow, his hot blood draining from him, Caesar saw Preacher drawing nearer to him, brandishing a freshly loaded crossbow. The injured ape glanced about desperately, searching for a viable avenue of escape, but there was nowhere to go. The grenades rested nearby, but not so close that Caesar could grab one before the human squeezed the trigger on his crossbow. Caesar could not help but note the irony that it would be Preacher of all people, not the Colonel, not Red, who ultimately ended him.

I had my killer at my mercy once, and I didn't even know it.

Preacher halted several feet away from Caesar. He peered unhappily at his victim, clearly conflicted, before raising the crossbow and taking aim at Caesar's heart. Caesar braced himself for the fatal shot, regretting that he could not try to save his people one last time. It was up to Rocket and Maurice and the other apes now.

Goodbye, Cornelius, my son. I pray I will not see you soon.

Prepared to face his death head-on, Caesar stared back at Preacher. Then a deafening blast stunned him, sending him tumbling into the snow. Preacher vanished in a heartbeat, blown to pieces before Caesar's eyes, leaving nothing behind but charred, unrecognizable fragments and a blackened crater.

Dazed, his ears ringing from the blast, Caesar blinked in surprise. It had happened so fast that it took him another second to realize that he was still alive and that Preacher was... gone.

He looked around in confusion and saw Red high on the wall, holding a smoking grenade launcher. The renegade gorilla gazed stoically down at Caesar, who could not believe his eyes.

Red? Red saved me?

The gorilla stood calmly on the wall, cradling the weapon, looking more at peace than Caesar had ever seen him before. For a second, he reminded Caesar of the loyal ape he had known years ago, before Red had thrown in with Koba and turned against Caesar and the other apes. Before he had sided with the humans against his own kind.

The gunner behind Red was notably less serene. With his ears still ringing from the explosion, Caesar could not hear what the soldier was screaming at Red, but the furious human was obviously shocked and outraged by what the gorilla had just done. Drawing his sidearm, he pointed the pistol at Red, who made no effort to escape his fate or to even look at the man about to execute him. He merely gazed down at Caesar—until the flash of a muzzle signaled his end.

The ape's massive form crumpled.

Caesar's back still bore the scars of Red's whip, but nonetheless he regretted the other ape's sacrifice. Red had to have known what would happen to him if he fired on Preacher, but he had done so anyway, trading his life for Caesar's when it mattered most.

Then the soldier who had killed Red swung his gun toward Caesar. Reacting quickly, the ape snatched the fallen grenade from the snow and sprang to his feet, despite the sharp pain caused by the sudden motion. Gritting his teeth, he pulled the pin and hurled it straight at the fuel-filled tanker beneath the wall.

The gunner watched in horror as the grenade arced toward the tank car, even as Caesar spun around and sprinted away from the tanker as fast as he could.

The entire tanker erupted like a gigantic fire bomb. Towering flames engulfed an entire section of the wall, consuming all the gunners in an enormous blast that dwarfed the one that had killed Preacher. The din from the explosion drowned out the world, including Caesar's own pounding heartbeat. Billowing black smoke, reeking of burning fuel, rose like a malignant cloud toward the sky. Blasted wooden logs, boulders, and slabs of pulverized concrete broke away from the wall, crashing down into the blazing wreckage where the tanker had been. The roar of the flames challenged the din of war.

Caesar felt the heat of the fire at his back as he raced into the adult pen, clutching his wounded side. Blood seeped through his fingers, but he knew he couldn't slow down. If everything went according to his plan, the tanker explosion was just the beginning.

Any moment now…

As he hoped, the tanker next to the flames exploded, too. An equally titanic explosion rocked the camp, sending up sky-high flames and smoke and shattering whatever windows remained in the barracks, as Caesar sprinted toward the tunnel entrance in the middle of the pen.

A third tanker ignited, adding to the conflagration, as a chain reaction set off one car after another, blasting the camp apart. Caesar tumbled into the tunnel, half-propelled by the shock waves ripping across the camp as the chain of explosions headed down the tracks, toward the depot at the base of the mountain. He tumbled into the tunnel right before a cataclysmic explosion destroyed the wall, the camp, and everything above him.

Rolling onto his feet and hands, he raced through the crumbling tunnels, which were already collapsing around him. Dirt and ice rained down, threatening to bury him alive. His feet and knuckles splashed through muddy puddles. Caesar had never navigated these tunnels before, let alone in the dark, so he gasped in relief as he spied a shaft of daylight shining down from the surface. Falling snow danced in the light as he rushed toward it and leapt for the ladder, scrambling up it only a few paces ahead of a wave of mud and dirt and broken timbers that came whooshing up the shaft after him, propelling him up and out of the pit as though he had been launched from a cannon.

He landed flat on his stomach on the icy plain above the tunnel, the impact triggering a stab of agony so intense that he had to catch his breath. Gasping and panting, he let the pain subside a little before lifting his head to see dozens of hairy simian feet pointing away from him. The feet belonged to a throng of apes whose backs were all turned to him. Rising painfully to his feet, he found his people staring out beyond the huge outcropping in awe. The air stank of smoke and burning fuel.

How much damage did I do?

Unable to see past the transfixed horde, Caesar dragged himself higher onto the rocks and was stunned by what he beheld. The escalating explosions had utterly destroyed the prison camp. The wall, the watchtower, the barracks, the empty pens, and the railway tracks and depot, had all been devastated by the earth-shaking blasts set off by the detonating tankers. A voracious inferno now blazed where the camp had been. Charred and flaming debris still rained down on the cratered canyon, which was now a funeral pyre of epic proportions, many times the size of the pyres that had once burned along the shore beyond the apes' fortress. The martyred apes had been avenged many times over. Caesar found it hard to believe that any of the Colonel's fanatical flowers had survived the fiery holocaust.

Alpha and Omega, he recalled. *The Beginning and the End.*

The Colonel had promised his soldiers both, but there would be no beginnings here. Only an end to his mad crusade.

Looking away from the burning canyon, he spotted Rocket and Bad Ape among the survivors, gazing up at him in shock and wonder. No doubt they had thought him consumed by the explosions as well, but they looked happy to be proven wrong. Rocket in particular appeared deeply moved to see his friend again after their poignant goodbyes back at the camp.

Caesar knew how he felt.

He was about to sign to his friends, and was looking about for Lake and Cornelius, not to mention Maurice and the girl, when the groaning of heavy machinery overpowered the fading echoes of the explosions. Turning his eyes to the north, Caesar was brutally reminded that the war was far from over.

The enemy army was still coming.

39

The Colonel and his troops were gone, wiped off the face
of the earth by an Armageddon of Caesar's creation.

But the Colonel's human foes remained.

Despite the damage that had been inflicted on the
advancing army by the camp's defenders, the convoy rolled
across the icy expanse. A column of tanks, troop carriers,
trucks, jeeps, and Humvees had been dispatched to rein in
the rogue commander and his death squads, only to find
the Colonel's base blown to pieces right in front of them.

You're welcome, Caesar thought grimly.

The convoy braked to a halt before the raging inferno,
less than twenty or so yards from the outcropping
sheltering the apes. Soldiers in winter gear—their faces
hidden by parkas, ski masks, and goggles—stared at the
devastation, their mission abruptly completed in the most
extreme fashion imaginable.

Just for a moment, Caesar allowed himself to hope
that the soldiers would assume that one of their own
mortar shells had set off the chain reaction and simply
turn around and head back north. Their objective
had been obtained; the Colonel would no longer be

eradicating every infected human he could find.

They can go home now and keep looking for a cure.

But he knew he was fooling himself. Hundreds of apes, even skulking in the shadow of the mammoth outcropping, were difficult to overlook. And indeed, within minutes one of the faceless soldiers looked away from the blaze and spied the teeming horde of apes over by the rocks. He pointed wildly as other soldiers noticed the apes as well, while Caesar remembered the Colonel's warning from before, that his enemies were no friends of the apes.

They all want to kill us.

The soldiers had many guns. The apes had one, and Caesar didn't even know how much ammo Rocket had left. The apes were without defenses; their only options were fight or flight. Caesar prepared to order a retreat. Perhaps some of his people would make it up into the hills alive.

A long, tense moment passed, as though the humans had to mentally switch gears before targeting a different enemy. They slowly began to raise their guns…

One more explosion, even larger than the earlier ones, tore apart the face of the mountain, throwing great chunks of woods and hillside flying. A thunderous boom, echoing off the crumbling walls of the canyon, jolted both humans and apes.

The old weapons depot, Caesar realized. *Under the mountain.*

The blaze finally reached it.

The colossal blast was almost immediately followed by a quiet rumbling that rapidly built in intensity. The ominous noise came from the snowy upper reaches of the mountain.

The solders turned toward the rumbling.

So did the apes.

A human voice cried out:

"AVALANCHE!"

Dislodged by the explosion, tons of packed snow and ice and rock streamed down the shattered slopes of the mountain, gaining speed and momentum at a terrifying pace. A billowing cloud of powder preceded a plunging wall of white that cascaded over everything in its path. Fractured slabs of ice the size of roofs knocked loose still more snow and boulders, feeding the avalanche as it came roaring down at the blasted canyon—and the wide frozen tundra beyond.

It's heading our way. It will be here in moments.

The soldiers knew that, too. Forgetting all about the defenseless apes, they scrambled madly to get away from the avalanche. Soldiers leapt from their vehicles and ran frantically in all directions.

They don't stand a chance, Caesar realized.

He saw another way. Acting on instinct, he hooted at his people, waving them on vigorously, as he did the unthinkable and charged at top speed toward the mountain and the avalanche.

His people followed him without any question. Moving en masse, hundreds of apes raced away from the outcropping and across the plain to the foothills beside the blazing canyon. They dashed at simian speed up the lower slopes of the mountain, despite the onslaught of snow and ice rampaging down to meet them.

Maurice worried about the others as he and Nova led the bulk of the children up the mountain. The first wave of the retreat had managed to make it across the expanse and into the hills before the fierce battle below had cut Maurice and his party off from the rest of the apes still stranded by the outcropping. Unable to turn back with so many helpless children in his custody, Maurice could only shudder at the gunfire and explosions he heard coming from the war being waged where his friends were. A gigantic fireball, climbing high into the sky, made him wonder if anyone was still alive on either side of the wall… if the wall itself was still standing. Along with the children, he stopped to gape at the rising smoke and flames.

And then they heard the rumbling.

Looking away from the smoke, Maurice saw a tidal wave of snow and ice, shaken loose by the blast, racing down toward them from high above the tree line. The deadly avalanche threatened to wipe him and the children from the face of the earth unless they got out of its path right away.

We have to do something. Now!

With only heartbeats to spare, his shrewd eyes seized on the soaring pines all around them. He took a deep breath to fill his voluminous throat pouch and bellowed at the top of his lungs. Dispensing with signing for once, Maurice leapt for the nearest tree, carrying Nova on his back. Instinct as well as intelligence spurred the other children to follow his example, the apes clambering up the trees as only apes could.

But could they climb fast enough?

Further down the mountain, Caesar and the other apes also launched themselves into the trees. They climbed as fast and as high as they could, rushing to get above the avalanche before it buried them alive.

It was a close race. Caesar was still scrambling up the side of a towering pine when the forefront of the avalanche struck, carrying a winter's worth of snow and debris down the slope at the base of the pines. A rising tide of snow chased Caesar and the other apes all the way up to the very tops of the trees until there was nowhere else to climb, even as the monstrous avalanche continued on down to the burning remains of the camp, dumping tons of snow onto the inferno, and kept on going. It swept over the wide frozen waste, plowing over the army from the north. Vehicles, hardware, and fleeing soldiers vanished beneath the unstoppable cascade.

Nature can wipe us out at any minute, the Colonel had said.

But sometimes we help it along, Caesar thought.

The rising snow began to wash over him as he clung to the treetop with every last bit of his strength. Freezing powder buffeted his face, forcing him to squeeze his eyelids shut. The endless rumble of the avalanche thundered in his ears as he fought an elemental battle against the surging ice and cold. The force of the avalanche tried to tear him from his perch, but Caesar wrapped his arms and legs around the tree trunk, refusing to let go.

Apes belong in trees, he thought. *It's what we are made for.*

For a moment, he flashed back to the first time he had ever climbed a tree, on that glorious day, nearly a lifetime ago, when Will and Caroline had first taken him to the forest and let him off his leash to climb... and climb... and climb... as high as he was able. Caesar sometimes thought his life had truly begun on that day, high in the treetops, with nothing but the sky above him.

It would be fitting if he died there as well.

The avalanche crashed against him like the end of the world. It seemed to go on forever, but then, almost as suddenly as it arrived, the tide ceased and a stunning silence replaced the roar and rumble of the cataclysm. Barely able to believe that the danger had truly passed, Caesar cautiously opened his eyes.

An opaque white haze blotted out the world and everything in it, so that Caesar seemed to be adrift in an endless cloud, not unlike the heaven imagined by the humans. For a moment he thought he was the only survivor. Then the floating powder began to disperse, clearing the air, and Caesar was able to see the breathtaking aftermath of the avalanche.

It was all gone: the camp, the enemy army, everything.

The entire canyon had been buried beneath a mountain of pristine white snow, which extended out onto the wide-open expanse beyond, where no trace of the northern forces could be seen. Caesar scanned the plain, searching for any surviving soldiers or vehicles, but beheld only endless white as far as his eyes could see.

It was as though neither the Colonel nor his enemies had ever been there.

Jubilant hoots and barks came from all around him and he was flooded with relief as he glimpsed countless other apes clinging to the treetops just above the crest of the snow. Chimpanzees, gorillas, orangutans, and bonobos… they gazed in unison at their leader, who had saved them all once again. A chorus of simian voices rose to hail Caesar, growing steadily louder and more exuberant. More voices answered from higher up the mountain, proclaiming that Maurice and the children had survived as well. The buried slopes rang with the triumph of the apes.

Caesar allowed himself a weary smile.

40

Caesar led his people down from the mountains in search of their new home, following the route charted by Blue Eyes before the war with the humans claimed his life. It pained Caesar that his firstborn had not lived to take part in the exodus, but he carried Blue Eyes' memory with him on the trek.

Your dream will live on, Caesar silently promised his son. *We will reach the haven you found for us.*

Rocket served as their guide, having taken this journey with Blue Eyes before. Caesar was grateful that his old friend had survived their trials and could now keep them heading in the right direction. Without Rocket, they would have been lost. Bad Ape had appointed himself as Rocket's new best friend and partner, which Rocket... tolerated.

The journey was a long one, taking them over the mountains and down the other side. Cold snowy wastes tested the apes' endurance, as did the scorching sands of the trackless desert beyond. The blistering sun and stark, barren vistas made them pine for the cool green forests they had left behind. Caesar knew that many of his people were tempted to turn back at times, to risk returning to the forest the humans had driven them from, but they trusted Caesar, who trusted the hope Blue Eyes and Rocket had brought back to them before. The Colonel had sought to murder that hope, as he had murdered Blue Eyes and so many others, but ultimately he had only delayed the exodus, not halted it. The apes would have their future, no matter how far they had to go.

And the humans?

Caesar could not help wondering whether they would find a cure to the mutated virus in time, or if this new plague would spread until all human voices were silenced. The question was a troubling one, with dire implications in either instance, but Caesar was in no hurry to discover the answer. Delivering his people to safety was challenge enough for the time being.

Let the humans deal with the plague. The apes would go on regardless.

The journey eventually took the apes past the edge of a vast wasteland that appeared to be completely devoid of life. The bleak, desolate vista chilled Caesar; even the brutal deserts they had traversed before had been home to plants and animals suited to that unforgiving environment—snakes, scorpions, cacti, and so forth—but nothing bloomed and scurried in this austere, forsaken landscape. Caesar sniffed the air, but smelled nothing living. Even the dry, dusty soil felt dead.

The decaying ruins of a forgotten nuclear power plant loomed in the distance. Its cracked cooling tower and breached containment dome were evidence of some long-ago catastrophe, no doubt resulting from the chaos that had accompanied the collapse of the humans' civilization during the original plague. Caesar had heard tales of such disasters. Unsupervised, the humans' dangerous technology had burned out of control, sometimes literally.

A large, rusted metal sign marked the border of the dead area surrounding the wrecked plant. Thick block letters spelled out an ominous warning:

FORBIDDEN ZONE

The sign troubled Caesar as he walked past it, Cornelius riding on his shoulders. He shot a worried look at Rocket, who shrugged and pointed at their actual destination: a tall desert volcano rising up in the distance.

A final steep climb up the black lava flows brought the apes to the crest of the dormant volcano. By the time they reached the top of the immense cinder cone, Caesar was on his last legs. With Cornelius still clinging to his back, he paused to catch his breath before stepping forward and gazing out over what lay before him. He gasped in wonder and relief.

A verdant green paradise was hidden within a deep crater more than a thousand feet across. Lush vegetation covered the gently sloping walls of the crater, which held a sparkling blue lake at its center. The crystalline waters looked like heaven after the apes' long, thirsty trek across the desert, while the entire crater was everything Blue Eyes had promised and more: a haven, a sanctuary, where the apes could finally live free from fear.

Not an end, Caesar thought, *but a beginning.*

His people ran past him, eager to explore their new home and taste its water, but Caesar was too weak and tired to go on. He sat down on a mossy, sun-warmed rock to rest his legs and take in the beauty of the hidden refuge, which seemed a fitting reward for all the trials and hardships his people had endured to get here.

You were right, Blue Eyes. This was a risk worth taking.

Maurice waddled over and sat down beside him. Nova

occupied her usual place upon his back; that she was the orangutan's adopted daughter was taken for granted now, accepted by the entire tribe, who had not forgotten the girl's part in rescuing their own children. Cornelius peeked curiously over his father's shoulder at Nova, fascinated as ever by the human child. She smiled shyly at him, just as a rambunctious troop of excited little apes ran past, jabbering and jostling each other playfully. Despite the rigors of the climb, they still had plenty of energy left over to run and tumble and explore this glorious new playground.

Let them enjoy themselves, Caesar thought. *They've earned this.*

Both Nova and Cornelius eyed the other children with interest. Nova hopped off Maurice, eager to join in the fun. She looked back at Cornelius and held out her hand.

Somewhat more hesitantly, the young chimpanzee climbed off Caesar and down to the ground, where he looked uncertainly back at his father, clearly torn between joining the other children and staying with Caesar. Since their reunion after the avalanche, Cornelius had seldom ventured far from his father's side. Caesar had understood and indulged him in this, but he knew that Cornelius could not cling to his side forever. His son needed to learn and grow and live free.

He smiled gently at Cornelius and nodded at Nova and the other children, encouraging him to go play. A pang stabbed Caesar's heart as the little chimp succumbed to temptation and took Nova's hand. Together they scurried off in search of fun and adventure.

Go, Caesar thought. *Be brave... like your brother.*

The two fathers remained behind on the rocks. They shared proud, paternal looks as they silently watched the children play together. That the little apes accepted Nova as one of their own pleased Caesar, who found the sight profoundly moving. He recalled the Colonel's dire prophecy of a planet of apes where humans were nothing but beasts. Such a world might still come to pass if the mutated virus spread unabated, but seeing Nova and Cornelius playing together, hand in hand, gave Caesar hope for a better world than the one foreseen by the Colonel.

Who knows the future?

Maurice also gazed at the children in approval. Smiling, he turned to Caesar… and was startled when Caesar reeled and briefly lost his balance, almost toppling from the rock. Grimacing, Caesar righted himself as the sudden dizziness passed, if only for the moment. His hand was cupped to his side. Blood seeped through his fingers.

The wound from Preacher's crossbow bolt had never had a chance to truly heal. Caesar suspected that he needed surgery, as he had after Koba had shot him years ago, but human surgeons like Ellie were in short supply these days, especially if you were an ape. Caesar was not surprised that the climb had torn open the wound again. The hot blood streaming from his side showed no sign of stopping, and he had little doubt that he was bleeding inside as well.

Maurice noticed the blood at last. His tranquil smile evaporated and a distraught expression came over his face as he grasped the truth. Caesar smiled sadly, confirming the orangutan's fears. They shared a long, silent goodbye before Caesar finally spoke for the last time.

"Don't worry… we are home now."

Tears welled in Maurice's eyes, but a look of contentment came over Caesar's face. The carefree merriment of the children drew his gaze again. His throat tightened as he contemplated Cornelius; he regretted that he would not live to see his son grow to maturity. Cornelius had lost so much already.

Maurice grunted softly to get his attention. Caesar

turned back toward his friend.

Your son will know who his father was, the ape signed. *And what you did for us.*

That would have to be enough, Caesar realized. His own eyes grew damp as he looked back at Cornelius. He knew he could count on Maurice and Rocket and Lake and Nova and all of his people to look after Cornelius in the days and years to come. His son would never be alone.

Apes together strong.

Darkness encroached on his vision, leaving only the memory of the idyllic landscape the apes had found at the end of their quest. The laughter of the children slowly faded as Caesar closed his eyes and drifted away.

No more war, Caesar thought. *Only peace.*

Peace for the apes.

Peace for Caesar.

ABOUT THE AUTHOR

Greg Cox is the *New York Times* bestselling author of numerous movie novelizations, including *Godzilla*, *Man of Steel*, *The Dark Knight Rises*, *Ghost Rider*, *Daredevil*, and the first three *Underworld* films. He has also written books and stories based on such popular series as *Alias*, *Buffy the Vampire Slayer*, *CSI: Crime Scene Investigation*, *Farscape*, *The 4400*, *The Green Hornet*, *Iron Man*, *Leverage*, *The Librarians*, *Planet of the Apes*, *Riese: Kingdom Falling*, *Roswell*, *Star Trek*, *Terminator*, *Warehouse 13*, *Xena: Warrior Princess*, *The X-Files*, *X-Men*, and *Zorro*.

He has received three Scribe Awards from the International Association of Media Tie-in Writers and lives in Oxford, Pennsylvania.

Visit him at:

www.gregcox-author.com

ACKNOWLEDGMENTS

I didn't see the original *Planet of the Apes* when it first opened in 1968. I was only eight years old at the time and my parents judged it too intense for me. Ditto for the sequel, although I did manage to snag the Gold Key comic-book adaptation, which thoroughly freaked me out with its bleak, apocalyptic ending. But by the time *Escape from the Planet of the Apes* opened in 1970, I was allowed to catch up with the entire series by watching a triple feature of the first three movies all in one afternoon.

Been an *Apes* fan ever since.

So when Steve Saffel and the good folks at Titan Books offered me a chance to actually write an *Apes* novel, based on the upcoming movie, I jumped at the chance. Many thanks to Steve and the crew for thinking of me, to Cat Camacho for editing the manuscript into shape, and to Josh Izzo, Dylan Clark, and the rest of the crew at 20th Century Fox for providing me with everything I needed to write the book in a timely fashion. And a shout-out to Greg Keyes, my fellow "Apes" author, whose prequel to this story should have also seen print by now. Needless to say, we touched base with each other fairly often on matters of simian continuity.

I also want to thank my agent, Russ Galen, for handling the business end of things, and my girlfriend Karen for letting me lock myself in my office for hours on end, listening to *Planet of the Apes* soundtrack albums, even though we were in the process of house-hunting at the time.

And our cat, Sophie, just because.